THE
DATING
GAME

Books by Kiley Roache

Frat Girl
The Dating Game

KILEY ROACHE

THE DATING GAME

ink
yard
press

Recycling programs
for this product may
not exist in your area.

ISBN-13: 978-1-335-01756-7

The Dating Game

InkyardPress.com

Printed in U.S.A.

For my sister.

part one
gamification

chapter one

Roberto

Is there a fun fact about me that might impress a billionaire? This is what I wonder as I sit in the first lecture for Professor Dustin Thomas's class. Which is actually my first college class, ever. At the beginning of the hour, he asked the class to go around and *say your name and a little bit about yourself.*

As the minutes click by and the chance to speak snakes through the room, getting closer to me, I have only a big, fat blank.

I'm beginning to think I might be in over my head. That applying for this class might have been a mistake. That applying for this *school* might have been a mistake.

The question has reached the guy sitting in front of me. He stands up, introduces himself as Joe. He takes a second to mention the place he was born before moving on to all the places he has interned.

I can't blame him. If I wasn't a freshman whose job experience included mowing lawns, scooping ice cream and sorting the book drop at the library, I would probably do the same. When else are you gonna find yourself in the presence of Dustin Thomas?

After all, he is not just a billionaire, but a billionaire-maker. A venture capitalist, Thomas was an early investor in companies like Instafriend. Yep, that Instafriend. He's the guy who helped turn a group of kids working out of a dorm room into tycoons.

Now he's pretty much retired and tells all the tech blogs that he just wants to teach one class a year about the work ethic required for entrepreneurship, and research how the study of human behavior can be harnessed for marketing.

We are all here pretending we care about those topics so that we can be in the same room as him. And maybe be around when he decides to come out of retirement.

The next person stands up. "Hi, I'm Megan, and I went to a little school in Cambridge, Massachusetts, before coming here to Warren University to get my master's." She winks, and points to her Harvard crew sweatshirt, just in case she was so coy that we didn't know what she meant.

I've seen one-upmanship like this all throughout orientation, and it's not that I don't find it irritating; it's just that I don't have time to care. Of course, I want to grab some of these kids by the shoulders, tell them how ridiculous it is to debate whether Exeter is better than Andover when so many schools in the US—including the one I went to for K–8—are straining to afford books and basic supplies. But I can't exactly do that.

If I want to carve out a piece of that golden pie for myself, and even more important, for my family, I know I need to operate in this world under their rules. In my notebook, I jot down a few things I could share, like my magnet school acceptance and the community service recognition I got at high school gradation. I stare down at the paper. Neither seems like enough.

"And, what was the last thing I was supposed to say—a fun fact?" Megan asks, tapping her chin. "Um, well last summer I received the award for best intern when I worked at Apple, so that was pretty fun!"

A small laugh erupts two seats over, but it is quickly concealed by a fake cough.

I look down my row. The guy who laughed reaches under his seat for a water bottle. Maybe to cover up more laughter, or maybe because he's hungover. After all, he's wearing sunglasses and a baseball cap inside the auditorium.

He slips the bottle into the side pocket of a backpack bearing the large seal of what I assume was his high school. The logo includes a gold shield and a founding date that means his school is older than the country. *Fancy.*

He leans back and props his feet on the chair in front of him. This guy is either so rich that he doesn't need this class, or straight up stupid.

"Hi!" A cute blonde shoots up like her second-row chair is on fire. She straightens her shoulders. "My name is Sara Jones, and I'm a freshman studying computer science."

"Great," the lounging dude mutters. "Hermione Granger is in this class."

I'm not sure if he's talking to me, but I kind of hope he's not.

I am actually grateful for Sara, the only other freshman who has stood up so far. At this point, it seems that most of the students are upperclassmen, if not graduate students. I am trying my best to remember everything my high school guidance counselor told me about not letting anyone make me feel like I don't deserve to be here because of my age or where I come from. It's a bit easier to do so knowing I'm not the only freshman. In that small way, I am not alone.

Sara collapses into her seat, as if that sentence exhausted her.

Professor Thomas gestures for her to continue. But Sara just looks from side to side.

"What?" she says, her voice even higher than before.

"Your fun fact," the dude next to me yells, still practically draped across the chairs. He looks like a heckler at a comedy show.

"Oh." She stands again and straightens her skirt with shaking hands. "I, uh…"

My heart sinks to my stomach on this girl's behalf. I know what it's like to feel intimidated, like everyone around you is summing you up, just waiting to academically eat you alive. I've been in rooms where I am the only kid who looks like me, the only one who speaks two languages at home, the kid who's "only" here because of a scholarship, who's from that neighborhood your parents tell you to avoid when you drive back from the airport. People find this out about you, and it's like they smell blood in the water.

Of course, I have no idea what this girl's story is, or why she looks like she might cry in the middle of this class right now. But I feel for that isolation.

"Um…today I learned that twin sheets do not fit on a twin extra-long mattresses." She forces a smile and sits down as a few people laugh, including, thankfully, Professor Thomas, who musters a chuckle.

I decide I like this strategy, to say something that isn't a thinly veiled résumé check. When it gets around to me I say, "Hi, my name is Roberto, but most people call me Robbie.

I am a freshman and will either major in computer science or electrical engineering. I haven't decided yet. And my fun fact is when the last *Harry Potter* book came out, I stayed up all night and read it in two days."

I sit back down. I guess that still was kind of a humble brag, depending on how you look at it. But it's from elementary school so I think it's okay.

When the introductions are over, Professor Thomas moves his coffee cup before sitting on the desk at the front of the room, a causal gesture at odds with the fiercely competitive atmosphere in the auditorium.

"People often ask me what makes an entrepreneur," he begins. "What sets aside the man who has the type of success where he enters an industry, climbs to the mid or upper-mid level and retires fine, with the kind of mind that alters an industry completely, leaving a mark for decades after he's gone? The kind of mind that takes an idea born in a garage and turns it into the kind of thing my colleagues and I trip over each other to invest in?"

At the HP Garage reference, half the room scoots farther up in their seats. It's Silicon Valley, after all.

"The answer is failure." He pauses dramatically. "Sure, all successful people experience setbacks. They are passed over for a promotion or don't get a job. But some successful businessmen can *make* it through good careers without experiencing terrible failure. Catastrophic failure—down in the gutter, debt piling up, not sure if you can keep the lights on another week failure—that is where an entrepreneur *lives*. If you are innovating, you are coming up with an idea that either people have tried and failed to succeed with before you, or is so ridiculous that no human has even thought of it before. You will be laughed out of rooms. You will spend hours, if not months, building prototypes that fall apart.

"You joined this class because you want to be entrepreneurs. But from what I could gather from the...illustrious introductions you all just gave, very few of you have ever failed. You've worked incredibly hard and jumped through the right hoops, checked the right boxes. But the thing about innovating is that you will work one-hundred-hour weeks, not for the six-figure checks you'd get if you went into established industry, but for doors to be slammed in your face. You don't work hard and then succeed. You work hard and then you fail, you fail and then you fail again. And then, finally, just when you want to give up for the three-hundredth time, you succeed more than you could ever imagine.

"I teach for *this* school and I make this class application-only because I don't waste my time with students who aren't worth it. I ensure that those who make it through my class leave having gained something, and I advocate passionately for my past students. But if they don't have what it takes— the intelligence and technical skill, yes, but also the willingness to fail—they don't get to have me as their teacher. You proved you had the first two in your application. Now let's see the latter." The professor stands up and steps away from his desk. "Over the next three weeks, you will form groups of three or four and come up with a product that you will pitch to me, as if I were a VC, the next time our class meets."

A murmur ripples through the room. The professor continues, unfazed. "There are no well-worn paths here. There are no test prep books or study guides for innovation. You must go forward, maybe for the first time in your life, with no clear direction set out for you. You can reach out to mentors, read books and do research, but in the middle of the night, when part of your project isn't working, you have just you and your equally blind teammates to count on. With that in mind, I hope you choose wisely." He walks behind the desk and picks up his briefcase.

"I expect you to sink, but try to swim. This is, after all, worth a third of your grade for the class. Go ahead and get working. I'll see you in a month." With that, he walks out the door in the front of the classroom.

The lazy dude sits up with a start at the sound of the closing door.

The rest of the class is in stunned silence.

A few rows up, Sara stands and looks around, a stricken expression on her face.

People begin to murmur to those around them, and there's an awkward laugh here, and a "Nice to meet you" there. Students start to stand and ask about being in the same group, for clearly there's nothing else to do but to assume Professor Thomas was being serious.

More and more students venture from their seats. They reach a critical mass and rapidly it seems like the whole room is power walking, introducing, teaming up and swarming together. They move like a school of fish rushing upstream, and I feel like a tiny minnow being tossed around.

"Are you in the MBA program?" A man in a suit pushes through two young women tyring to reach another guy wearing a tie.

"Who has a master's?" a brunette woman yells into the crowd.

My mouth feels like sandpaper. I slide my notebook into my backpack and reach for my water.

Down the aisle, the lazy dude stands and turns to the row behind us.

"Hi, Braden Hart." He reaches out his hand to a be-spectacled, white, hipster-looking guy, who has teamed up with an olive-skinned, preppy-dressed girl in the row behind us.

"How many languages do you know?" the guy asks, skipping any introduction.

"Three." Braden crosses his arms with confidence.

The hipster guy raises his eyebrows. "Which ones?"

"French, Span—"

"Coding languages, you idiot," the girl snaps. The hipster guy just blinks at Braden.

"Oh." Braden steps backward. "I don't really...uh..."

The hipster guy scoffs. "Get out of my face." He holds up a hand.

I slide out of the row and walk up to a group of older-looking students. I could've tried for the group behind me—I do know three coding languages—but I don't want to work with anyone that rude.

A girl with a pink stripe in her hair smiles as I walk up.

"Hi, I'm Roberto." I clear my throat. "Robbie," I add.

"Hey, I'm Rebecca," she says.

"Chad." The guy reaches for my hand, and as I shake it I can't help but notice he's wearing both twine bracelets and a Rolex.

They ask me about my skills, and I nod along as I walk through my experience. They seem less interested when I mention my passion for social impact, but they don't tell me to get lost or anything.

"Do you have any experience at a start-up?" Rebecca asks.

I start to answer, but my attention is pulled away. On the other side of the room, Sara is speed walking from group to group, her heels clicking. She barely makes it a few syllables through her high-pitched introduction before she is turned away. And turned away. And turned away again.

I bring my attention back to the people in front of me.

"I don't, but I was in the prebusiness club at my high school," I say.

Rebecca nods. She leans over to whisper to Chad.

Around us, groups lock together and push upstream toward the exit like mini tornados, probably trying to get from the classroom to the library without losing any members.

"We're really sorry, but my thesis coadvisees want to join and that would make us five," Chad says. "You're the only undergrad, so it's only fair if you're the one we cut."

"Sorry!" Rebecca shrugs sheepishly.

I nod and say thanks anyway. Looking around the room, I count group members, looking for any that have an opening. But in a flurry of business cards and iPhones, the room has thinned. Just as quickly as it exploded with sound, the auditorium is quiet. Practically empty.

Sara is stalking a group of three headed toward the exit, yelling her high school GPA as the door swings shut in her face. She turns on her heel, her shoulders falling.

I stand in the aisle, mystified.

Braden, who has taken a seat in one of the last rows, looks up from his phone, "Well, I guess it's just us then."

chapter two

Braden

I stand slowly and make my way toward the other guy. The hot blonde is charging toward us, crossing half the auditorium in the time it takes me to move past a couple of rows.

"Sara Jones," she says, sticking out her hand for a firm shake as if this is a job interview. I half smile in return, unable to tell yet if she is overenthusiastic but tolerable, or going to be a real pain in the ass.

She pivots to the other kid, who seems rattled by her wall of energy. "Robbie," he responds quietly. He is broad shouldered, and definitely over 6', since he's significantly taller than me, and I'm exactly 5' 10 and 3/4".

I straighten my posture, not wanting to lose any height to slouching.

"All right then, looks like we're a team." She punctuates her sentence with a sharp nod and a smile.

I roll my eyes. *As if we aren't the intellectual equivalent of the last kids picked in gym.*

She pulls something out of her Longchamp bag and thrusts it into my hand. I turn it over. An honest-to-god business card.

Sara Jones.

Co-Founder: EduConnect.

"EduConnect?" I look at her, studying her face closely.

"My school used that," Robbie says, taking a card as well.

"Half the schools in California do," I mumble, looking back at the card. I read an article awhile back about the students in some place in the Midwest, Wisconsin or Minnesota or something, who quadrupled the efficiency of their high school's software system, then refused to sell their work, instead donating it to every school in the country. My father sent me the article. Asked why he was paying so much for my private school education when public school kids were doing that. Public school kids like my new partner, it seems.

Sara shrugs. "I was sick of how inefficient my school's online grading system was, so I helped fix it."

"You got some game," I say, shoving the card in my pocket.

"I uh..." She blinks at me for a second. "Thanks."

She blushes and averts her gaze to the small pink notebook in her hand. She flips it open. "I think we should get brainstorming as soon as possible. I could schedule an ideation session for later in the week? I think we need like three packages of sticky notes?" She pauses, her pen resting above the page. A drop of ink falls, staining the otherwise immaculate paper. "Yeah." She scribbles something. "Three hundred or so is enough for the ideation stage. We— *Shit*, we also need to decide on a scheme for color coding..." She continues to scribble away.

"Ideation?" Robbie turns to me.

I shrug, *I have no goddamn idea.*

Sara's head snaps up. "Ideation," she says. "You know? Like, the creation of ideas. In the design thinking process."

"Sorry, babe, I don't speak tech buzzword." I shrug.

She wrinkles her nose. "Whatever you call it, we need a plan of attack." She pauses. "A structure for development."

"Don't we need an idea first?" Robbie asks. "Like, how can we have a strategy for growing something when we don't know what it is yet?"

She looks from him to me, but I just grunt in agreement. He's making more sense than she is. She's making up words, for God's sake.

"We can't just wait around," she says. "There has to be a strategy we can use, some sort of technique. To optimize the creative process."

I brush my hand across my face so she can't see me laughing. "Isn't that the point? That you can't optimize it—isn't that what makes it *creative*?"

Her mouth freezes in a little O and her pen hovers.

I decide I'm done with this for today. I shove past her as I start up the aisle, my footsteps echoing in the now-empty auditorium.

"Wait, where are you going?" I hear the clacking sound of her shoes behind me.

"To take a nap!" I yell over my shoulder. "I'm hungover as fuck."

"What! You can't just—"

"You're cute, Blondie, but you've got to learn to calm down." I don't look back as I push through the door.

She releases a noise that barely sounds human. But before she can continue, there is the sound of the latch clicking.

★ ★ ★

I walk from Main Quad back to the more residential part of campus. I enter my dorm with headphones on, avoiding small talk with the nerds playing some sort of dragon and princess game in the lobby.

The generic dorm furniture, some sort of cheap wood covered in a plastic-y coating meant to make it look like slightly less cheap wood, is still piled up outside my room. A bright yellow notice has been taped to it, letting me know I will be fined if it's still in the hallway by a certain time tomorrow. I crumple the note and push open my door. I toss the paper onto my new desk, and it slides across the stainless steel.

It's almost noon. Which means it's three in New York. And eight in London. I sigh. I really don't like calling my parents when I'm still struggling to think through the remnants of last night's booze, but if I don't soon, I'll be in much more trouble.

I climb onto my bed, its ridiculous thread count beige linens wasted on a captain's height twin extra long mattress. I try to get comfortable, rearranging the white and tan throw pillows, which are covered with embroidery and anything but cozy, but with this hangover it's no use—it feels like someone is stabbing me with no less than three tiny knives. I pull out my headphones with a click and dial.

"Hey sweetie!" my mother sings over the phone. "Give me one second, I'll patch in your father…"

I clear my throat as the dial tone sounds again. I picture the sound bouncing across a map, from a California dorm room to a sitting room in Hyde Park, and then ringing in a busy office on Wall Street.

"Hart and Smith," the voice of one of my father's many assistants says over the phone. I used to know their names, when I was six and would come visit his office, dragging Matchbox cars across grand windows, pretending they were driving along the streets of downtown Manhattan so far below. But then came boarding school for me, and his promotions that meant there was a rotating team of high-heeled blondes when I came by his office once a year.

"Hi, yes, this is Marcy. His wife. I'm on with our son, Braden. He should be expecting the call, if you wouldn't mind patching us through?"

"One moment," her voice singsongs. The phone rings again. I stare at the cracked ceiling, the one part of the dorm room that my mother couldn't replace.

She does this every time. The furniture thing.

I don't want it to look like a dorm, I want it to look like your home, she said. Like I had any conception of what a stable home was.

"Hello." My father sounds tired, as usual.

"Hi, Dad."

"What's going on?"

"Nothing, I, uh, just got to school yesterday and wanted to call." I reach for the string hanging from the blinds covering my small, square window. "Sorry to call you at work. Mom's in London so..."

"Hey there!" my mother interjects.

"...I didn't want to wait until it was too late."

"Right, of course," my father says. There is the mumbled sound of someone talking in the background and then he says, "Yes, as long as we have it before five."

I wait for him to return his focus to the call, knowing better than to try to talk over whatever is happening in New York.

"Did you get moved in all right?" he asks. "How were the new movers?"

"Fine." I sigh. "They still need to come back to pick up the old furniture and bring it to storage though. They were supposed to this morning while I was at class, but it's still here."

"God," my mother says. "It's as if nothing can get done without ten follow-up calls. I'll have Katherine ring them tomorrow."

"I don't need your assistant to do it. I can call my own moving people." I scoff. "Jesus, I've been in boarding school since I was nine—I think I've got it."

"Braden," my father says. "Don't be rude to your mother. She's just trying to help."

I exhale and lie back on my West Elm pillows. "Sorry, Mom," I mumble.

My father might as well have been scolding me for pouting about not getting a cookie until after dinner. Going to boarding school somehow means both growing up at hyper speed and never growing up at all. On one hand, you have immense freedom at an early age. But at the same time, your parents haven't interacted with you day-to-day since you were a child, and when you do talk to them, a lot of those old mannerisms still remain. They don't know how to parent a teenager, so they offer some sort of combination of parenting for a ten-year-old and for a thirty-year-old.

"You better behave yourself out there," my father says. "I do not want a repeat of last time."

I make a small sound in the affirmative, my throat suddenly too dry to form words. I should've known those sort of threats wouldn't have been left behind in high school. That he would never let me forget that, despite all the privileges I'd been given, I was still dumb enough to be caught drinking in my high school dorm. And that the only reason I wasn't expelled like the other kids with me that day was that my father, in addition to all the tuition he'd paid, made a six-figure donation to the school. He'll never let me forget that, if I misstep again—get in trouble for partying or fail a class—I will not get off so easy.

"How are your classes?" my mom asks, always one to avoid confrontation at all costs.

"Okay." I clear my throat. "I've only been to the Dustin Thomas one so far, and it is a little rough." I sit up. "Get this, it's the first day and he wants us to pitch in a few weeks. I'm one of only three freshmen, so of course all the grad students cliqued up. I'm stuck with kids whose greatest stress in life has probably been who will make homecoming court—"

"Well then, you'll just have to lead." My father cuts me off. "I don't want to hear it. You know when I first started my company, it's not like we were nabbing the finest natural talent of the corporate world. I had to make do with people who didn't know anything about business. You just have to find the untapped potential, the unpolished drive, and teach those people how to work. As long as people have the right leader, you can bring out potential you never would have known was possible..."

I roll my eyes. I don't have time for the spiel my dad gives at charity luncheons and leadership conferences full of hungry MBAs across the country, pretending he didn't work in a simpler time. When he started out, oil technology was a pretty safe bet—and yes, he did a lot to make it more efficient, but it's not like he invented the idea that, hey, people might need gasoline.

"…it's about hard work and dedication, son…"

By this point, I can practically mouth along to the words of the speech. My father has a strict understanding of the type of success his child should achieve, and how it should be achieved.

My phone buzzes against my face. I glance down to see a banner alert for an email from Sara Jones. It's a When2Meet request.

I put the phone back to my ear, but my father hasn't noticed I was distracted. I close my eyes as he rambles on.

Sometimes I wish I had the type of parents who encouraged me to try my best and told me it would all be okay. Who dropped me off at college themselves. A mother who tried to hand me my stuffed animal that I told her I wouldn't need but was a little glad she brought anyway. A father who patted me on the back, trying not to cry as he called me young man and wondered who would play catch with him on Saturdays now.

But if that were my reality, would it have still been *Warren* I was moving to?

He continues. "…identify a problem, brainstorm solutions, test, evaluate, repeat…"

I know they've given me opportunities most parents only dream of supplying their child. The fancy schools, camps every summer at elite universities, travel sports teams, trips to major world capitals and exotic islands. But sometimes I wish they could've just given me their time instead.

The international boarding schools and multiple vacation houses were great. But it would be nice to have a home to be homesick for. One house and one school and one place I am from. Now I'm left just feeling sick.

By the time the call winds down, ending with my mom

demanding I call once a week and not-so-jokingly insisting
that my dad do the same, I am ready to be alone with my
thoughts. My skin feels itchy from the inside out.

I hang up and am staring at the dark-screened phone in
my hand when it buzzes for the second time. Please respond
ASAP, the subject line of Sara's second email reads.

"Jesus." I toss my phone aside and pull one of the extra
throw pillows over my face.

chapter three

Sara

Only 5 percent of Silicon Valley start-ups are run by women.

I read this statistic in a *TechCrunch* article last year, but it's all I can think about when I walk into my Advanced Computer Science lecture, and am greeted by an auditorium full of men—most of them white—many of them in hoodies and sipping overpriced energy drinks.

The harsh, industrial cleaner smell that seems to permeate the engineering quad burns my nose as I make my way down the aisle. I sit alone in the first row and slide my laptop out of the polka-dot Kate Spade case my little sister got me for high school graduation.

Class won't start for another five minutes, but many people are already coding away. The click of fingers hitting keys is sometimes interrupted by chatter as the boys talk amongst themselves. No one talks to me.

I check my email. Robbie responded already, saying how nice it was to meet me and thanking me for setting up the

When2Meet. He seems nice. I friended him on Facebook, and it turns out he lives in my dorm too! I'd feel bad I never met him before, but with three hundred students, there are plenty of people in Dawson hall that have yet to cross paths.

I send back a smiley face emoji.

Braden, on the other hand, has completely ignored my message. I can already tell he's gonna be one of *those* project partners. The ones that expect the work to be done but do none of it themselves. Not to mention way he talked to me today—calling me *babe* and making fun of design thinking. What a piece of work.

The door near the front of the room swings open, and a girl with a heart-shaped face walks through. She has glowing brown skin, big curly hair and fierce eyes lined with charcoal makeup. Even in the terrible florescent light of the classroom, the highlighter across her cheekbones shimmers.

Around me, the chattering fades, and guys look up from their screens to gawk at her, their mouths hanging open. The girl sips the iced Venti Starbucks in her hand and doesn't look at any of them as she walks over and settles into the seat behind me.

I want to talk to her, but she is just so *cool*. I glance over my shoulder, reaching up to scratch my head so that I can half hide behind my arm. She's leaning back in her chair, her legs propped up on the back of the empty seat next to me. She is wearing light-washed ripped jeans and Gucci sneakers and looks like she could be on the cover of a magazine, or at the top of my Instagram Discover, an influencer with thousands of likes, more than she fits in the fashion wasteland that is the Computer Science building. She unfolds her computer on her lap, the back of which features a sticker for Instafriend and another that says Code-Blooded Bitch in swirling pink writing. I want so badly to be her friend. I want so badly to be her.

My stomach tightens and I turn back to my own screen. I have no idea what I could possibly say to this girl that might impress her. I don't know why *she'd* want be friends with *me*.

Our professor shuffles in, clicks on the PowerPoint and starts class at the hour on the dot. And just like that, my anxiety fades and is replaced with dull sadness. I lost my chance.

I type along in OneNote as the professor makes his way through an introduction to machine learning. I raise my hand for every question—I did all the reading assigned over the weekend and this lesson is straight from those pages—but am called on only once. He does pick me to make sure the attendance sheet makes it all around the room, though.

He ends a few minutes early, and I am still saving my notes when someone taps my shoulder.

I turn around, and the smell of vanilla tickles my nose. Cool Girl smiles at me. "Hey," she says.

"Hi!" My voice is too high.

"You a freshman?"

"Uh, yeah." I tuck a piece of hair behind my ear.

"Thought so. At this point I know most of the girls in the program. All twelve of them." She rolls her eyes. "I'm Yaz. Sophomore."

"Sara. No *h*." Right after I say it, I regret it. Like she cares.

But she seems amused. "Yeah, this is not how you spell my name either." She holds up the Starbucks cup that says *Jazz* in Sharpie.

I laugh. Not sure what else to say but not wanting this conversation to end, I point to the sticker on her laptop. "Did you work there?" It might be awkward to ask, but I can't help but wonder. I am *addicted* to that damn app.

"Oh, uh, yeah." She glances at her computer, like she forgot the giant advertisement was there. "I would not recommend it." She shakes her head, closing the laptop and slipping it into her bag.

"Really? It's like a dream job for me."

"Yeah, I mean they paid well and it's a great résumé builder." She stands and pulls her bag over her shoulder. Pausing, she looks at me. I realize she is waiting. I quickly dump everything into my bag and pop up to follow her.

"The culture was just pretty brutal for women," she says. "Full of bro-grammers. I would lead my group and then never get picked for projects. Was mistaken as an assistant like three times."

We make our way out of the now-half-empty auditorium.

"One night I was working late and someone thought I was there to take out the trash."

"Oh God, that's terrible." I squint as we step out into the sunlight .

"Yeah, it's unfortunately not unique to Instafriend either." I cringe.

"If I can give you one piece of advice, kid—start your own company. I think that's the only way women are going to advance in tech, by doing their own shit. You need to strike out on your own, by any means necessary. That's what I'm tryna do."

I nod vigorously, taking mental notes. She spikes her cup, now just ice slightly stained a coffee color, into the recycling bin.

We are approaching the split between the main academic quad and the turn toward my dorm. I don't know which way she's going, but I don't want this conversation to end.

"Do you want to go to the library or something?" I ask. "Work on the homework?"

"I wish I could." She checks her watch. That's how cool she is—she actually wears a watch. So vintage. "But I have to get going. I have this wine-night thing with my dorm-mates from freshman year."

"Is that a thing?" My eyes go wide. "Like, drinking on a school night?"

"I mean, not finals week, but week one, sure." She pulls her phone out of her bag. "It's gonna just be upperclassmen tonight, but here, let's exchange numbers and hang another time."

We type in our numbers, and when she hands my phone back she says, "I'm glad there's another brave soul with me in this class."

I wonder if that comment should make me feel good or bad for my whole walk home.

chapter four

Roberto

"But how would you make it profitable?" Braden interrupts Sara, who was midway through pitching an idea. She pauses, her marker halting on the dry erase board.

"What do you mean?" She stares at him, eyes like daggers.

"How would it make money?" Braden asks again, drawing out his words, as if the problem before had been him speaking too quickly.

I look away to keep from laughing. We've been here for three hours now, in the Engineering Center, working inside a replica of the Palo Alto garage where William Hewlett and David Packard created, you guessed it, HP, when they were just a few years out of Stanford. This version of it is made of glass and filled with group worktables and dry erase boards. I've started to feel like our workspace is mocking us, and Braden's dumb, cynical sense of humor makes more and more sense every minute.

She makes a face at him. "Why does everyone keep asking that?"

"I mean," I say before Braden can get another sour word in. "It *is* a class on entrepreneurship."

She giggles and I am grateful. I'd feel bad if my teasing tormented her the way Braden's seems to—but the joke was right there.

She runs a hand through her hair. It looks nice slightly disheveled in this way, almost better than when she floats into the room and it's perfectly in place. "So what do we have then?"

I scan my notes. It's Friday, and we've met twice now since we were given the assignment on Monday. "Well, we repitched Facebook accidentally, discussed a biomedical technology idea that would take years of R & D, discussed an emoji keyboard made entirely of puppies doing different things, and then finally you suggested an emergency alert app that would not make money."

"So we're nowhere." Braden rests his head on the table. "Fabulous."

"Do you think he'd really fail us?" I ask. I picture an F on my transcript, the first grade below A I would've received since the fifth grade. It feels like someone is wringing out my stomach.

"He couldn't, right?" Sara looks at me with wide eyes. My heart twinges. She falls into the chair across from me, tossing her dry erase marker onto the table.

"I definitely think he would," Braden says, face still on the table. "I think that was the whole point of his speech." He raises his head, his hair now askew.

"What would that do to our GPAs?" Sara starts to crunch numbers in her notebook.

"Well, considering this is our first semester, we're starting at zero," Braden says, "and assuming we are each taking a standard load of classes, and get As in all of them, which will be no easy feat… We would have a GPA of 2.66 by Christmas."

"Yikes." Sara sets down her pen.

I look at my own notebook and the list of ideas that have been scratched out one by one.

The silence in the room is palpable.

I click my phone to check the time. "Yo, guys, I'm sorry, but I have to go soon."

"What?" Sara says. "But we don't even have an idea yet!"

"I know, I'm so sorry, but—"

"It's the first weekend of the year." Braden cuts me off. "The kid wants to actually go to college, Blondie."

She bares her teeth at him. "*Don't* call me Blondie."

"I'm sorry, Sara, I really am." I swing my bag over my shoulder. I leave before she can reply.

I step onto the engineering quad, strictly organized with its rectangular buildings and perfect, half-circle hills. I hop on my bike and head toward the Cal Ave train station.

When I'm at school, I'm not far from home, at least as the crow flies. But it is quite the journey on public transportation.

I pop headphones in my ears as the train pulls up to the station. It takes me a while to find a seat among the young employees of Silicon Valley. Twenty-somethings who prefer to live in bustling San Francisco rather than the sunny suburbs near the tech campuses, they usher through a sort of reverse commute every day.

When the train gets to SF, I hop off the Caltrain in favor of the BART, which is faster but has far less seating, to cross the Bay. Outside the window, trendy places with purposely misspelled names like Flur and Cheeze that sell artisan rugs and fifteen-dollar truffle-infused grilled cheeses give way to chain stores, diners named after their owners and taquerias with pictures of the food on the wall.

Telephone wires run overhead and street art and tags start to pop up on the sides of buildings. It feels like I'm thousands of miles, not a few zip codes, away from where I started. Here, a yard is a decent patch of grass in front of a house that looks like the kind you'd have drawn as a kid—a solid square with a triangle on top. In Silicon Valley, yards are rolling, professionally landscaped hills surrounding castles the likes of which I'd seen only in picture books or episodes of *My Super Sweet 16*.

I know we are leaving the "nice neighborhoods," the ones people move to "for the schools" and brag about by underlining their zip codes on envelopes or tagging their location on every Instagram post. But there is something more real about the towns that pass outside the window now. Everything is less polished, sure. And yeah, grass springing up from cracks in the concrete is less aesthetically pleasing than cobblestones. But at least it's a sign of life.

This is an actual neighborhood. A town people have lived in for a while.

The buildings here did not just spring up with the influx of Google employees during the second "gold rush" in Northern California. Here, people know each other. They grow up and work hard here. They have first birthday parties with paper cups of soda and homemade piñatas, first jobs with aprons, and first kisses on dares. They didn't swarm in after college with a degree and a résumé, take from the land and swing back out to retire young. They establish roots here, or at least, they do as best they can.

"Coliseum Station," the staticky voice informs the BART

passengers as I hop off the train. The sun is setting, sending streams of light through the fog gathering close to eye level. It's only a few blocks to my house from here, and even now I feel relieved. The first week at school has been great, but also an overstimulating amount of new things. It feels nice to be somewhere familiar.

I walk the few blocks to my street quickly, anticipation building the closer I get to home.

As soon as I round the corner onto my block, I hear a young voice call out, "Robbieeeeee!"

I take out my headphones and turn to see my seven-year-old neighbor, Mateo.

"¡Hola!" I say.

He smiles a gap-toothed grin as we do the secret handshake we perfected when I babysat him last summer.

I ruffle his hair. "Man, you need a haircut."

"You sound like my *mom*. She's been saying that all week."

I laugh. "Well, your mom knows what's up."

He wrinkles his nose.

"Hey, I brought you something!" I swing my backpack to my front.

His eyes light up as I pull out the Warren University T-shirt I got him from the bookstore.

"Awesome!" He grabs it from my hands and stares at the blue letters for a second before pulling it on over the T-shirt he is wearing. It covers up half his basketball shorts, looking almost like a dress on his small frame. Well, an adult small was probably not the right decision. I should've shopped the kid's section.

"It's a little big, but you can grow into it." I ruffle his hair.

He nods vigorously. "I can wear it when I go there!"

Behind him, the front door swings open. "Roberto, I thought I heard you!" Mateo's mom waves as she steps outside.

"Mom, look!" He points to the letters on his chest.

"¡Qué bonita!" She smiles. "Did you say thank you?"

"Sí." He turns to me and shakes his head. "Gawd, who does she think I am?"

I laugh. His mother just looks at me and shakes her head, smiling in a tired but amused way.

"I'm here to see my dad," I tell Mateo. "And you should go in for dinner, but I'll see you tomorrow, okay?"

He nods and gives me a high five before sprinting inside. *Oh, for the days when I ran everywhere I went.*

Mateo's mother pats him on the back as he races past and waves at me before she closes the door.

"¡Hola, Papa!" I say as I push open the door to the house where I grew up. My key gets stuck as usual, but after a few tries I get it loose. I close the door and then click the lock back in place.

"Roberto!" My father steps out of the kitchen. He pulls me into a big hug. I breathe in the smell of his aftershave and home.

"¿Cómo estás?" He steps back, hands still on my shoulders, and examines my face. "¿Te han dado de comer en la universidad? Te veo muy flaco! Do you need food? Something to drink?"

I laugh and shrug him off. "Sí, I've been eating." I step into the kitchen. "I'll take something to drink though." I grab a Jarritos Lime from the refrigerator. It's been my favorite flavor since I was five, and he always buys it. As the door closes, the photograph of my mother, smiling as she holds me just days after I was born, swings up before settling back into its spot.

I feel a pang in my heart. My dad has had this picture up for years, but the effect on me never really goes away.

Next to it, my Warren acceptance letter is tacked on with a magnet.

I remember the day he put it there. The whole block came over to party when I got in. A few kids who used to call me a nerd and throw things at me from the back of the classroom even timidly offered a *That's really cool, man.*

I sit down at the light wood table. Across from me, where my father must have been sitting, a newspaper is open to the crossword, half-done. A pencil lies across the top, and along the margins, the Spanish translations of words are written in my father's clean, plain handwriting.

He sits down and pushes the paper to the side. "How was your first week at school?"

I start into stories about dorms and classes, and he asks if I've met any nice girls.

I know it isn't exactly a typical college move, to come home the first weekend. But I also know my father is lonely. My mother has been gone almost ten years now.

About three months from the ten-year mark, actually. A fact we've been keeping quite a close eye on.

It all started when I was seven, so young I barely understood what was going on. One day my mom went to work and didn't come home. It wasn't until a few hours after she was supposed to be home, and my dad was pacing a hole in the kitchen floor, that we got the call.

There had been an ICE raid on the restaurant where she worked. Unlike my dad, who was born in the States after his parents emigrated, my mother's parents had crossed the border when she was three. Oakland was the only home she remembered, but that meant jack shit to the immigration officers.

She wouldn't be deported for two more years. But that was the day it felt like they stole her from me. They detained her, held her for a five-thousand-dollar bail we couldn't immediately come up with. For two months, she was held in county jail. I remember that time in flashes of pain. I try not to think about it, but images come up. Waking up with screaming nightmares, sweating through Spiderman pajamas. The strange kitchens and living rooms I'd go to after school, staying with a rotation of moms from church who offered to watch me so my dad could work extra shifts to put toward bond.

And the sterile room for visitors to the jail. Once a week, for an hour, timed so exactly, so harshly, so inhumanely. Seeing my mom, but knowing she wasn't coming home with us. Watching the clock on the wall loom and click past the minutes, getting closer to when they would take her away again.

And even when we finally had enough saved and got her out, it hung over our heads, that clock. We were reminded of it every week, when she had to check in with ICE. Every minute we were moving toward the day of her hearing.

Two years after she was initially apprehended, her court date arrived. They said she had a right to a lawyer, but "at no cost to the state." Since my parents still owed money to family and friends who helped with bond, that "right" didn't mean much. There was no translator either, and this was before my mom had much English. The whole thing lasted five minutes, and then they deported her, sending her back to a country she had no memory of, to live with extended family she'd never met. Taking her away from me.

I had never been to an airport before that day. I'd always imagined going under different circumstances, heading on an adventure overseas or to Disney World. But I did not want to go there like this.

To stand in that big concourse, bustling and sterile, and say goodbye to my mom. I was at an age when I thought it wasn't okay for boys to cry, and I had told myself on the way there I wouldn't. But of course I did. I cried harder than I ever had, and ever have since. I screamed and clutched her jacket and, when the time came, had to be pulled away from her. At eighteen, I still have nightmares about that day.

Once she was deported, she had a ten-year bar before she could try to come back to the States. Because my dad was a citizen, we heard we could apply for a waiver. So instead of trying to come back to us under the radar, my mom stayed in Mexico, saved money and waited. And then she submitted an application, and waited some more.

And then a bureaucrat decided that since my dad could work and I was doing okay in school and physically healthy, her absence did not create "extreme hardship" for a US citizen, and denied the waiver. As if birthdays and Christmases and Mother's Days and first days of schools passing without my mom wasn't extreme enough hardship. As if three or four trips a year to visit her, knowing she couldn't visit us, wasn't extreme enough hardship. As if breaking our family up across an invisible line wasn't extreme enough hardship.

After the waiver was denied, the only thing we could do was wait.

So not getting to stay and party the first weekend of college? There were much more unfair things.

"I've started seeing more of those buses on my way to

work, going to those tech places," my dad says. "Los veci-
nos are mad."

I nod. I'd read the articles and Facebook posts complaining about the buses and the gentrification they represented.

"Is it bad that I keep thinking I can't wait to see you go by
in a bus that says Google on the side?"

I laugh. "It might be. I do the same thing though."

"At least you will wave to me when you pass through the
neighborhood, instead of clutching your bag like some of
these people."

"Dad, if I make it onto one of those buses, you won't be
living in this house anymore."

He smiles faintly. I have been talking about buying him a
big house with a pool and granite countertops since I got the
magnet school letter in eighth grade.

"Ya veremos..." he says. "I don't mind it here too much
though."

I nod and think of Mateo and the rest of the neighbors.
I know what he means, but I also know I will work until I
don't have to read news reports on shootings with my heart
racing, hoping not to see my neighborhood, my cross street
or, God help me, a name I know.

My father prepares me food even though I tell him I already
ate, and then we sit in the living room and watch his shows.
He tries to explain all the backstories and relationships between the characters to me, and I don't have the heart to tell
him I watch this only with him so he really doesn't have to.

During commercial breaks he asks me about school and I
ask him about work. He still watches TV live, so we can't fast-
forward. I've tried to explain that we can stream Netflix on
my computer if he wants. But I think he likes to watch shows

as they air. It gives some structure to his week, each show associated with an evening. Mondays and Wednesdays are *Law & Order SVU*. Thursdays are *Grey's Anatomy*, and then a call to my mother to discuss the episode to pieces. Sundays and Mondays mean the guys coming over for the game. Television is an event for him in a way it just isn't for my generation.

There is a wonderfully comfortable silence as we watch. The TV set hums slightly, and sounds echo from outside, so even when there is no dialogue or music it's not silent. After a week of orientation, small talk and overzealous introductions, I find it relaxing not having to fill every second with talking.

When the shows end at eleven, we both get ready to sleep.

"I'm so proud of you, mijo," my father tells me, standing outside the bathroom door in his slippers as I brush my teeth.

I'm just getting started, I think as I shut off the light in my childhood room and climb into the twin bed I have slept in for the past seventeen years. Someday, I'll do something to truly earn that pride.

Just as I am about to drift off to sleep, my phone *pings*. It is a new alert sound, not a text, but my Warren email. I roll over and swipe open my phone. The message is from the financial aid office, congratulating me on my first week of college and sending me a number of reminders about work study and book vouchers.

And then, halfway down the email is this line: Remember that to qualify for continued aid you must be in good academic standing, retaining a GPA of 2.75 or higher.

I sit up in bed. Braden's words from earlier, about getting a 2.66 if we fail, echo through my head and are interrupted by the memory of Professor Thomas saying he intends to flunk half the class.

I click the Lock button and watch the screen turn black before setting the phone back on my nightstand. I hope that, when I wake up, I will have thought of a project that will please Professor Thomas. Everything I've done—everything my parents have done—depends on it.

I barely sleep. And when I do, I dream about code.

chapter five

Sara

Since our meeting ended sooner than I expected, I work for a while longer on homework by myself and try to soak up any inspiration I can from the HP Garage replica. I finish my CS assignment and head straight back to my dorm. It's not like I had any other plans tonight. Or any night really.

From a building away I can see people are already milling around the lawn outside my dorm with red cups in their hands. I smile as I walk past, but they don't say anything to me.

I walk inside and can hear the music as soon as I step into my hall. I'm not sure which room it's even coming from, but the floor is practically shaking from the bass.

As I get closer to my room, it gets louder. The door before mine is slightly ajar. I pause in front of it. Through the crack I can see that the suite is crowded. There are people sitting at the kitchenette table and piled on the couch, three on the seat and another on the arm. And even more people are standing. They're drinking and talking and laughing and flashing smiles and tossing hair over shoulders with a wink.

It's not just one person playing loud music. It's a party.

They have the overhead lights off and shades closed, and a little disco ball on the table throws multicolored light across their trendily clothed bodies.

I recognize Colleen McGregor, one of the residents of the room, who is also in my Intro to Rhetoric class. She is standing over the table, a drink in one hand and a cell phone in the other. A cord runs from the bottom of the phone to the disco ball.

She is speaking rapidly to another girl, who is looking at the phone too. Probably debating the music.

Colleen looks up from the screen and right at me. I step backward. I hadn't realized I had been standing here for a while and was blatantly staring at this point. *Crap, she's going to think I'm so weird.*

I practically run to my door, unzipping my Longchamp as I go. I scrounge around for my keys among the Post-its and pens and lip glosses. *Why aren't there pockets in this damn thing? Who thought one giant sack was a good handbag plan?*

"Sara!"

I turn to see Colleen standing in the hallway. She tucks the red cup in her hand behind her back. Her face is sort of shiny but her makeup is still in place, if a bit smudged around the edges. It's her eyes that betray her drunkenness the most. Well, that and the cup she's not hiding well.

"Yeah?"

"Have you done the assignment yet? The reading response thing?"

"Oh, um, no," I adjust my skirt. "Not yet." The statement

is both true and not: I had done most of the assignment today in the library, but I still had one question left.

"Great!" Her eyes light up. "I haven't even opened it yet and was worried I was, like, totally behind." She exhales dramatically, her entire chest rising and falling. "Do you want to go to the library tomorrow, work together on it? Maybe grab Starbucks before or something?"

I nod. "Sure. That sounds fun."

"Cool!" She grins, and I notice a bit of red lipstick has migrated to her teeth. "See you then."

I swallow the lump in my throat and nod as I reach for my door handle.

"Oh and, Sara, I almost forgot."

I spin around so quickly I curse myself for seeming overeager. "Yeah?"

"Def let us know if the music bothers you. We'd be happy to turn it down." She's back in the room, the door slamming between us, before I can think of a reply.

I step into my room and set my bag on the kitchenette table. I really lucked out being placed in the new building, with suite-style quads.

The other bedroom door is closed, with sweet smoke and trance-y music radiating from the cracks around the frame. Not really my scene.

My roommate—the one I share a bedroom with—Tiff, is sitting on our couch, the bluish light of her MacBook illuminating her round face.

"Hey!" she says. "How's your day been?"

"Well," I say, stepping forward. "My first class was—"

She turns and pulls an earbud out of her ear. She wrinkles her nose at me. "I'm Skyping my boyfriend," she says definitively.

"Oh…sorry." I pick up my bag and go into our bedroom, closing the door quietly behind me.

I step over a hot pink bra, an empty Red Bull can and a history textbook as I make my way to my side of the room. I hang my bag on its hook and kneel on my pink shag rug as I place my loafers under my bed, in their spot between my Sperrys and black pumps.

Movie night? I text Yaz.

Using my step stool, I climb onto my captain's height bed. I scroll through Instafriend while I wait for her to respond. The pictures tonight are mainly sunny skies, palm trees and backpacks, mixed in with red cups and low-cut dresses and eyes tracking just left of the camera. First week of school pictures have a little more variety in college.

I fall back onto my bed, cuddling my stuffed dolphin toy and setting my phone on my stomach.

Buzz. It vibrates again and I almost drop it flipping it over so quickly.

Yaz: sorry can't. On a date!

My heart sinks.

Yaz: Thought you had to work all weekend. Did you guys figure out your project?!

I stare at the text for a second before sending a quick **no worries and no luck yet** and standing up. On the other side of the wall, the opening bars of "Sunday Candy" ring out. The room reacts immediately, mostly with "oohs" and "ahhs" but also with a single male vice that yells "Overplayed!" He is immediately met with boos.

I hum along as I peel off my clothes and hang up my skirt in the wardrobe, then place my shirt and bra in my hamper.

I pull on my pink-and-white polka-dot pajamas. They're the old-fashioned kind that button down the front and make me feel very put together and glamorous. At least, they usually do.

I pad across the room to the sink. There is one shower and toilet for the whole apartment, but each room has its own sink and mirror.

I set my phone on my little shelf below the mirror, where my skin products are arranged.

Tiff has only a toothbrush—mysteriously, no toothpaste to be seen. *Is she using mine?*—and a bar of soap, sans soap dish.

I sigh and grab a scrunchie, then pull my hair back and turn on the faucet. I scrub my face in circular motions, staring at myself in the mirror. The glass vibrates slightly from the music next door.

I splash water on my face, carefully apply toner, and then moisturize.

After setting a timer for two minutes, I brush my teeth.

"Shots, shots, shots!" they chant next door. I spit toothpaste into the sink a little too aggressively. I fix all the bottles so they are labels out and then pick up my phone and scroll to my RA's contact.

Me: hey can you please ask them to quiet down. Room 212.

Greta (RA): Hi! I am not around the dorm right now, but maybe try whoever's on call

Awesome, even my RA has more of a life than me. I shut off the light and get under the covers, pulling my comforter around me to make a little cocoon.

I sigh and open Snapchat. I click through the flashing images: of beer pong games and concerts downtown, of girls laughing over dinner and boys shotgunning beers at the count of one, two, three. There is even a Syllabus Week filter, so it is definitely, like, a *thing*. I watch grainy videos that pan around rooms like the ones next door. Girls wink at the camera and guys flip it off and everyone seems to be having a grand old time.

An alert flashes across the top of my screen and my heart betrays me by beating a little faster.

I have a Snapchat from Chris Miller.

I take a deep breath and open it. It's a selfie in a car that features only part of his face and the boys behind him in the backseat.

Boys night the caption reads. He looks good. His eyes sort of sparkle from the flash.

It makes me want to vomit.

Even so, I swipe to the side to reply. I sit up and give my best "disinterested and beautiful" pose. My face looks good in the camera. A tiny bit of remaining eyeliner still darkens my eyes, and I'm glow-y from the moisturizer.

I hover over the center button that would take the picture. Behind me, you can clearly see the stuffed animals and books on my shelf. And the clock on the top of the screen says nine-thirty.

I exit out of the camera.

And although I know it will just make me sad, I check

anyways. And sure enough, right there in his Snap story, the boys' night picture.

I put in my headphones and lie back down. *Since I'm already being masochistic enough…*

I open iMessage and click on his name. I scroll past the most recent stuff, the messages that were weeks apart: when do you leave for college? and happy birthday sorry this is late and how have you been?

I go back to the good stuff. The talk every day, your mom asks who you're texting during dinner, losing sleep staring at your phone until four, everything they say is perfect, stuff.

We met at a party. It was my grade school best friend Claire's seventeenth birthday. Claire and I went to different schools after eighth grade, and by the time this party rolled around, our friendship had diminished to getting Caribou Coffee every few months and our moms talking to each other about how each of us was doing. So I'm sure my invite was more out of obligation than anything.

But I went anyway. By that point in high school, I think my parents had started to worry about the number of nights I spent in my room, making chem flash cards and streaming *Grey's Anatomy*. So I wasn't about to turn away an invite to a Real High School Party.

It was over the summer, and one of those days that stayed hot, even after the sun went down. The warm Minnesota summer reminding us of how much we had wished for the heat all winter.

The event was in her backyard, with twinkly lights strung overhead and country music radiating from an iHome. And vodka in a water bottle hidden behind the swing set.

When Chris came up to me, I was sitting alone, watching

the fire crackle, while most people clustered together, talking in groups of three or four.

I had lingered near one cluster for a while, but no one stepped back to let me in, and I was too self-conscious to push forward. So I took a seat and drank the orange soda that I was too scared to spike and thought about how I should've just stayed home.

"Too good for us?"

"What?" I looked up to see a tall, skinny boy with hair that looked like he put effort into. Effort that paid off.

"You're sitting here all alone." He gestured toward my bench.

"I, um, I'm just shy." I twisted the tab of the soda can around. It was partially true. Sure, I could speak in front of hundreds at a Model UN conference, no problem, and didn't even blink before speaking up in class. But a party—a party with alcohol and kids who went to parties a lot... That was a bit different.

He sat down next to me. "I can be shy sometimes too."

I nodded and kept my eyes on the fire.

"You got a name?"

I smiled and turned to him. "Sara," I said. "With no *h*."

He looked at me, confused.

"At the end," I clarified.

"Ahhh." He said. "I'm Chris Miller. There is an *h*."

"Nice to meet you." I looked back to the fire.

"Well, Sara without an *h*, would you like some?" He held out a can of Sprite.

"Is there...um...?" I looked at him.

"...booze?"

"Yeah." I blushed.

He grinned, and I noticed his smile was kind of crooked. "Yeah."

I pursed my lips.

"If you don't want—"

I grabbed the can from him, bringing it to my lips and taking the smallest sip possible.

"So what's your favorite subject in school?" I said as I handed it back.

We talked until the end of the party, and I kept taking sips of vodka Sprite so small that I hoped they didn't count any more than church wine.

When I got home, I had a Facebook friend request from Chris Miller. I accepted it, and got a message within a minute.

Glad you told me there was no h. Otherwise I wouldn't have found you.

I could see the reflection of my smile on the screen as I typed my reply.

Facebook turned to iMessage and summer turned to fall. We were talking every day, and the texts were getting flirtier and flirtier.

One night, hours into clever back-and-forths, he messaged **damn I wish we went to the same school so we could hang out.** A week later he said **homecoming is coming up and I don't know who to ask.**

Both times I stared at the text until it was burned into my brain, but was too nervous to push further, to say that we could hang out anyway, or that he could invite *me*.

I was hoping that if I was just funny enough over text or pretty enough on Snapchat, he would figure it out himself.

I thought we really had something, or at least were building to something.

A few weeks into school, I had lunch at the mall with Claire.

"Do you want to look around a bit?" she asked, after we paid for our fancy mac and cheeses and strawberry lemonades at the Cheesecake Factory.

"Sure!" I slung my Michael Kors purse over my arm and we made our way toward one of the department stores.

We talked about the social media posts of people we hadn't seen since eighth grade as we waded through the semiformal dresses in the Juniors' section.

Claire picked a dress up off the rack and held it up. "This one would look really cute on you. You have the boobs for it," she said. "I wish I did." She adjusted her T-shirt.

"There's nothing wrong with your boobs," I said as I walked over to her.

She rolled her eyes. "You say that, but you don't know I'm wearing a bra with two cup sizes of padding."

I laughed and examined the dress. It was lavender with a sweetheart style neckline. I took the hanger from her.

"I did already buy a dress, but this one is really pretty." I mentally counted the babysitting money I still had after lunch. "And if I end up going to two dances, it would be nice to have a different dress."

"Two dances?" she asked, not looking up from the rack as she pushed a bunch of dresses over, the hangers making a loud screeching sound.

"Well..." I bit my lip and looked at the dress, not her. "Maybe I if I go with Chris, to um, your school's." I looked up, wanting to gauge her reaction, in case he'd said anything to her about me.

Her head snapped up. "Chris, like Chris Miller?"

"Um, yeah."

"How does he even know you exist?"

I flinched. "We talked at your party. And we've been texting since. We have a Snapstreak."

"I don't know." She picked up a dress. "That might not mean anything. He talks to a lot of girls."

I put the dress back on the hanger. *I don't think he talks to a lot of girls as much as he talks to me.*

Heck, there would be no time left in his day. I was falling behind on sleep and deadlines talking to him, and there was definitely no one else in my picture.

By the time I pulled into my driveway after the mall I had a text.

Chris: Why did you think we'd be going to hc together?

I stared down at the screen, the radio still playing and the engine still running, and suddenly it felt like my heart was in my butt.

Me: I didn't mean to assume anything

Me: I just thought with how much we've been talking

I sighed and turned off the engine while I tried to formulate my next text, explain to him what I thought he was a part of. What I thought we were.

My phone buzzed in my hand.

Chris: We don't even go to same school or have same friend group

Chris: Don't get me wrong it's fun texting with you. But I don't want you to think this is something it's not.

In my dorm more than a year later, I stare at the text that made me cry for twenty minutes while sitting in my driveway.

It wasn't the first time I'd made up love in my mind. Listening to Taylor Swift as I lay in bed, staring at the ceiling, imagining dates and cute moments and a life with a person, just because he had a nice smile or said I was pretty one time.

It was a fun sort of bittersweet pain. Easier than the dull ache of loneliness was the drama, the saga of unrequited love for someone who was half real, half your own imagination. But it was kids' stuff.

I plug in my phone in and set it on my shelf. Framed next to it is the poster I bought on Etsy that says Who Run the World?

I don't have time for distractions anyway.

chapter six

Braden

My phone buzzes against the table, again. Sara looks up, sending daggers my way.

I shrug and read my message. It's not my fault; it's Friday night.

She sighs. "Could you please take this seriously?"

"What?" I don't look up from my phone. "I didn't text myself." I set my phone down and meet her gaze, daring her to say more.

Robbie starts to chuckle but quickly masks it with a cough when she turns her Stare of Disdain in his direction.

"Ugh." She types something on her computer rapidly, her many bracelets jingling as she researches God knows what dead end or already-done idea. Or maybe she's just documenting all the ways I annoy her.

I fold my arms over my chest. It's not like I wasn't worried about this too. I realize how royally fucked we are. More than halfway to the deadline with zero done. But it's not like sitting here stressing and running through her weird improv design games—or whatever they're called—is gonna get us any closer. I might as well be getting drunk somewhere.

Another text lights up my phone, almost on cue.

I lean back on the couch and put my feet on the table. We're in the lounge of Sara's and Robbie's dorm this time, sitting on half-worn-through cloth couches, as people wander around us, playing foosball or discussing some nerd TV show. A group walks by laughing loudly as they drag a keg toward their dorm room.

Sara, in her latest email analysis of our progress, had mused that maybe working in the HP Garage was putting too much pressure on us. So far we aren't having any better luck here.

She's staring at her screen now, fingers poised above the keys as if she's waiting for something to happen.

"Maybe if you flip upside down the creativity will fall to the top of your brain," I suggest.

"Ha-ha." She makes a face at me. "Thank you for finally contributing to the group."

Next to me on the couch, Robbie is ignoring us, clearly checking his email.

"No, I'm serious," I say. "I learned it in *my* 'design thinking' class. East Coast style is different."

She sticks her tongue out at me, a surprisingly young reaction from someone who likes to pretend she's already thirty. It's so out of character that it's kind of charming.

"Are you making fun of me?" she asks.

"Not at all." I smile slyly. "It's a real technique."

"Okay, fine." She looks at me with *I dare you* in her eyes, closes her laptop carefully and sets it on the seat next to her. She flips over, swinging her legs up to rest against the back

of the couch, her head hanging off the end, blond hair pooling on the floor.

I snort, and Robbie looks up from his email, confused,
before breaking into the biggest smile I've seen on him since
we became part of this godforsaken group.

For a second I almost forget how much I don't want to be
here. My phone buzzes again. *Almost.*

I stand without a word and start packing my bag. Maybe
they won't notice I'm gone if I make my exit stealthily.

"What are you doing?" Sara's eyes narrow.

"Uh, leaving." I continue to pack my things.

Her jaw drops, or, I guess lifts, as she is upside down. The
amusement of a moment ago pops like a soap bubble. She
scrambles back up to sit normally.

"You've got to be kidding." Her voice is angry, but in a
calm way. She doesn't yell. "You take three follow-up emails
before you respond to anything, you show up late to meetings to shoot down ideas and call me *babe* and *Blondie* more
often than my name. And now you want to leave early, two
weeks before we're presenting? Give me one reason why we
shouldn't kick you out of our group right now."

"Because I'm all you've got." I sling my messenger bag over
my shoulder. "You need three people in your group, and no
grad student is going to join two freshmen without an idea,
no matter how many 'ideation' charts you make."

Robbie sighs. "He's right."

"So you're really going to leave?" she asks.

I check my phone, quickly responding that I'm on my way.
"What?" I shrug. "It's the biggest party of the year—you don't
expect me to stay here, do you?"

"And yet you expect us to?" she snaps back.

I raise my eyebrows. A daring move, but an empty threat I'm sure. I think of all the project emails I got from her between 10:00 p.m. and 3:00 a.m. last Saturday. "No, I don't. You're welcome to come with."

Sara crosses her arms, "Well, maybe we will."

"We what?" Robbie looks from me to her and back.

Sara stands, brushes a piece of lint off her dress pants and looks me dead in the eyes.

"I mean," Robbie says, looking down at the crumpled papers in front of him, "I want to give up for the night as much as any anyone but—"

"No," Sara says, eyes unwavering. "Braden is right—we are stuck with each other. And if we have to work with him, he has to party with us. We're in this together, whether we want to be or not."

She's daring me to sit back down in a huff, to admit that if they aren't doing the work for me, I'll see the need to do it on a Friday night. But I'm not about to give her the satisfaction. "Fine, but the buses leave in an hour and I want to have at least two drinks at the pregame, so I'm only gonna give you fifteen minutes to change."

"Buses?" Robbie asks.

"Change?" Sara asks, looking down at her ensemble.

"Yes." I turn to Robbie. "To the club in the city. And—" I look Sara up and down, blouse buttoned up to her neck and form-concealing pants, and laugh "—yes. Change."

I wait outside their dorm and smoke a cigarette. The door behind me clicks and I turn to see Robbie.

"What's up?" I nod my head.

He waves.

"Smoke?" I ask.

He shakes his head.

I nod. "Most West Coasters don't. I'll never adjust to the looks I get, like I'm killing kittens or something."

He hops onto the little brick wall I'm leaning against. "A lot of my friends did in high school." He stretches his arms above his head, yawning. "I just don't see the appeal." He re-adjusts the way he's sitting. "It doesn't seem worth it to me. But I don't...judge you or anything."

I nod and look at the ground. I flick some ash off the end of my cigarette and watch it as it flitters toward the pavement, then take another drag.

"Although..." He half smiles, his eyes lighting up mischievously. "Cats can get lung cancer, especially if their owner smokes, so you, uh, kind of might be killing kittens."

I laugh and cough out the rest of the smoke I was blowing. "I guess I really am the devil then."

He turns and looks toward the dorm behind us. "Depends on who you ask."

"True." I pause to take another drag. "You know, I really am willing to do my part. I'm not trying to get you guys to do all the work. I just can't deal with all the sitting around stressing. Running through the same ideas that will never work, pretending to move forward and wasting time."

"Yeah, I know." He clears his throat. I can't tell if he's being honest or just trying to be nice. "And I get that Sara can be a little high-strung or, like, overzealous sometimes. But I don't know if pushing her buttons is the best way to deal with that."

"But it's just so fun." I put my cigarette out on the stone bench.

As I look over my shoulder at the dorm, the front door swings open. Out steps a blonde, her hair reflecting the light from the streetlamp. A tight black dress hugs her curves, and when she steps forward it is with a grace few can manage in stilettos that high. Her makeup still looks natural but is slightly darker and smokier near her sparkling eyes, and there's a dash of bright red across her lips. Sara looks hot.

Heat rushes to my face and I avert my gaze, realizing I've been staring—gaping, practically the entire time she's been walking toward us. And so has Robbie.

"What?" she asks. Like she genuinely doesn't understand our reactions. "Am I too dressed up?"

"No, you're perfect—I mean, fine, you're fine." I stalk forward, "We're just late." I take off down the street.

The preparty is in full swing by the time we arrive at the Sigma Alpha frat house, one of the ones that hasn't gone coed yet, ignoring the trend that's been sweeping campus since some girl pulled a stunt last year and pledged a fraternity. Loud music—the most recent chart-topping pop song—emanates from the house. Through the window, colored lights swing through the crowd, lighting up people dancing or sipping from red cups. The entrance is jammed with students trying to get through the door, which is guarded by a member of the house. They reach past each other, yelling, positioning themselves to get closer. Warren's out in full force since undergrads—or at least undergrads not in Professor Thomas's class—haven't been assigned much work yet.

"Looks unlikely we'll get in," Robbie says.

"Don't worry about it," I say. "Just follow me."

He shrugs. "Whatever you say—it's your night, man."

"Excuse me." I push through the crowd. I stand tall, like I'm meant to be there. Like I'm there all the time and annoyed at the sudden crowd. People step aside for me, my confidence separating our group from their desperation like oil in water.

Glancing behind me, I see that Sara is just feet behind but Robbie has been cut off from us by the shifting crowd. "Yo, hurry up," I yell back to him.

He pushes himself through the crowd.

When I turn back, Sara is already through the door, looking back at us and waiting.

I try to step forward and an arm reaches out to stop me. "No freshmen," the frat member playing bouncer tells me.

"Yeah, yeah." I nod. "Connor invited me. I'm a potential pledge." I pull out my phone and show him the texts from my high school friend who is now in Sig A. I remember Robbie. "And he's with me."

He examines the messages, grabbing my phone to look more closely.

"Yeah, okay." He nods and steps aside to let us through.

"What was that about?" Sara asks.

"We're dudes," I answer.

She seems confused, but I don't have time right now to explain the way the world works. We make our way down a hall, through more people, some of them leaning against the walls, flirting while casually sipping drinks, others loudly and excitedly telling stories fueled by alcohol and Syllabus Week excitement. There is a roar of noise, music and conversation, but no words are discernible.

I turn to Sara and watch as she takes it all in, her analytical mind probably trying to figure out what decision-making strategy the fraternity brothers used to choose the music and the cheap booze.

Speaking of, at the end of a hall there's a table with a few open boxes of wine and 30s of beer. I pick up a Rolling Rock and examine it, wondering if the taste is worth the 5 percent alcohol content.

"Braden!" I set down the beer and look up to see Connor rushing toward me. He is still wearing his hair in that over-done boy-band-wannabe way, and his face is already flushed and sweaty from the party.

"Hey!"

He pulls me into a hug.

"These are my...friends, Sara and Robbie," I say. "And this is Connor—he was my prefect at boarding school."

"No way!" Sara's eyes glow. "Like *Harry Potter*. They really call it that?"

Connor laughs. "Yeah, they really do." He reaches out to shake her hand, then Robbie's. "Nice to meet you, guys. Can I get you anything?" He turns toward the table and picks up a box of "sunset" flavor wine, then examines the label. "Ah come on, y'all shouldn't be drinking this shit." He sets it back down. "I'm so sorry—we are terrible hosts."

"Eh, we're freshmen," I say. "I'm just happy to be inside the party."

"Come with me, I'll help you guys out," he says. We follow him past the dance floor and toward the stairs, where a scene similar to the front door is playing out. A Sigma Alpha brother guards a mob of people trying to explain why they should be able to get upstairs.

The guy waves when he sees Connor, and tells people to let us through. We make our way up the stairs and down the hall to the door with his name on it.

Connor swings it open to reveal a room crammed with three beds—two bunked and one raised above a desk. The furniture is the standard-issue kind provided by housing, the kind finally picked up by my movers. On the desk are a few books about international relations and computer science as well as a bottle of Patrón with about a shot left and a collection of squished limes. There's also a half-empty bottle of Grey Goose.

"Help yourself to any of that." He gestures toward the desk. "Or we have this if you prefer." He pulls a bottle of champagne from his mini fridge. I take a swig of the Goose and throw him a thumbs-up. "Here, you'll need these." He holds out a handful of wristbands.

I set down the bottle and grab them, shoving them in my pocket.

We bring the champagne with us as we head outside to load the party buses. The front lawn is chaos, as those heading from the house to the bus merge with the crowd that never made it inside.

"Sara!" someone yells from behind us.

I turn to see a redhead flying toward us and hug-tackling Sara in the classic drunk-girl way.

"Oh my god, how *are* you?" she asks, like she hasn't seen Sara in years, rather than since, let's be real, probably lecture this afternoon.

"Uh… I'm pretty good." Sara stumbles back a bit, confirming my suspicion that this greeting was a bit overzealous.

"Can you believe this bullshit? They're barely letting anyone on the buses! I tried to pay them but they wouldn't take my money."

"Pay them?" Sara looks confused. "You don't need to do that. It's a party for Warren students."

"Yeah I know, but *'it's a private party though.'*" She does a voice for the second half—Generic Dopey Drunk Dude, I think it is. "I guess the house rented the bus so they can pick who they invite."

"Here." I pull the colored wristbands Connor gave me from my pocket. I hand one of the orange strips of paper to her, and she squeals. *Okaaay then.* I give the other two to Sara and Robbie, who take them more calmly.

"Oh my god, thank you." The girl stares at her wristband like it's Cartier. "What was your name again?" Now she looks at me like *I'm* Cartier.

"Braden."

"Braden." She steps a bit closer. "Thank you. I'm Colleen."

She carefully steps around Sara and closer to me, her arm brushing against mine as we file toward the front of the line. As we climb onto the bus, she leans over to take my hand. "Let's sit together, *Braden*."

chapter seven

Sara

When Braden had said buses would come to take us to the city, I'd pictured the big yellow kind that used to bring us on school field trips, with brown pleather bench seats that split to reveal foam that everyone would pick at, and those windows that slid down when you pinched the sides. Or maybe even one of those coach buses, like the ones that took us to work events at my internship last summer, with plush seats that had real seat belts and high ceilings with luggage storage.

I had definitely not pictured *this*. The inside of this bus glows purple from the lights on the ceiling. The sides are lined with black leather seats, like couches. Above them are big mirrors, interrupted only by large speakers. Along the back is a bar and a cooler, which was empty save for ice but is quickly being filled with beer and liquor by the boarding students. In the middle of the bus are three large silver poles. *Stripper poles.*

"Interesting way to get around," I say to Robbie.

He just nods, the back of his neck turning red.

I step around the stripper poles quite deliberately and take a seat.

"Oh my god, Sara." Colleen plops down on the other side of me, flipping her fiery hair over her shoulder and sending a breeze that smells of perfume and whiskey my way. I'm surprised that she's sitting with me, considering how she's treated me in the past. Maybe it's just because Braden is busy haggling with the driver about the aux cord. Though maybe that's not fair. Maybe I judged Colleen too soon. "This is *so cool*. Thank you so much for getting me on here—you are *so cool*."

"Uh, no problem." I smile.

"So, this guy Braden..." She leans in closer to me, but doesn't do a very good job of lowering her voice. "Is he, like, *in* Sig A?"

"In what?"

She looks at me sideways. "Sigma Alpha. The frat, silly, the one whose party we were just at."

"Oh, uh..." I look around for Braden, but he's still on the other end of the bus, talking to a girl who is leaning against one of the stripper poles. "No...he's rushing, I guess, so maybe he will be soon."

"He knows someone in it though?"

"Yeah from high school. His old prefect."

"Oh." She considers this, turning to look at him again. She snaps her head back toward me. "Prefect?"

I am about to say *Yeah, I know! Like Harry Potter!* but she charges forward with the conversation.

"So he went to boarding school? Do you know which one? Exeter? St. Paul's?"

I shake my head. "Sorry, I honestly don't know."

She nods, lost in thought again. I look at the wristband fastened where my watch usually is, and then glance at the doorway where people are still petitioning to get on. *This is so weird.*

I was never popular in high school, or middle school, for that matter. I had some friends for sure, people I cared about and spent time with. Someone to talk to during class or sit with at lunch and hang out with a couple times a month. I think I was liked well enough. But I was no homecoming queen. I didn't play the cool sports or go to the cool parties. My friends and I had movie nights and got pizza in town like once a month or so; we didn't sneak out or throw parties in our basements or caravan to music festivals or crash parties at nearby colleges.

Honestly, I was fine with that. I liked that my friends were nice people, and while it might have been fun to do some of the things the cool kids did, I didn't ever feel the desire to be "cool." I knew it was totally arbitrary, why some people were considered popular and others not. It was bullshit.

But there was a tiny part of me tonight that felt a thrill when I got to walk past crowds wanting to get into the house and on the bus—wanting to go where I was going. Part of me felt proud when Colleen thanked me for helping her get here too.

I hated that I liked it.

"Sara, you want to help with this?" I look up to see Real Life Percy Weasley—Connor—holding out a bottle of champagne. Excitement surges through me.

"Yes! I've always wanted to do that!"

He hands me the bottle. "Okay, you take the little cage

thing off, yeah like that, and then twist the cork and pull it out—but don't aim it at anyone."

I begin to twist the cork and it shoots off just as the bus jolts forward. I squeal as champagne spews into the party bus full of party people, who laugh and smile at me. So many people are looking at me, and they are not staring, not wondering why this girl is talking so much in class or bossing around the group project. They are looking at me like I am pretty, like I am fun.

I take a sip of the champagne right out of the bottle. It tastes great, like Christmas dinner and New Year's Eve and weddings. Not sour and bitter like the other alcohol I've tried.

It's much easier to drink when you aren't cringing at every sip, and by the time we get to the city, I find myself laughing more easily and swaying with the motion of the bus.

We finally arrive at the club and disembark. I thank the driver as I wobble down the stairs, not sure if it's the champagne or my shoes making it such a problem. I reach for Robbie's arm, to balance myself.

"Are you all right?" He turns to me with concern in his eyes.

I swallow and nod, suddenly speechless.

We line up at the club. Colleen and Braden somehow make it to the front of the line right away, but Robbie and I hang back, not wanting to cut anyone. We get our hands stamped by a large man in a tight black shirt and head inside. The club is rapidly filling, and colored lights sweep over the dim downstairs dance floor. Across the room is a bar and a DJ stand that is currently emanating a remix of a Drake song while the DJ holds a headphone to his ear with one hand and pushes buttons with the other.

Above my head, a sort of balcony circles the room, accessible by a sweeping staircase at the edge of the dance floor. On the balcony are big leather booths and tables with sparkling chandeliers hanging above them.

People rush by me, some heading straight to the dance floor, others swarming the bar.

I see Braden across the room, and the flash of a credit card being handed over before a bouncer moves to let him upstairs. Colleen is on his arm, and following close behind are a number of girls in similarly tight, short dresses. I guess she's done with me then. It stings, but what did I really expect, given how she's treated me these past two weeks?

"Look at Braden," I turn to Robbie and say.

"Yep." He shrugs. "Classic. Want to get a drink?"

I follow him through the crowd circling the bar, everyone trying to get the bartender's attention. He's a young guy, not much older than us, in a gray T-shirt and tattoos down his arm. Like most bartenders I've seen, he's quite good-looking; I wonder if that's a requirement for the job.

Then again, most bartenders I've seen have been on TV.

I watch him pour translucent gold liquid into a line of shot glasses. *Tequila.* My stomach turns over just thinking about the smell. I wonder if it's bad to order wine at a club like this. Or champagne, for that matter. Most of the people around me seem to be taking shots.

"Do you think they have a cocktail menu?" I ask Robbie.

"Hmmm." He examines the crowd in front of us. At the other corner of the bar, two girls lean forward, extending fistfuls of cash toward the bartender as they try to get his attention, half their chests hanging out of their dresses. "I'm gonna go with probably not."

The bartender looks toward us as he moves one of those silver shaker things. Robbie waves his hand and smiles. The bartender nods and holds up one finger.

"Oh jeez," I say. "Decision time. What should I get?"

Robbie laughs and the sound makes me smile. It makes me proud that I am the reason for the laugh, even if I am sincerely a bit worried about ordering. "Well, what do you want?"

"That's the thing." I feign an exaggerated look of distress. "I don't know!"

"Do you want shots? Or a G and T, maybe a Long Island Iced Tea?"

"Iced tea?" I am a huge fan of Arizona cranberry iced tea; I would love an alcoholic drink that delicious and refreshing.

"Yeah, there's like five different kinds of alcohol and—"

"Oh." My eyes go wide. "Definitely not that."

Suddenly, the bartender is in front of us. "What can I get you?" And just like that, time is up. My heart starts to race. It's like walking into a class and realizing there's a test you haven't prepared for. Truly a nightmare scenario.

"I—uh—" I stammer.

"I'll have a beer." Robbie swoops in to save me. He names some brand.

The bartender reaches for an amber bottle and pops the top off with expert grace before handing it to him.

"And you?"

I keep my voice as low as I can, considering the blaring music. "Do you have anything that has alcohol but doesn't taste like it does at all?"

He laughs, but not in a mean or mocking way. More like he thinks I'm a lovable idiot. "I got you." He starts to fill a glass with ice.

A few seconds later, he hands me something pink and sparkly that costs twelve dollars. I take a sip; it tastes like something they might have served at Libby Lu back in the day. Worth every penny.

Robbie and I lean against the bar, sipping our drinks and watching the revelers. Across the room, I spot Braden and Colleen on the balcony, leaning against the railing and looking down at the dance floor. He taps her shoulder and points. I follow his hand to see a waiter walking toward them with a large bottle of alcohol on a silver tray, a sparkler burning from the top, sending glittering embers into the air, floating for a moment before delicately burning out.

Her eyes light up as Braden gestures to the waiter to hand the sparkling bottle to her. She kisses Braden's cheek before taking it.

"Do you think she's with him because he got us in?" I ask.

"What?"

I turn to Robbie, who's staring at the DJ stand. "Them." I nod my head toward the lovers on the balcony.

"Oh. Maybe." He examines them. "Or maybe it's because his watch is worth more than our tuition."

I try to focus on the hardware on Braden's wrist from across the dance floor. It looks nice, but I can't imagine how a watch could be *that* nice.

"Maybe it's his charming personality." I take a sip from my drink.

Robbie laughs.

I move the glass away from my lips. "He can be kind of funny though, in a sarcastic way." I watch him talk to Colleen. "That is, when he's not making me pull my hair out." I turn back to Robbie. The colored lights of the club dance across his face in the shadows. I never really noticed how nice a jawline he has. I briefly wonder if he's ever thought about modeling, or if anyone has ever approached him to sell products on his Instagram. I worry in my tipsiness I've been looking for too long.

I set down my glass, now just ice, on the counter.

"Another?" the bartender asks.

"Sure—actually, make it two," I say, still not knowing what it was. I turn to Robbie. "On me, for being the only team-mate I can tolerate."

"Thanks but…I can't drink that," he says.

"Why not? It's delicious." The bartender sets two cocktail napkins and then two beautiful pink concoctions in front of us.

"All right." Robbie sighs and picks up the drink. He takes a sip and raises his eyebrows. "You know, masculine pride is bullshit anyway."

One frosty pink drink later, I am trying not to blush as people start to grind on the dance floor a few feet away. I look down at the bar. At my hand, which is just inches from Robbie's. Goose bumps tingle up my arm. I don't know if it's the drink, or seeing him outside the library, but I find myself making an effort to remember that Robbie is just my friend and class partner, and it would be inappropriate to hold his hand.

"People are so wild." I look up. Robbie has evidently not been thinking about, or looking at, me. I turn to see what he is talking about. The dance floor is full of couples and clusters of friends.

A girl in a pink dress so cute that I want to ask her where she got it is dancing with her friends when a dude walks up behind her and grabs her waist. But instead of slapping him in the face or walking away, she giggles and starts grinding on him.

I turn to Robbie and say, "I wish there was a way to meet someone that wasn't so bullshit. Somewhere besides a party."

He shrugs. "There's online dating."

"Yeah, but, like, how do you know someone's not a serial killer?" I sip whatever drops of my drink are left among the ice at the bottom of the glass.

"Hey, maybe that could be our start-up," he says. "A serial-killer-free dating app." He waves his arm, as if to paint a picture of this visionary idea.

"Ha-ha, quite funny." I smile and look away, not wanting to get into a conversation about the project, even a facetious one.

Across the dance floor, a large bouncer moves the red velvet rope for a moment to let Braden and Colleen down while fending off the requests of the crowd haggling to get upstairs.

They walk toward us.

"Hey, guys," Braden says as soon as they are close enough for us to hear. He then turns to Colleen, "Looks like the bathroom's right over there."

She smiles and looks past him to me. "Hey, Sara." She wiggles a hand at me.

I wave back halfheartedly before she disappears toward the ladies' room.

"Women," Braden says, like I'm not one. "This girl acts like she can't make it to the shitter without me."

"You're disgusting," I say.

He doesn't care. "May as well order while I'm down here" He waves at bartender. "Save on tip."

"I'm pretty sure you still tip if you order at the bar," Robbie says.

"Why?" Braden asks, not looking up from the bottle service menu. "They barely do anything. Just hand it to me."

Braden leans over the bar and inquires about ordering another bottle. I overhear the guy saying it'll be an extra fifty for the sparkler, and Braden countering that the upcharge was only twenty before.

"It's all so made up," I say in Robbie's ear. "Who can go in the house, who can get on the bus, who is a VIP. People are idiots."

"What's that?" a voice says.

I turn to Braden. A disco light flashes behind him, shining through the edges of his hair like a halo. *A halo on the devil, how ironic.*

"I was, um, saying—"

"People aren't stupid," he interrupts, seeming to have actually heard me just fine. "They just know the game. You get to sit at the cool kids' table if you bring the class cookies. You get to go to the prom after-party if you buy the limo. Bottles and tables at clubs, the red rope—they're just the grown-up version," he says. "People know there's value in being wanted, and that it's the kind of value you can count in Benjamins."

A waiter taps him on the shoulder, and he signs a bill after barely glancing at it. "Yes, the boundaries are arbitrary," he says. "But they *are* real. People sell them."

Before I can say anything in reply, Colleen is back and they are gone.

"I mean, kind of," Robbie says to me as they walk away. "They've monetized around status but no one has really sold it directly. They sell hair products and perfume and expensive clothes to make you seem wanted, but no one has formalized selling, like, acknowledgment of social status directly."

"What would that be? A sticker you can put on your forehead, saying you're a ten?"

He smiles and my heart flutters. "Something like that."

I just shrug and sip my new drink.

The sun burns my eyes when I open them the next morning. I guess I forgot to close my blinds when I got home last night. I sit up only to realize I also forgot to change into my pajamas; I'm still wearing the tight black dress. At least I remembered to take off my shoes, even if they are just tossed on the floor and not placed neatly in their spot. In fact, I think I may have taken them off on the walk back with Robbie and Braden, who ended the night with us since Colleen went home with Connor. I shudder when I think about how dirty the sidewalk must have been, but at the time my drunk brain could only think about the pain of my heels.

I rub my eyes, and my hand comes away smeared with black eyeliner. *Great.* I hope my skin doesn't break out because of this disruption in my cleansing and moisturizing routine.

I peel off my dress and throw it in the bright pink hamper, then pull on athletic shorts and a Warren sweatshirt. I place my shoes under my bed quietly, so as not to wake the still-snoring Tiff, and head to the main room to make coffee.

The two girls from the other room are early risers, so I'm expecting to see at least one of them when I open the door.

Instead, I see Robbie sitting on my couch, dark circles under his eyes, typing rapidly into a MacBook. Heat rushes to my face, and I cross my arms. My sweatshirt is thick, but I am not wearing a bra. Plus, I'm a wreck. Not that I should care; it's just Robbie. Robbie, whose eyes look dreamy and romantic, even though he is looking at code on his computer. I don't know what's getting into me lately.

"What are you doing here?" He lives in the same dorm as me, so I know how he got in the building, but what's he doing in my room?

He looks up. "Oh good, you're up. We've got a lot of work to do."

"How did you get in here?"

"Your roommates let me in," he says, a little more *duh* in his voice than I'd prefer. "I didn't want to bother you, since you had quite an intense night. So I thought I'd just work until you woke up." He says all this while still typing, only slightly slower than before. "But I wanted to catch you as soon as you did, so I thought I'd work here."

I pad across the room and take the spot next to him. "Work on what?"

"This," he says, turning the laptop toward me. I examine the code. The style is probably less elegant than what I would write, but it's easy enough to read.

"What exactly did you do…?"

The front door swings open before I can finish my thought, and none other than Braden Hart saunters in, carrying a tray of coffees and a box of doughnuts.

"We formalized it," he says, holding out a latte to me with that stupid, cute smile plastered across his stupid face.

chapter eight

Roberto

"What does that even mean?" Sara looks at me and runs a hand through her blond hair, which is still slightly disheveled. Even with sleep in her eyes and last night's makeup on her face, she looks beautiful.

She turns to Braden, who is still holding the coffee out to her. She rolls her eyes but takes it.

"Well," I say. "Last night, after Braden and I walked you back from the frat house, we got to talking about all that social status stuff you and I discussed at the party and—"

"It's a dating app!" Braden's eyes glow. "But instead of being for creeps and losers who can't get dates in the real world—"

"Braden!" Sara looks appalled.

I shake my head and reach for my laptop, hoping that if I show her more of the code she will be less appalled by the way he is pitching it.

"Sorry." He shrugs. "Instead of being like that, the selling point is that the *most desirable* people in the area are on it."

"How?"

"Well, Sara, I'm glad you asked." He sounds like he's hosting an infomercial. "Like on Tinder, users of this app can swipe yes or no for the profiles of other users, but *unlike* Tinder, the rating doesn't *just* affect whether they match with the person, but contributes to an overall score, which determines someone's overall rating—platinum, gold, silver, or unrated."

"I don't know." Sara wrinkles her nose. "This sounds like an asshole thing to do. Rate humans like that. And it's misogynistic to award one girl 'platinum' status over another because, what, *more strangers think she's hot*?"

"But the ratings don't just apply to girls," I counter, inserting myself into the conversation before Braden destroys all the work I've done so far. "You said yourself you hate that you can't tell whether guys on these sites are creepy. With this system of girls rating guys back, none of the creeps who spam girls' in-boxes will make it more than a few minutes without getting a rating so low they're knocked out of the system."

"Hmmm." She considers this.

"It's just like we talked about last night—the serial-killer-free dating site. It could be great."

"Plus…" Braden looks up from rooting through the doughnuts. "There's a week until the presentation, and it's the only idea we have."

So we get to work. Posting up all week in Sara's suite, we skip some of our less important classes and shower less often than we probably should. Fueled by coffee and takeout, we start to assemble the skeletal version of Perfect10.

And by *we*, I very much mean me and Sara. Braden "big ideas" Hart does a lot of "supervising."

★ ★ ★

"How have we been looking for the same bug for *two hours*?" Sara lets her head fall to the table. We are sitting in her tiny kitchen, staring at a screen full of code while a rerun of *Jersey Shore* blares in the background and Braden sits with his feet up on the coffee table, laughing along.

I exhale. "I'm asking myself the same question." I examine the code again.

"You know what." Sara's head pops up. "We don't have time for this. We have to start working on building the profiles tonight." She pushes my computer away from her and stands up. "I'll get my laptop from my room, and you and I will start on that.

"Braden." She turns toward the couch. "I need you to take Robbie's computer and fix this bug."

I grimace, thinking back to the first day of class and realizing that when the people in that other group asked him how many coding languages he knew, Braden never really answered. I hope to God he at least knows some Swift.

"Oh, I, uh…" Braden stretches his neck over the edge of the couch, but doesn't sit up. "I can't do that."

"I don't care if you think it's beneath you." Sara looks exasperated. "We just need it done right now."

"It's not that I think it's beneath me." He looks at the remote in his hands, turning it over to examine it more closely. "I just…don't know how to do it."

"What do you mean?" Her tone is ominous.

He sits up slowly. "I, uh, can't code."

"You *what*?" Sara's face goes red.

I just laugh. Because, what else can I do?

"What the hell do you mean you can't *code*? We're *building an app.*" She starts to move toward him, and I wonder if she's going to hit him. I wouldn't blame her, honestly. "Don't you think you should've mentioned that sooner?"

He shrugs. "You never asked."

"Are you fu—" Sara stops herself, almost shaking as she closes her eyes and breathes deeply. She continues more quietly but through gritted teeth. "Just leave."

"What?" He stands up quickly, and the remote clatters to the floor.

"Just get out of my room. The grown-ups need to get some real work done."

"Fine." He picks up his bag roughly. "Like I need any more reason to waste my time here." He storms out and the door slams so hard that it shakes the wall.

"Well then." Sara plops down on the seat next to me. "Back to it, I guess."

"I mean…" I check the time. "Is it really that bad if the text doesn't line up on such an obscure part of the settings page?"

"Yes." She seems shocked I would even ask.

"The odds that Professor Thomas will trigger it when testing it out…"

"It doesn't matter." She draws the computer closer to her. "It has to be perfect just because…" She shakes her head. "Because when I put my name on something, I want to know I did all I could to get it as perfect as possible."

I exhale loudly, but she just keeps typing.

"It's fine the way it is," I say.

"No, it's not." A little crease appears at the top of her nose as she studies the screen. "Wait!" Her eyes go wide. She clicks one button, testing the code, I assume. "Yes! Oh my, that's it." She hops out of her seat, the biggest smile on her face. She sorts of jumps up and down, giggling, she is so giddy.

I lean over to see the screen and the perfectly lined-up sample text, and I can't help but smile as well.

That's the weird thing about someone who is so overzealous about things that seem unimportant. Yes, a lot of times you find yourself shaking your head at how seriously they take the stupid shit. Annoyed at how on your ass they are about using a coaster even when your cup is foam, or scheduling when you will meet to pick the perfect font for your project.

But then you find yourself getting excited along with them when things go right, when they align perfectly. It makes you more passionate. You start rooting for the little details, because you know it makes their heart soar, and the dumb stuff starts to make you happy too.

The next day, Sara lets Braden come back to work, if you can call it that, but forbids him from watching TV.

He starts texting instead.

Two hours into us coding, he looks up from his phone. "So how are we presenting this thing?"

Sara doesn't even look up from her computer. "We need to know what it is before we try to sell it."

"No, we don't." He sits up.

"Uh, *yes, we do*," she says.

"I thought you might say that." Braden grabs his backpack and saunters over to the counter. He unzips his bag and starts rooting through it.

"Oh, he came prepared," I say, without thinking. I'm sure he thinks I'm being sarcastic, but I'm genuinely shocked.

Sara looks up. "What?"

"Do either of you know what this is?" Braden puts a small piece of paper on the fridge with a magnet. It's some sort of company logo, but he has replaced the name of the company with stylized text of the word *logo*.

"Uh, no," I say.

Sara shakes her head.

"This one?" He pins up another piece of paper, with another logo on it.

We both shake our heads.

"That's what I thought." He reaches into his bag again, this time pinning up the classic apple with one bite out of it.

We both laugh.

"Well, of course I know that one," Sara says.

"I mean, dude." I gesture to the two open MacBooks sitting in front of us.

"That's what I'm talking about. Most people don't know what computer is the fastest or has the most storage or capability. Both of you are CS majors and neither of you even knew what company these were without the name—you surely couldn't tell me if they make better computers." He pauses, I'm assuming for effect. "Because what most people know isn't the gritty details in the code and wiring of the thing they're buying. They know which company had the 1984-themed commercial about beating The Man, or which one told them to Think Different in 1997. It's a computer that's advertised with sexy close-ups and displayed in stores with glowing counters like it's a damn modern art gallery. It's Justin Long, while these ones you don't recognize are the old dude whose name you don't remember." He punches the Apple logo with his finger. "They know a simple logo for a simple concept—Mac is sleek, it's smart, it's free and it's young.

People remember that and they open their wallets for that. That's what's important."

"Nice speech." Sara crosses her arms over her chest. "But we aren't presenting to the 'average person,' unfortunately for you, Braden. We are presenting to an expert in tech, and he will know whether it's the fastest, or whether, you know, it works at all, which is the risk we are facing right now. So, if you'll excuse us, Robbie and I need to go back to coding."

"We are presenting to an expert in the tech *business*. He wants to know we can sell—it doesn't matter what we're selling."

Sara scoffs. "Says the guy who refused to work until we had an idea. Thanks, but I'm going to keep coding."

He sighs and joins us at the table. "Then at least put me in charge of the presentation."

"I'm not so sure I want to put you in charge of anything." Sara makes a big show of turning back to her work.

"I think we should let him," I say.

"What? Why?" She looks at me like I'm betraying her.

"Because he just sold me on the idea of becoming a graphic design major for half a second, and I don't actually want to do that at all. If he can talk like that about logos, I trust him to talk about our project well."

"Fine, whatever." She grumbles. "Braden's in charge of the presentation then."

"Great, thanks!" He throws his backpack over his shoulder. "I'm gonna go for a walk. Get the creative juices flowing."

"Do whatever you want," Sara says.

"Thanks, Mom." He kisses the top of her head and is out the door in an instant.

"Useless," Sara sighs, scrubbing her head as if to get rid of his cooties. "I can't believe he gets to put his name on this project too."

"I know." I reach for my water and take a sip. "But hey, maybe we will get to fill out one of those things at the end." I set back down my glass. "Group evaluations where we say who did what and how well, so we can set the record straight."

"Trust me," she says. "I've been writing mine since day one."

chapter nine

Sara

"Dude, it's time to go to sleep," Braden says. He slides the cup of coffee, now cold, away from me.

I hold up my hand to signal this is not an option, not taking my eyes off the screen. My fingers are poised above the keyboard, at the ready. "There has to be some way to make it better."

"Dude, it's due at midnight, and it's—" Braden checks his stupid diamond watch "—eleven-thirty. If you try to 'fix' something, you could ruin the whole damn thing. Just let it go."

He doesn't need to tell me how close we are to the due date. I keep looking from the clock on my microwave to the clock on my computer, as if one might be different.

Braden tilts back the chair he is sitting in and rests his feet against my kitchen table in a way that seems dangerous.

I'd tell him to sit up, but I'm not sure I'd be sad if he fell. "But—"

"Sara." Robbie shakes his head.

I slump into my chair. I expected negativity from Braden, but if Robbie is saying it, it might be right. "I just…" I turn the computer toward them. "It looks like a Myspace page or something."

"Well, yeah, it's not pretty," Braden says. "But I can BS that in the presentation. At least it works."

Robbie and I share a look.

"What was that—?" Braden sits up, his chair making a loud noise as the two legs return to the floor. He narrows his eyes. "It *does* work, right?"

I look toward the ceiling. "Well…"

"Most of the time," Robbie clarifies. "It just, well, it crashes very easily."

"How easily?" Braden is indignant.

Robbie bites his lip. "When there's more than five users."

"What?" Braden looks back and forth between us. "Don't you think he'll test for that kind of thing?"

"Hey," I say, my voice stern. "Those who don't code do not get to complain."

"Jesus Christ." Braden grabs his laptop and swiftly closes it, then slides it under his arm. "I need to go work on my presentation. It's gonna be quite the task to pass this literal piece of shit off as gourmet chocolate."

He storms out. Robbie and I stare at each other as the sound of the slamming door rings in our ears.

"That was a pretty gross metaphor," I finally say, standing up to get a glass of water.

"Yeah."

I lean against the sink and sip my water. "Are we totally screwed?" I ask.

Robbie considers this. "Maybe he will reward us for the ambition of the project we took on."

I make a face. "He said he wanted to fail people. I don't think he's one to give points for trying."

"Yeah." He examines the Chinese menu on the table in front of him.

"Do you want to go with me tomorrow when we have to change majors?" I ask.

"It's a date," he says.

I smile. And I feel warmth in my heart, a sort of relief, that I can smile despite how screwed we are. That he can make me smile.

The next day, I file into the classroom along with the other students who arrived before the doors were unlocked. I pace for a while until I spot Robbie walking through the doors. I cross the aisles toward him.

"Where would you like to sit?" I ask.

"Wherever you want."

I point to three open seats in the fourth row. He nods and walks toward them. I look around. "Of course Braden isn't here yet."

"Well, at least he's consistent," Robbie says as he sits down.

I manage a small smile. "It's tough to spin that boy positively." I take the seat next to him and breathe deeply, trying to calm the nervousness running throughout my body. It feels like there are Pop Rocks in my blood. I set my bag down at my feet and adjust my skirt.

I always try to dress extra nice for presentations and tests. *Dress for success*, as they say. Or in this case, I'm dolled up for my own funeral.

Other groups file in, some carrying big signs and posters for their projects. Most are talking to each other quickly and loudly, the whole group eager and engaged, like a well-oiled machine. Few look worried.

My phone buzzes.

Yaz: Good luck today, superstar!

I smile. I had mentioned how busy we were with the project, especially with midterms for other classes coming up. I start to type a reply to explain how bad things have gotten, then sigh and delete it. I decide on a simple **Thanks we need it** instead. Her typing bubble pops up right away, but I click my phone on airplane mode before she sends the reply. I can't handle disappointing Yaz right now, on top of everything else.

I will just text her after.

"I think I may throw up," I whisper to Robbie.

"Really?" His eyes go wide.

"Yeah." I half laugh. "You might want to sit far away from me."

"Nah." He smiles. "Just, you know, try not to."

My eyes flicker toward my lap, and he reaches for my hand.

At his warm touch, my heart speeds up. A different kind of nervousness. The emotion is so overwhelming and unfamiliar that my initial thought is to pull my hand away. To use it to cover my now-red face. But something about the stakes of the day makes me bold. Instead of pulling my hand away, I lean over and rest my head on his shoulder.

"It's going to be fine," he says. "You're brilliant, and you built something brilliant."

"*We* built it," I correct. I look at his hand, woven in mine, and suddenly my nervousness starts to dissipate.

"Yeah, let's just hope Braden remembers to present it though," he says. "There's only five minutes until class starts."

Aaaaand the nervousness is back. "I'm going to kill that boy." I look back toward the door. "You may actually witness a murder."

"Witness? Who says I wouldn't help you?"

Seconds before class starts, the door in the back of the classroom swings open, and Braden saunters in, wearing a suit but no tie and holding a laptop under his arm.

"Didn't want to cut it a little bit closer?" I ask through gritted teeth.

"I like the suspense," he says, shimmying into our row. He stares at our still-interlocked hands as he passes. "All right then." He raises his eyebrows.

The back of Robbie's neck turns red and he pulls his hand from mine. My heart sinks. *Is he embarrassed of me?* I use that hand to tuck a strand of hair behind my ear, hoping the stinging tears in my eyes aren't visible.

I can barely focus through the first few presentations. I keep glancing at Braden, hoping to see him studying slides or flipping through notecards like everyone else in the auditorium seems to be doing. But he just watches the other speakers, as calmly as if he were watching a TV show and not about to go up there himself.

As the third presentation ends, I lean forward to see Professor Thomas's reaction. His face remains blank and his arms stay folded across his chest, just as he was at the end of the other presentations. We are royally screwed.

Eventually, our names are called and Braden saunters up to

the front of the room. He takes his time setting up, fiddling with the adapter as he plugs his computer into the projector. He has no note cards.

"There are seven billion people on Earth," Braden begins. I hold my breath. He clicks a remote and a slide appears— a picture of the globe. "More than half of those people are women. You would think, with odds like that, I wouldn't be single, and yet…" He opens his arms. "Believe it or not, ladies, I am."

Heat rises in my chest. What the hell is he doing? But to my surprise, a number of people laugh. I sit a little taller. And something magical happens. In this auditorium of upperclassmen and business school students, Braden's smug, annoying demeanor comes off as confidence.

Braden grins. "But seriously, our world is faced with a disconnect. As populations grow and more and more of us live in large cities, we somehow become less connected, lost in the crowd. In a world of seven billion, you can't know everyone, and without direction, it's hard to know who you should be getting to know—who is worth your time.

"Take this example. You're a young woman, and your friends invite you to a bar after class. You're wearing a nice outfit, and you hope you might meet someone. Maybe you end up chatting with a few people at the bar, and one of them is an absolute dud, and another is not bad, just okay."

He flips through stock images of smiling men. "Maybe when your friends are leaving, the just-okay guy asks you to stay for another drink. You could stay, or you could go to the next bar with your friends. How do you know if you should stay, or if another guy, a *better* guy, is at the next bar, or the other one down the street, or even at the 7:00 a.m. yoga class you were going to attend tomorrow, had you gone home early? There are 16,000 bars in New York City alone and on a Friday night, roughly half of them are filled with guys like the one you are taking to. You have no way of knowing if the guys in the bar with you are the best people, or if the girl or guy of your dreams is just down the street at the Irish pub, or any of the other thousands of places."

A slide comes up, featuring hundreds of headshots of people, young and old, attractive and not so attractive.

"Of course, you could try online dating." He takes a step away from the center of the room. "Dating apps aren't much better at letting you know who the crème de la crème is. They narrow the size of the 'room' you're in, but not necessarily by quality. After all, just because someone's favorite movie is *Ferris Bueller's Day Off* and yours is too doesn't mean they're the person of your dreams.

"But I ask you." A flirty smile plays on his lips. "What if there was an app that could take you to a singles bar, where the party is big enough that you're drawing from the whole world but small enough not to overwhelm you...because, with the flip of a switch, you can block out all the noise. Now you're in a room with *only* the most charming, the most attractive and the brightest of all."

He clicks a button, and most of the headshots on the screen fade to black, leaving only the supermodel-level hot people.

Around me, note cards are folded into laps and computers are closed. There is barely a sound in the auditorium besides Braden's voice. He has captivated the room.

"So without further ado, I would like to invite you to the most exclusive party around. Ladies and gentlemen, you are invited to sign up for the most exclusive dating app in the country. You are free to find out whether or not you are—and whether you deserve—a Perfect10."

A logo I have never seen before comes up on screen. And I must admit, it's not half-bad.

I lean forward to see Professor Thomas more clearly. He unfolds his arms. Turning his head to the side, he studies Braden with his chin resting on his hand.

Braden begins to present the actual app, and what he shows bears little resemblance to the mess we turned in. He certainly avoids the holes of Perfect10 by putting up still pictures of what certain screens *might* look like and painting a picture of how one could use that page, instead of showing them how it works and revealing how much it glitches.

"Thank you." He clicks the slide remote, and the screen goes to black. He heads back to his seat.

Professor Thomas raises his eyebrows and claps.

A few students join in, and others look conflicted, probably debating whether applauding our project will make theirs look that much worse by comparison.

I feel dizzy, and blood rushes past my ears making it hard to hear. I reach for my armrest to stabilize myself. To make sure this is real.

Braden collapses into the seat next to me. I just nod and smile awkwardly at our fans.

"How'd you fix the formatting?" I whisper. "I thought you couldn't code."

"I didn't. I photoshopped the screenshot."

Oh my gosh.

The class goes long, since a number of presentations do not stay within the time limit. When it is finally over, Professor Thomas walks to the front of the room.

"I'm posting the grades from today," he says. "If you got below a C, don't bother coming back. I'll see the rest of you next week." He pegs a piece of paper to the board and walks away without another word.

As soon as the door closes behind him, people shoot up from their seats, running toward the front of the room. We push through the crowd.

"C-plus! Thank god," a girl close to the paper exclaims.

Another girl pushes her way in front of the paper, running her finger down the list to find her group's name. I spot a D scribbled where her finger comes to a stop.

She lets out a shriek and falls to the floor. Her group members pick her up and *shh* her, practically dragging her out of the way and creating enough space for me to step forward.

I scan the list quickly, looking for our names. There are a lot of Cs and about a third of the grades are Ds or Fs, so this will be a bit of a bloodbath.

Finally, I see it.

HART, JONES, DIAZ   **A+**

"Ohmigod ohmigod!" I jump up and down, my heels clicking on the floor.

Braden does a Tiger Woods-style fist pump.

Robbie stands totally still, eyes on the paper, as if in awe.

"This is unreal!" I say to him, grabbing his shoulders, "Last night we were praying for a C!"

"I know," Robbie says, his voice hoarse.

I turn away from the list and practically skip as I head up the aisle, which is still clogged with people.

"Sorry, excuse me," I say, swimming upstream and stopping when I can't weave around a girl who keeps inching right when I go left and left when I go right. "We saw ours—we're just trying to leave."

The girl blocking my path looks confused. "Oh, I'm not trying to see my grade. I'm trying to talk to you guys." She adjusts her glasses.

I'm taken aback. "What? Why?" I take a step back and bump into someone behind me. I already know it's—

"Braden Hart." He reaches past me to shake her hand.

Someone else taps my shoulder, but when I turn around I am met with a wall of classmates, not just one. People say my name and thrust business cards at me as if they're asking for autographs.

"That was great!" a guy in a button-down says.

"Best project I've seen!" says one of the girls I recognize as having rejected me from her group the first day.

"When will it go live?" another girl asks as she throws her Louis Vuitton bag over her shoulder.

My eyebrows furrow. *What is she talking about?* This was just a class project. I begin to respond, "Oh, we're not—it's just for—"

"Before the end of the month!" a voice interrupts me. Braden reaches past me again, this time with his business card. "Send me an email and we'll let you skip right to gold." He flashes her a winning smile.

I feel like I might throw up.

The girl giggles and blushes as she puts the card in her bag before spinning around and walking away.

"What exactly do you think you're doing?" I whisper to Braden.

"Her dad works at the biggest venture capital firm in the

Valley," he replies through teeth locked in a smile. He waves to the girl as she glances over her shoulder. She smiles and tucks the card into her purse, throwing up a call sign with her thumb and pinky.

"This, Sara Jones," he says when she is through the door, "is how million-dollar stories begin."

part two

move fast,
break things

chapter ten

Roberto

"I just don't know." Sara sighs. "It's a miracle we pulled this off as a class project. You can't exactly photoshop demos in the real world." She stares at her drink.

We are toasting with red cups of cheap champagne in the main room of my suite to celebrate this morning's success.

"Dude." Braden is already on his second cup. "This could make our careers."

She considers his words. "I have dreamed of starting my own company. And there are so few female founders... A dating app isn't exactly what I pictured, but then again, Whitney Wolfe is one of my heroes, and she made Bumble."

"Exactly." Braden's eyes are bright. "This is your chance to be like her—a trailblazer. Plus, we could be talking millions."

"Really?" I ask. I picture buying my dad a big house in Atherton. Hiring the best lawyer around and figuring out a way to get my mother back to the States. Helping the people back home. I turn to Sara. "I think we should do it."

"But people are interested in a product we don't actually have." She bites her lip.

"Could we have the app working by the end of the month?" Braden asks.

She runs a hand through her hair. "I mean, maybe." She looks to me. "Do you think we could do it?"

"We'll make it happen," I say. I'm not sure it's possible, but if this is a million-dollar chance, we have to take it.

"Yes!" Braden raises his glass toward us.

"Easy to celebrate when you don't have to build the thing you made up today," she says.

"Fair enough. Although you have to admit..." Braden extends his arms proudly. "I saved us all. MVP performance for sure."

She makes a face and mimics him, repeating his tone back in nonsense words. I laugh and take a sip of my drink, oddly happy our little group will stay together for a while longer.

The next day, Sara and I get to work trying to put together an app that actually does what Braden said it would.

"Ah, my computer's about to die," I say just minutes after setting up at Sara's. I pull the charger out of the bag and cross the room to plug in.

As I head back to my seat, I have a good view of Sara's screen. I notice the familiar blue-and-white homepage of Instafriend, rather than the black screen with white characters that would take up the window if she is coding.

"Ooops." She clicks the red *X* in the corner of the screen.

I sit down across from her and plug the charger into my laptop. "What?"

"I swear I was only checking my feed for a second."

"Dude, do you think I care? Braden watches *Jersey Shore* while we work—heck, he's not even here right now. You can check your Instafriend." I spread my arms in a grand gesture, mocking Braden. "We are our own bosses now."

She laughs. "Okay, cool. Because for some reason my brain is hardwired so that a step from not working to working is going on that damn site."

"Dude, I know!" I say. "It's like I go to my computer to work, open a browser to get my homework assignment, start typing, and boom, no matter what homework site I meant to go to, my fingers just type Instafriend."

She shakes her head. "I know. It's nuts."

"Maybe we should try to work there, even if we do become millionaires from this. See if they'll let you in on whatever mind control they did to make that happen."

"I'll consider it." She laughs. "Oh, hey," she says, "look at this." She turns the computer so that I can see the invite page of an Instafriend event. The picture is a bunch of smiling kids holding computers. "I've been meaning to ask you, can I send you an invite to an information session on this program I do? It's a coding camp for kids who might not ever have the chance to learn CS in school. I did it last year over spring break, but this time I'm a team recruiter too."

"Yeah for sure," I say.

She smiles and turns the screen back toward her. "Okay, I'm sending it."

My phone vibrates in my pocket.

She taps her hands on the table. "Time to get to work." She turns back to her computer and immediately melts. "Awww. Okay, we'll work in a second, but there's this video of a puppy inside a watermelon, and it's *eating* its way out of the watermelon and it's so tiny and omigod."

Warmth spreads through my chest just watching her react to the video. "You think that's cute? Have you ever seen Otters Cuddling While Floating in a River?"

Her eyes light up. "No!"

"Fantastic film." I quickly exit from my work and pull up YouTube. "Should've won the Academy Award for cuteness, really. Got robbed." I turn the screen toward her and hit Play.

She covers her mouth with her hand and makes a squealing sound.

"I know, right?" I say.

"It's official." She shakes her head. "Otters are cuter than puppies."

I laugh. "There doesn't have to be a ranking. Not everything has to be a competition."

"Um, but then how will we know who should win the Academy Award for cuteness?"

"A valid point." It makes me happy to hear my own joke returned by her in this new way. What seemed lame when I said it somehow seems cool now.

For a beat there is silence. We are both still leaning in close, like we had been to watch the clip, our faces just inches from each other. I notice that her eyelashes are kind of blond too. My breath catches.

Then the door swings open. "How's it going?" Braden bursts in with a tray of coffee.

I clear my throat and lean back in my seat.

"Hard at work?" he asks. "Building the best app of the century? Making me rich and successful?"

"You're already rich," Sara says.

He considers this. "All right, so just successful then. Are you making me that?"

She shakes her head.

He presents us with the tray of cups. "Coffee for you, my gorgeous CS genius?"

Sara side-eyes him, but takes a latte.

I grab the other one. "Gorgeous?" I raise a hand to my chest. "Braden, you flatter me."

Both of them burst out laughing.

There are a lot of disadvantages to being a quieter person, like being picked on in middle school or losing credit for an idea at work that was actually yours when someone repeats it during a meeting. But one great advantage is that when you *do* make the perfect snarky comment, the wit combined with the surprise that *you* were the one who said it blows the roof off the place. That's every class clown's folly really; they throw out a hundred jokes a day, hoping for the one that knocks the room off its collective feet. But the only way to really do that is to also have the shock value.

Braden walks us through his presentation, and I take notes on all the promises he made that we now have to deliver on. I start to get nervous when I get to the tenth item, but I remind myself that there is no option for quitting when it comes to a million-dollar opportunity. Sleep be damned.

"Oh, and one more thing," Braden says as he stands to leave. "We're doing an interview with the *Warren Daily* to-morrow night. I have a dinner, but it should be over by—"

"What?" Sara says. "No, we are not."

"Yeah, we are." Braden takes his phone out of his pocket and pulls up his email. "They contacted me this morning."

"And you didn't think to check with us before you answered?"

Braden is taken aback. "I didn't think I'd need to. Why wouldn't we say yes?"

"Um, maybe because we're trying to hide the fact that we don't actually have an app yet? And inviting the freaking press in here doesn't exactly help with that?"

"That's a good point." I point to Sara.

"Don't you think hiding from them makes it more suspicious?" Braden challenges.

"No, I really don't. You know why? Because they would never expect anyone to be stupid enough to pitch a product they haven't actually made."

I laugh despite the awful truth of it.

Braden snaps back, "Is this your first day in Silicon Valley then, or...?"

"Oh, shut up." She gestures toward him. "Let me see this email." She turns the phone so that I can read as well. "'...would love to speak to you about your company,'" she quotes. "Great, now it's a company."

"Of course it is." Braden rips his phone from her hand and stuffs it back in his pocket.

"There isn't even a product yet, let alone a company to sell it." She shakes her head. "No, we can't do this. We'll worry about selling it when we know what it is."

Braden shakes his head. "You're making a big mistake." He turns and leaves, slamming the door behind him.

chapter eleven

Braden

I stand outside my dorm and wait for the town car to pick me up. I don't know why my dad still uses the same car service our family had pre-Uber. It seems stupid to have an assistant make a bunch of calls to get me a ride when I could summon a private car with just the push of a button on an app.

I remain silent during the whole ride, enjoying the calm before the storm.

The driver takes me to the parking lot of a Japanese steakhouse. In classic New Money, California style, the high-end restaurant is down the street from a Panda Express and across from a gas station.

I mutter a quick "Thank you" as I hop out of the car. My parents are already waiting when I step inside, so we greet each other for the first time in months in front of the hostess.

"Braden!" My mom pulls me into a hug, her shawl wrapping around me like a blanket.

"Hi, Mom," I say.

"Good to see you," my father says, extending his arm.

I nod and shake his hand quickly.

"They refused to seat us *until the entire party was here*," he says, cutting his eyes at the hostess, who is about my age and probably not the one who wrote that policy.

"We're ready now," he says more directly to her.

"This way," she says shyly, grabbing three menus. The restaurant is light and airy, with large windows opening to a garden and luckily not the gas station that would be visible if the windows were on the other wall, which is covered in bamboo. The tables are draped in immaculate white cloth and have weird sculptures as centerpieces.

After the first two tables are deemed unacceptable, we are placed near the window at what is meant to be a six top. I wonder briefly if being too close to the door or too near to the air vent was really the problem, or if he just wanted a table big enough that he could sit more than an arm's length from my mother.

We silently read the menu for a few minutes. I decide quickly which cut of meat I'll be getting—it's the same as when we came here when I visited Warren as a senior in high school, but I continue to pretend to read so that I don't have to be the one who breaks the tense silence.

I reach for my water, and my mother seems to take this movement as invitation for conversation.

"Everything looks very delicious," she says. "Doesn't it, Jared?"

My father nods.

"It reminds me of that place we went to, years ago, when we were in Japan, that place the Williams took us. Do you remember what it was called?"

"No." My father shakes his head. He looks around. "Where is the waiter? I would love to order a drink."

My mother presses her lips together and looks at her menu. I await her next attempt at "normal family conversation."

The waitress comes by, and my father orders dinner for all three of us.

I study the reflection of the light on my glass. Sometimes, being in a room with both my parents is like being trapped inside a play. One of those perverted Levittown nightmare kind, the sort that peel back the glossed-over 1950s American Dream, exposing the hell that it really was. When conversations about what's for dinner and how the kids are doing erupt into screaming matches and threats. Except, my parents perform only the first act when we're all together, and wait for the explosion of anger when they call me from opposite sides of the earth, wanting me to convey to the other what they think about the models brought back to hotel rooms or a boat purchased without calling to check first.

It would almost be better if there was screaming and yelling. If, right now, they started throwing drinks and voicing all the thoughts that must be racing through their minds as their lips weigh the pros and cons of various appetizers. Sure, it would make quite a scene in this eerily quiet and stuffy restaurant. But then everything would be out in the open. And then, maybe issues would be dealt with and changes would be made.

Instead, I'm supposed to go along with this charade, like I don't mind talking about the weather or passing the bread when there is so much pain.

The infidelity, the threats of extortion if divorced, the

games of control over bank accounts and properties... It makes me want to scream.

Sometimes when I'm with them, I feel like I'm drowning and trying to scream but no one can hear. With no outlet, my body is destroying itself from the inside out.

"So how are your classes going?" my mother asks as the waitress sets down our food.

I blink, and it takes a second for me to realize she's talking to me. I clear my throat. "Uh, good, actually." I squirm in my seat. "You know that one with Dustin Thomas? Our project went really well." I adjust the napkin on my lap. "We got an A-plus, the first in the class's history, and our professor recommended that we pursue the idea outside of class. And Thatcher Bell's daughter is actually in the class and showed a lot of interest, so hopefully we'll be able to meet with his firm."

"Are you going out to any other firms?" my father asks. He doesn't look at me as he speaks, focusing on cutting his steak.

"Uh, um, no, we don't really have the resources for that right now. At this point I just feel very lucky that she—"

"It's not about luck." He stops cutting his food and looks up, piercing blue eyes on me, knife and fork still in his hands. "What's your strategy? Angel investors don't actually come down from heaven, Braden." His voice is stern.

My mom drains her wine. "Why don't we talk about something else? Are you making friends?"

"No," my father interrupts. "It's important that he understands that this is not an opportunity to waste. An A-plus in a class is nothing if you don't play this right from here on out. He's made a mockery of what I've paid for his education before—I am not going to let him do it again."

I push my food away from me. I've lost my appetite.

I was stupid to think that a man who's made the Forbes list would be impressed by a leading grade in one class. Stupid to think he would see me as anything but the kid who was almost expelled from boarding school.

"Excuse me for a moment," I say, setting my napkin on the table as I stand up. I pull out my cell phone as soon as the restroom door swings closed behind me.

"Hello?" the voice on the other side of the line says.

"This is Braden Hart. I'm calling about your article. I'd like to give you an exclusive interview."

chapter twelve

Sara

GROUNDBREAKING APP COMES OUT OF WARREN CLASS

PALO ALTO—The first ever A-plus was awarded this week in Professor Dustin Thomas's famously brutal class, Econ 214: "Becoming an Entrepreneur." But that is just the beginning of the enormous success expected from Perfect10, CFO Braden Hart said.

"This is going to change the face of dating throughout the United States, if not the world," he told the *Daily*.

The app, which allows users to rank other singles resulting in a cumulative score that decides a user's status as platinum, gold, silver or unranked and lets other users block certain groups, will go live next Friday.

"The vote of support from Thomas is huge," Hart said. "Especially since he's a venture capitalist by trade himself. We expect great interest in the project."

Hart went on to say that he would be shocked if there weren't one million users on the app in three months' time.

"Braden!" I pound on the door in front of me, the half-crumpled newspaper in my other hand.

Finally, it swings open. Braden rubs his eyes and looks down at me. He's wearing only boxers and his hair is a mess. He looks really good. Like he definitely works out—he has a six-pack and even those little triangle things by his hips that seem designed to draw the eyes downward.

My face gets warm and I avert my eyes. I will *not* be distracted from my rage.

"What's up?" he asks, half yawning.

"I'm going to kill you." I hold up the paper.

He smiles crookedly. "Pretty great, right?"

"CFO?"

He leans against the door frame. "Since clearly I'm the only one who understands the business side, I thought it made sense."

I throw my copy of the *Warren Daily* at his dumb washboard abs. It falls to the floor.

"You can't just make up a title for yourself! You…you can't just make up a *company*, for God's sake. Not to mention—" I exhale. "It will *'change the face of dating throughout the United States, if not the world'*?"

"Right?" He smiles as he leans over to pick up the paper.

"I swear to God, Braden Hart—"

"Have you checked your email?" he asks. He holds the paper against the wall and smooths out the wrinkles with his other hand.

"Don't change the subject." I push past him into his room. I am momentarily distracted by the feeling that I have left campus. Furnished more like a house than a dorm, the room is full of grown-up furniture. And not the type I'd even expect actual grown-ups to own. From the decorative clock to the stainless steel desk, it's like a room out of a magazine. I shake my head to dispel the distraction.

"One million users?" I ask. "Not only is that an absolutely bonkers number, but predicting the number of users is the most arrogant metric. We have no idea if that's even possible."

"It's totally possible. Instagram had one million in two months."

"Why the hell do you think we're Instagram?"

He sets the newspaper down carefully on his desk. "Why do you think we're not?"

I press my fingertips to my temple. "We're supposed to roll out the app in a week, and we're still not done building it. And now you've set the expectations higher than we could ever possibly meet."

"That's so much better than us unveiling a perfect app to no one listening."

I raise my hands like I'm about to literally pull my hair out. "Says the guy who doesn't code!"

"Hey now, I just signed up to take CS 101 next semester," he says.

"I—" I lunge toward him, but he grabs my wrists to hold me back.

"Seriously, Sara, just check your email."

I force myself to take a deep breath and lower my arms. "I don't see why…" I shake my head as I pull out my phone.

Ten new emails pop up as soon as my in-box refreshes. All of them are addressed to me, Robbie and Braden with subject lines about the app. They're from *Business Insider*, *TechCrunch*, the *Huffington Post*…

"Wow." I look up.

"Yeah." He raises his eyebrows. "This is going to be huge."

"Holy shit, holy shit." I skim some of the emails. "Okay, will you get on answering these? I have to… I have to go finish an app."

Suddenly there is no time to be mad. A part of me is even excited about this, and *maybe* even grateful to Braden. Not that I'd ever let him know that. I race across campus to find Robbie.

That night, when the clock strikes twelve, we're still in the common room of Robbie's suite, working on the app.

"I am so hungry and so tired," I say. I turn around to lie upside down on the couch. It's become my usual restless position. "Is it really worth a million dollars to keep going?"

"Good question." He laughs. "But look at it this way— think of all the naps you could take if you were your own boss, not to mention the doughnuts you could buy if you had all that money."

"Doughnuts you say?" I raise an eyebrow.

"Yeah. There's this place in Palo Alto that has amazing doughnuts. Open 24-7 too."

"Really?" I spin around to sit upright.

"Yeah, you wanna go?" he asks. I'm already looking for my keys.

I practically skip downstairs.

"You know," I yell across the dark courtyard as I look for my bike. The yard is filled with row upon row of bike racks, two wheels being the preferred way to get around the largest college campus in the United States. "We're probably too hungry to work anyway. So really, getting food is the productive thing to do."

"Exactly." He walks toward me, navy bike in tow. He takes in my light blue beach cruiser, complete with large white basket and bell. "Nice bike."

"I always wanted one like this." I blush. Fumbling with my key, I try to unlock the bike, but it's as if there's something wrong with my hands all of the sudden.

"Here." He reaches for the key. His hand brushes mine, sending electricity through my body.

He doesn't seem to notice. "This happens to mine after the rain—you just have to wiggle it." He unlocks it with ease and hands me the key. Stepping back to examine his work, he smiles and says, "It's a very Sara bike. I like it."

I try to talk but make a series of mumbling syllables as I hop on my bike. My head feels fuzzy all of a sudden. *Pull it together, Sara.* I take off pedaling, not looking back. I'm too embarrassed to meet his eyes right now.

He catches up to me before the first stop sign but doesn't say anything. Everything's a lot quieter than it is during the day, and it almost feels like we have the whole campus to ourselves.

Streetlights glimmer every few yards, popping up between some of the hundreds of palm trees that line our path from Main Quad into town, so that we are constantly in and out of darkness. The breeze blows back my hair and I breathe in the air, which still smells like summer here, even though it's late fall.

I feel so free. That's what I really love about college. The freedom of it. And I don't mean drinking or being allowed to have a boy in my room if I want to. Sure, that would be nice.

But I'm talking about not having to ask anyone when I want to leave the house. Not having anyone telling me it's time for bed, or that I'm not allowed to have a doughnut at

1:00 a.m. if I want one. It's a sort of happiness I didn't know I was missing.

"Do you ever feel guilty?" Robbie breaks the silence. He veers off slightly into the empty road so that he's riding next to me.

"About what?"

"Perfect10. Like, I'm not sure it's the best thing for the world, you know, to have people rank each other. And we're building it."

"We're making a dating app," I say. He's biking faster now, and although his breathing sounds totally normal, I'm struggling to keep up. "It's not like we're running an oil company or, like, killing puppies to make coats."

He laughs, but not as fully as I hoped he would. It was more polite than anything. "I'm not saying we're Cruella de Vil. Maybe we aren't doing something *that* bad—I'm just not sure we're doing something good, you know?"

I consider this as we reach an empty intersection and stop at the red light even though no one's around. I've been so busy trying to make the app work properly that I haven't thought about this sort of moral dilemma for the past few weeks. It felt like we kind of already made our decision when we pitched our project to Professor Thomas.

"Like..." Robbie says as the light turns green. He kicks off the ground and pedals forward. "What if we designed the app *not* so you end up with the 'most desired person around,' but, like, the best person for you? Those are probably different things, right? For different people?"

"Yeah, I guess so."

"So why don't we help people find that?"

"Well, I feel like the competition is the thing that will keep people on the app, right? That will make them obsessed with it? If they find their soul mate and leave, we lose a customer."

He laughs heartily this time, from his chest. But I wasn't joking. "You sound like Braden."

My stomach twists. That's the last comparison I want to hear.

"I'm just thinking like a businesswoman," I say. "I don't have time to be nice—the VCs certainly won't be."

We turn onto a main road, and there are a few cars, so we have to ride one behind the other in the bike lane.

He doesn't say anything for the rest of the ride.

We arrive at a cute little shop with a neon pink doughnut sign, the only place in town still open on a weekday at this hour. As we lock our bikes, I see people through the window. Rowdy college students who have pulled way too many chairs up to one table and tired-looking middle-aged people in various uniforms, clearly night shift workers on a break.

A soft bell rings as we enter. An impossibly-cheerful-for-the-time girl in a pink apron greets us at the counter and takes our order with a feathered pen. I assumed we would get one doughnut each, but Robbie insists we share a half dozen.

"You can't just have one doughnut," he says. He turns to the cashier.

"Tell her."

"That's true." She nods seriously, blinking her heavily lined eyes.

We settle into a booth and Robbie sets down the box in front of me. My eyes go wide as I open it and examine our bounty. There are two chocolate-frosted doughnuts with rainbow sprinkles, one with no hole that's filled with frosting, a plain glazed, a half-chocolate-dipped glazed, and one with peanuts on the outside.

I carefully remove a chocolate sprinkle doughnut and take a bite. "Mmmmmm." I close my eyes. "This is heavenly." I lick the sugary frosting on my lips.

Robbie nods as he bites into the peanut one.

"You know…" I say. "My mom would kill me if she knew I was eating this." I rip off another bite. "She never let me have doughnuts as a kid. She was all about 'breakfast is the most important meal of the day it has to be healthy blah blah blah.'" I take another bite and consider which doughnut I will have next. "I was always sooo jealous of the kids at school whose parents would buy sugary cereal and all that." I take another bite and keep speaking, even with my mouth full. If I'm breaking one rule, I might as well be a full-on wild child. "And she still tries to micromanage my diet, calling to ask what I ate in the dining hall and so on."

Robbie is quietly eating his doughnut, and I realize that I've been rambling, something I do that I hate. "How about you?" I ask. "Is your mom like that?"

He exhales and looks away. "My mom, uh…" He turns back to me. "My mom lives in Mexico." He pauses to take a sip of his coffee. "She was detained, and then deported a few years ago. So, uh, no. She doesn't give me input on breakfast. I mean, I call her as much as I can, and we talk about lots of things. But doughnuts aren't usually one of them." He laughs in an uncomfortable sort of way.

"Oh no, I'm so sorry," I say. The words seem to fall flat as soon as they're out of my mouth, hitting the table between us with a hollow thud.

What are my stupid words of sympathy in the face of something so unbearable?

But he smiles gratefully, like I've actually said something helpful.

I feel an overwhelming need to fill the silence. "That was rude of me, I shouldn't have asked, I—"

"Nah." He waves his hand, dismissing my second apology. *Great, now he's comforting me. What kind of friend am I?* "How could you have known? I usually just say something vague or avoid the subject. But... I don't know." He fiddles with the plastic lid of his coffee. "Something made me want to be honest with you."

I nod, and we're quiet for a moment, sipping our coffee and watching people walk in and out of the door, listening to the light sound of the bell ringing.

"Tell me about her." I turn back to Robbie. "What does she like to do?"

He smiles, and this time it reaches his eyes. "She really likes music. She *loves* dancing," he says. "She would lead me around the kitchen, making me dance with her while she cooked." He blushes. "I used to love that, and then I thought I was too old, even though I wasn't."

I nod and take a bite of my doughnut.

"And at night, she would listen to ballads and sometimes show tunes. She liked songs that told stories," he says. "Likes," he corrects himself.

"She sends me videos now," he says. "Of herself singing." He pulls out his phone and searches for one. "It's ridiculous," he says, but his smile betrays his real feelings.

chapter thirteen

Roberto

Every few seconds, I check the clock, as if I'm half-afraid it will have jumped forward a few hours and we'll have royally messed up. I'm standing over Sara's shoulder as she types, hunched over the keyboard. I'm supposed to be helping her fix the bug, but I'm probably just making her more nervous. My eyes dart to the chair across the table, but I can't bring myself to step away from the screen and do nothing. Even if I'm not much help right now.

We've been up most of the night, trying to fix the last few hiccups before the scheduled launch of the app in—I check my watch—two hours and thirty-seven minutes. *Jesus Christ.* I run a hand through my hair and attempt to take a deep breath.

"All right," Sara says, leaning back in her chair. "I think... I think that's it. It should work." Her voice is faint.

"Well, test it." I take three paces in the small kitchenette before turning around and heading back toward her.

"It works!" she says. I walk up and lean over her shoulder to see for myself, and she is right. It works. It finally works.

"I can't believe it." She stares at the screen. "It's done."

"I can," I say, falling into a chair. "It feels like we've been working on it for centuries."

She laughs. "We made it *literally* just in time."

Just then the door flies open. "All right, you guys." Braden charges in. "We go live in just under three hours—it's game time." His voice is commanding. He sets down two computer bags on the chair and takes out his cell phone. "Okay, this is what we need to do…" He reads from a list, but I am only half listening, and honestly understanding only half the things I hear. "…and then there's the announcement on various other social media—Reddit, Facebook and Tumblr—which need to go out. Not to mention the press release. Speaking of, I need to get on the phone for an interview in—" he checks his watch "—five minutes."

As he continues to pace and ramble, Sara slowly stands up from the table and walks over to the couch. She pulls her legs onto the seat and drapes a fuzzy blanket over herself.

"Uh-huh." She nods along to what he is saying, her eyes fluttering closed.

I try to hold in a laugh as I follow her and take a seat on the opposite side of the couch.

Braden keeps talking, going on about an article on some blog.

"Oh really? That's interesting." I have no idea what he had just said. I adjust the pillows behind me.

He gives me an odd look, but continues with his speech.

His ringtone blares through the room, interrupting him. He jumps and clicks his phone.

"Hello, yes, this is Braden from Perfect10 Enterprises, thanks so much for making the time to talk to me!" He holds his hand over the receiver. "Reporter," he says to us. "I'll be right back, hang tight."

Sara gives him a lazy thumbs-up, I just smile. He brings the phone back to his ear, laughing as he opens the door to take the call in the hallway.

"I think," Sara says, after the door closes, "that it might be our turn to be the deadweight."

"Jersey Shore?" I ask.

"You know what?" She reaches for the remote. "I think so."

So we relax while Braden finally does his share of the work. We both end up falling asleep at some point in the afternoon, and I think I might have actually napped through the exact moment our app went live, although I'm not sure. I might have been listening to Snooki rant at that moment. The point is, for the amount of our lives that we've poured into this thing for the last two months, the actual afternoon of the launch was anticlimactic. Well, for me and Sara.

"Will you two wake up?" Braden shakes my shoulders.

I rub my eyes and sit up. He walks over to wake Sara as well, but as soon as he touches her shoulder, she sits up.

"Who's there?" She flails an arm, smacking Braden in the face.

He lurches backward, his hand going to his noise. "Ow."

I laugh so hard that I snort.

"What the hell, Sara?" Braden says.

"Sorry." She shrugs, which then morphs into a stretch with an accompanying yawn.

"You guys gotta at least rally for the launch party," Braden says, walking to the kitchen. "We have four hundred RSVPs yes, and I've rented out a restaurant for the whole night. Of course guests will have to download the app to get in the door.

And then get to platinum level to get in the VIP room with the open bar." He picks up the toaster and examines his face in the reflection. "Luckily you didn't leave a mark," Braden says. "I need to look good tonight."

"Ugh." Sara stands and lets the blanket fall to the floor. "How much time do I have to get ready?" she asks.

"Forty-five minutes."

"What?" She finally seems awake. "Why didn't you wake me earlier? Do you even know what it's like to be a girl?" She races into her bedroom and reemerges with towel and shower caddy in hand. "That's barely enough time to dry my hair, let alone style it," she says, before heading out into the hallway.

"I guess I should go get ready, too," I say. Although my routine takes about fifteen minutes, so I'm in far less of a rush. Regardless, hanging out alone with Braden doesn't appeal.

I'm ready with twenty minutes to spare, so I do what I usually do when I have a few extra minutes. I pick up my phone.

"Hello?" My dad's voice sounds like home.

"Hey, Dad," I say. "How are you?"

"I'm doing well," he says, the same response I always get. "Work is fine, friends are good, the house hasn't fallen down. How are you, though, college man?"

I smile. I keep telling him not to call me that, that it's embarrassing. But a few kids from my high school who were first-gen college students as well have told me about their parents being bitter or mad at them for having opportunities they couldn't have dreamed of. I'll take overly proud any day.

"I'm doing pretty good," I say. "It's been a pretty crazy week, but I had a free moment so I wanted to call to update you on the app launch."

"Thank you, but you know I don't understand any of that tech stuff." He laughs. "I'd rather hear more about this girl."

"What? What girl?" I say. My gaze darts to the door of my suite, which I left half-open. Although it is unlikely Sara will be ready yet, and she probably won't be walking down my hall anytime soon, I kick it closed.

"Every time you call to talk about the app," he says, "it's, 'Sara said this, Sara said that, Sara is so brilliant.' What's going on with that? Have you told her you love her?"

"No! Dad, what?" I pace the common room. "I don't love her, okay?" I'm speaking rapidly now. "She's my partner in this company, and she's very smart, that's why I said my *professional* opinion is that her ideas are brilliant."

He clicks his tongue. "Nope, I don't buy it. You love her."

"Dad, you're not getting it—"

"No," he says. "I think I am right."

Of course you do, I think but don't dare say.

"If you care about her, you should tell her," he says.

"It's not that simple," I say. "We work together, after all. And she is one of my closest friends here. My best friend."

I actually had been thinking about it—telling her. A few nights ago, I started tinkering with some code, building a cute game filled with inside jokes that would tell her how I felt. At 2:00 a.m. it seemed like the type of thing a guy would do in a movie, and something that Sara, who has a bunch of Nora Ephron movie posters on her wall, might appreciate.

I woke up the next morning and immediately dragged the game into my trash. It was way too intense. She'd probably never have talked to me again if I'd sent it to her.

"True love is simple," he says.

I exhale. "Will you please just let me tell you about this project? I'm excited about it."

"Yes, yes." I can picture him nodding. "I'm sorry, go ahead."

"Okay, thank you." I shake my head. "So basically, it's an app that helps people meet people, like to date…"

"Oh, the irony," he says. "You two, building an app you don't need."

"Dad!"

"All right, all right," he says. "Last one, I promise. Tell me about your computer stuff."

I do, and he dutifully doesn't bring up Sara again. But even after I hang up, I can't help but wonder if the way I feel about her is *that* obvious. And if so… *Has she noticed, too?*

chapter fourteen

Braden

I wake up feeling like a zombie. The launch party was a success—well, at least, the parts of it I remember. My mouth tastes like I licked an ashtray, and I vaguely remember smoking a cigar the night before. *Water, I need water.*

I roll over and my brain screams.

"Rough night?" my roommate asks from his desk. He's working on homework and has clearly been up for hours.

"A little bit." I fumble for my water bottle and take a long sip. I reach for my phone and detach it from the charger so that I can use it without getting out of bed. After checking my texts to make sure I didn't send any bad drunk messages, I click on my email.

There's the usual spam from various companies I've bought stuff from online, daily updates from the various newspapers I subscribe to and dorm-list server messages. The usual.

But one message stands out. The subject line is Re: Perfect10.

It's a reply to one of the blind inquiries I sent out yesterday to venture capitalist firms.

I sit up, my brain rattling against my skull. I click on the email.

From: mike@WilliamsBrownandMoore.com
To: Bradenhart@Warren.edu
Subject: RE: Perfect10

Hi Braden,

I'm interested in hearing more about this endeavor, but my schedule is pretty booked. We had a cancellation on Friday at 1 p.m., if your team is willing to meet then.

Tell your dad I say hello.

Best,
Michael

Oh fuck. Today is Friday.

I check the time—it's twelve. And their office is at least twenty minutes away.

I spring out of bed, texting rapidly. I stalk to my wardrobe and yank it open, then tug on pants with one hand while I text with the other.

Me: Angel investor wants to meet exactly one hour from now on Sand Hill, you need to get ready ASAP

Sara: what?!!?

Robbie: damn okay

Robbie: hopping in the shower now

Sara: are you kidding me?! There's no time!

Sara: Should we still go?

Sara: Are you ready for this?

Sara: Braden?!!!!!

Sara tries to call me, but I click Decline and instead scroll through my contacts.

"Hello?" Professor Thomas answers on the second ring.

"Hi, Professor, this is Braden Hart from your class and I'm one of the founders of Perfect—"

"I put my phone number on the syllabus for emergencies. Could you maybe just stop by office hours?"

"It *is* an emergency," I say. "We just launched yesterday and someone from WBM emailed and wants to see us today. I wanted to get your advice, like how should I pitch, what should I make sure I say in the meeting."

"You shouldn't go."

Feedback crackles over the otherwise-silent line. My heart drops into my stomach. "What do you mean? This is a huge opportunity for us—"

"It's not worth it. You should apologize for reaching out prematurely, say you don't want to waste their time and will contact them when the company is further along."

"What if we don't get a chance like this again?"

"I know it's tempting." He sighs. "And maybe an experienced entrepreneur could pull off pitching on the fly, but you are eighteen years old and have never pitched a company to investors before. It's not worth the risk."

My mouth goes dry. He sounds remarkably like my father.

"Thanks, I guess." I hang up the phone.

The sinking feeling in my gut turns into a burning fire. I text Roberto and Sara the address and hail an Uber for myself. I'll need this time to myself to formulate my pitch.

I've finessed and rehearsed my speech to journalists, but I thought I'd have more time before I'd actually be trying to sell a part of the company. This is the type of meeting I would have prepared for weeks in advance, if I'd had the chance. Instead, I am jotting ideas in the Notes section of my phone as the car speeds across town.

"Can I have one of these?" I say, taking a water bottle from the cup holder of the car. I unscrew the cap before the driver can answer. I chug it, hoping to drown this hangover a little bit.

"Thanks," I say, setting the empty bottle back in the cup holder just as he pulls up to the office of Williams, Brown and Moore.

Sara arrives at the same time, also pulling up in an Uber, although not a black car.

She's putting in her right earring as she steps out. She's wearing a professional-looking wrap dress and flats, and she seems to have showered since last night, which is more than I can say. Her eyes catch mine.

"I'm going to freaking kill you!" She charges forward and swats my arm.

I can't help but laugh, because even in her moment of un-bridled anger, she still can't bring herself to swear, opting for the kindergarten teacher–style replacement instead.

"Why are you smiling like an idiot?" she asks. "We're to-tally screwed."

"It'll be fine," I say, but my voice is shaky. "It's all about confidence."

"You smell like bourbon."

"I didn't have time to shower." I look away so that I don't have to see her reaction and wave to Robbie as he hops out of a car driven by another student.

I check my watch. "Five minutes to go... We might as well head in."

We take an elevator to the third floor. The office is light and airy, with big windows, stainless steel furniture and light blue accents. The modern, clean look should create a soothing atmosphere, but my stomach drops as I step off the elevator. I feel like I'm having the dream where I'm in a play I forgot to rehearse for, or when I show up to school naked.

"Williams, Brown and Moore," a pretty receptionist says into a phone. She narrows her eyes at us. Sara takes a seat in the waiting area and taps her foot on the floor. Robbie paces behind her.

"All right." The receptionist types into the computer. "I'll get him the message, thanks." She hangs up the phone with a click. "Can I help you?" she asks us.

"Yes." I step forward. "I am Braden Hart—we're from Perfect10."

She flips through a schedule in front of her.

"Our appointment is at one, but we might not be on there—there was a cancellation."

She nods. "Have a seat. I'll let him know you're here."

I sit next to Sara.

She leans over and whispers, "Please tell me this is like the class presentation and you've secretly been preparing a perfect pitch."

"I wish I could." I wring my hands.

"Hey guys." A fortysomething man in dark jeans and a button-down steps into the room.

We shoot out of our seats.

"I'm Michael." He shakes each of our hands. "I'm looking forward to hearing about your project. Let's head back to my office."

He leads us into a large room. There is a huge window against the back wall with a beautiful view of the foothills and in front of that, a grand desk.

Three tiny chairs are lined up near the door.

He offers us water, which none of us take, and then tells us to sit down. I settle into the seat farthest to the right. The florescent lights from above bear down on me. I can't help but feel like I'm about to be interrogated.

Why is it so bright in here?

"So." He folds his hands on the desk in front of him. "Tell me about this app."

I lean forward to the edge of my seat. "Well..."

I launch into a version of the speech I gave in class, explaining the thought process behind the app, what it does and why people will want to use it. He smiles and nods as he listens, and even throws in a pensive look here and there. About halfway through, he starts to scribble notes on a legal pad. I'm shocked to feel like things might actually be going well. I sit a bit taller in my chair.

"...and eventually, as the app grows successful, we can start monetizing by limiting how many times people can check their score to three times a week, and then charging 99 cents to check it."

"That's a really interesting idea," he says, skimming his notes. "I'm impressed."

"Thank you," I say.

"So how many users do you have?" he asks.

I look to Sara. She's looking from Robbie to me and back.

"What?" Michael asks. "What's going on?"

I clear my throat and turn back to him. "We're not sure."

"What do you mean?" He looks at Sara. "You didn't build a way to gather that sort of information?"

"We did," Robbie says. "It's just..."

"We haven't checked it yet," Sara admits.

"You haven't checked it?" Michael looks back to me, disbelief in his eyes.

"The thing is," I say, "we just launched yesterday."

He stands up. His face is red, and he seems to be holding himself back the best he can, his calm, cool, Californian demeanor gone. He closes his eyes and takes a deep breath. I didn't know an exhale could sound that angry. "So tell me exactly *why*—besides the obvious fact of who your father is—you are in my office right now?" His gaze digs into me.

"Well...I knew it could take months to get meetings, so I sent out a few feelers yesterday." I'm speaking too quickly, almost tripping over my words. "I didn't know we'd be asked to meet today, I thought it'd be in a few months and we'd be in the perfect position to pitch by then." I pause, weighing whether I should say what I want to next, knowing Sara will want to kill me. But things are already spiraling rapidly and the Hail Mary pass is my only option. "We're hoping to hit a million users in three months."

He shakes his head and walks to the door to pull it open. "Well maybe you should spend more of your *time* building your product and less planning for what you're going to do when it's magically the next big thing. Either way, you should definitely stop wasting mine."

Sara and Robbie stand quietly and walk out the door with their tails between their legs.

I stay back for a second. "Sir, I—"

"Get out of my office." He throws the notepad down on his desk. "It's ridiculous you even had this appointment."

chapter fifteen

I stare at the elevator doors, which remain closed. Robbie and I practically ran out of the office, only to get down to the lobby and realize we had no idea where to go.

Across the vestibule, Robbie is talking into his cell phone, I think to the guy who drove him here.

Braden has still not made it down. I can't imagine what he could possibly be saying, what he's thinking, staying up there.

I've never been so embarrassed, so *ashamed*, in my entire life. It felt like if I'd spent one more second in that man's view, my skin would burst into flames.

"Sorry about that," Robbie says as he hangs up. "It's a pickup with no backseat, or he'd give you a ride too."

"No problem," I say. "I Ubered here, and I was planning to do the same back."

He nods.

We are silent, and all I can think about is the giant Williams, Brown and Moore logo behind him. It dwarfs us by comparison.

I sigh. "I can't believe how terribly that went. Like, I wasn't expecting an offer. But I thought we'd be politely declined, not yelled at." I run a hand through my hair. "What do we do from here?"

"Get back to work." Robbie shrugs. "I don't think these sort of things usually happen like lightning striking," he says. "It's more step by step."

"I just thought this was *it*, you know?" I look out the glass doors at the overcast sky, which seems to hover low over the foothills in the distance. "Now I just feel stupid."

The elevator dings and the doors spring open. Braden steps off, radiating negative energy.

"Hey," I say.

He bumps into my shoulder as he passes, sending me stumbling backward, and pushes briskly past without a word.

The glass door slams closed behind him.

Oh, that is the last straw.

I push through the door, holding it open for Robbie, who is close behind me. Braden is on foot, turning right onto the road just as Robbie's friend's pickup pulls into the drive.

"Go on home." I turn to Robbie. "I'll take care of the drama king."

"Are you sure?" He looks from me to the boy who is taking off down the street on foot like he is filming a melodramatic music video.

"Yeah, we don't both need to waste our time."

I wave goodbye and head after Braden, almost running to catch up. My shoes pinch my feet, and the wind picks up, blowing my hair wildly, turning it into a tangled mess, I'm sure.

"Would you care to explain what the hell happened in there?" I say when I am within earshot.

Braden glances over his shoulder, but then turns forward without a word, continuing down the street. There is no sidewalk, just the quiet, winding road surrounded by trees. The branches rustle in the wind and the sky gets even darker, making it look more like dusk than midafternoon.

"Braden!" I yell.

"What?" He stops walking and spins around. "What could you possibly want now?"

"Don't talk to me like that." I'm taken aback. "You are the one who was supposed to handle the businesses side. I built the damn thing—you're the 'CFO.'" I mimic him with a goofy voice. "Remember? Why the hell would you send us into a meeting with zero preparation?"

"I didn't think they would get back to me that quickly. I—" He grabs his head, digging his fingers into fistfuls of his usually perfect hair. He turns to the side and paces into the road.

Raindrops fall around me, a few at a time. One drops directly on my head, feeling almost as if an angel was tapping me with her finger.

"No, that's not fair," I say. I straighten my shoulders, building up my nerve. "Don't act ignorant. You could have waited until we were ready, but you didn't want to."

He turns back around and stares at me, his mouth agape.

"You want *so badly* for this to be huge. Saying it was ready when it wasn't, talking it up to the paper, setting expectations waaay beyond what we could hope to achieve." I laugh, even though it's not funny at all. "You don't build anything—all you do is screw us over."

"You think I don't know that?" His voice cracks. "You

think I don't know that I am not the one who comes up with ideas or knows how to build them?"

He sits on the curb and clasps his head over his knees.

"Oh…" I was going to tell him not to sit, that the mud will ruin those expensive pants. But he's on the ground before I can warn him.

I purse my lips, trying to find the words to respond. I wasn't expecting Braden, of all people, to be so *vulnerable*, but that doesn't make me less mad at him. Or maybe it does. I don't know. Pity and anger swirl inside me, like red and green smoke competing for room.

I stay silent and just look up and down the road, watching as a Tesla races past in the opposite lane, headlights cutting through the ever-increasing rain.

Braden looks up at me. "Do you know why they talked to us fuckin' months before I would've expected them to?"

I shake my head.

"Because his partner recognized my last name. He even said in the email to 'say hello' to my dad." He rolls his eyes. "Classic."

"Are you…complaining about your dad helping you?" I think of my own parents, who were overjoyed about Educonnect but had no idea what it did. They have no way to help me in this field, but would give just about anything to be able to.

He laughs. "God, I must sound like such a brat."

"I wouldn't say that…" I say.

"That's because pageant girls know not to be rude to your face," he jabs.

I smile at his joke even though it's kinda mean.

"It's just…" He starts again, the vulnerability back in his

voice. "So many people at this school have built themselves from nothing. They were the top kids at their high school, the pride of their hometown. And I'm sure that they feel like, you know, if they can make it this far, they can make it. Because they know how to help themselves."

I tug the hem of my dress as I take a seat next to him. Water starts to soak through as soon as I make contact with the wet pavement, and I cringe at the thought of ruined fabric but try to push the concern out of my mind and focus on the teary-eyed boy in front of me.

"Do you know what my dad said when I got in here?" he asks, not waiting for an answer. "'Good, I've sure as hell donated enough.' There was no excitement—for me, it was like, if I *hadn't* gotten in here, it would've been an embarrassment. How the hell am I supposed to make them proud if nothing I do will ever be impressive?"

I stare at him as the rain picks up even more. The sky seems to open up, and my dress is soaked through in seconds. I'm sure my makeup is running down my face like charcoal tears.

They say it's sunny three hundred days of the year in Santa Clara County, California. Today seems to be one of the other sixty-five.

"You want to know why I'm so anxious to be part of something huge? Because every year I'm not doing something earth-shattering is another year I fall behind where my father was when he was my age."

"That's *so* unreasonable," I say. "Being a millionaire under thirty shouldn't be the bar."

"It is to my parents."

"Aw, c'mon. They can't actually think that."

"Sara." He shakes his head. "I've been going to schools with at least a fifty-thousand-dollar yearly tuition since preschool. Do you know how successful I have to be to return on that investment, to not be a loss to my parents?"

"But you're their son, not a stock. And sure, they've helped you, but you've worked hard too. They might be hard on you, but of course they're proud of you."

"I think you assume they're better people than they are." He turns away from me, looking into the grove of trees that lines the road. I turn to look too. Many of the branches are yellow or gray, and I suspect the trees are probably appreciating this break from the seemingly ceaseless California drought.

"Fifty-thousand-dollar preschool?" I ask.

He nods.

"That must have been just insane," I say.

"Yeah," he says. "The point is to be a feeder into elementary school and then high school. After that we had the highest rate of acceptance into Ivy Leagues in the country."

I raise my eyebrows. "I'm sure." I try to imagine what it would be like, for a letter from Warren or Harvard to be the expectation, not cause for celebration.

"We, uh…" He clears his throat. "We also had one of the highest rates of suicide."

My heart drops.

"Not to mention eating disorders, drug abuse." He shakes his head. "It's so much pressure, you know." He wipes a tear from his eye. "My close friend, he was, um… He passed away. I think—I think—" He stumbles over his words, letting out a sob.

I move closer to him, putting a hand on his back.

He takes a long, shaky breath. "I think he started to feel

like if he couldn't be perfect, he didn't want to be alive. Which makes no sense, you know? Because it's impossible to be perfect, and—" Tears run down his face. "And he was such an amazing guy. He made so many people so happy. I mean his laugh… Goddamn, I'd do the stupidest shit to make him laugh because it was just such a happy sound—it was contagious, you know? And that's the thing, he had all these things in his mind he thought he had to be, but damn it, if he was just here right now, and I could talk to him and make him laugh about something stupid? That would be the best thing in the world."

I lean forward, pulling Braden into a hug. He wraps his arms around me, slowly at first, like he is unsure. But then I feel his body give in, falling into mine. I can feel him shake as he sobs into my shoulder, trying to catch his breath.

"It's okay," I whisper. "Just breathe. It's okay. Just breathe."

chapter sixteen

Braden

The email from UCLA comes while I am at the student union working on homework. I prefer to work here between the food court and the big shady patio. The library is too quiet, like a tomb, my room too easy to nap in, and the dorm lounge too rowdy and filled with people wanting to offer you a beer. Here, with the smell of Subway bread, and coffee brewing at the ever-crowded Starbucks, there is the perfect amount of activity for me to concentrate.

I type a reply quickly.

We are considering a number of candidates to be included in the next round of school launches and will get back to you as soon as possible. If you have interest in being the Campus Rep for your school, which includes automatic promotion to gold status, please send along a complete marketing plan, along with your résumé as soon as possible.

Best,
Braden Hart
CFO, Perfect10

I'm only sort of lying. We wanted to launch to the next ten schools on the same day and were hoping to announce which schools by the end of the week. The problem is that we received requests from only eight, or I guess, nine, now. So the competition wasn't exactly as fierce as I might have let on.

UCLA is one of the ones we want most—being a public school, it will bring up our number of users substantially but maintain an aura of exclusivity because it's also a top university. But I don't want *them* to know that. We want each school to be hyped they were selected and feel like they won out against huge competition. Same for each campus ambassador.

"Is that Perfect10?" a female voice says.

I reach to close my computer slightly before looking behind me. But the girl isn't looking at my screen. She's looking at the phone of the girl sitting next to her. They seem to be here together, sitting at the same table with the same pink Starbucks drinks in front of them.

The second girl, a pretty brunette in a purple dress, blushes. "Yeah, I just got it today."

"Dude." The first girl pulls her phone from her bag. "I got it a week ago, and I am literally addicted." Her voice bounces over every syllable of the word *literally* as if to add emphasis to her already-hyperbolic use of the word.

"Did you hear…" Girl One leans in as if to tell her purple-clad friend a secret, although her voice loses none of its volume. *"Joe Fitzpatrick* is on it?"

"The quarterback?" The purple-dressed girl's eyes go wide.

"Yeah." Girl One smiles, seeming pleased with the reaction to her information.

"No way!"

"I know, right. Last year I would spend entire Friday nights trying to find what party he was at. Now I just have to get to platinum."

Great, I think. *We are assisting stalkers.*

Well, only if this chick makes it to platinum. I look her up and down. And without some really creative photo editing, she won't.

"Have you chatted with him yet?" Purple Dress leans forward.

"No, not yet, but I will soon. I've already made it into an *exclusive level*." She flips her hair. "Silver."

"Oh, that's really cool," Purple Dress says innocently. "I'm not sure how to check mine."

I make a mental note to make the status check button more obvious. After all, if people don't know where they stand, they won't be driven to change it. Maybe we should move it to the main page—or, uh, Sara and Robbie should move it to the main page.

"I mean, you probably don't have one yet." Girl One laughs. "But here, I'll show you," she says with pride, taking Purple Dress's phone. She swipes and clicks a few times confidently.

And then the smug look falls from her face. "That can't be right."

"What?" The other girl leans forward, worry in her eyes. "Am I in the totally ugly one or something? Oh my god, *am I not in one at all*?"

"No." Girl One sets the phone down on the table. "You're in Gold. How the hell are you already above me? *You just got the app.*"

"Really?" Her eyes light up, and she reaches for the phone. "I'm gold!"

"Yeah whatever, it's just a stupid app." Girl One puts her phone in her backpack and zips it closed with purpose.

Although *stupid app* seem like terrible words to hear about the thing I have dedicated the last few months of my life to, this is actually the best possible conversation I could have overheard.

Excitement is one thing. I know people are excited by the app from all the press we're getting. But people read an article or see a commercial about a product, get excited about it, mean to check it out later and then forget to buy it *all the time*.

But this girl is frustrated. From her slouched shoulders to the frown on her face, she is visibly shattered that she hasn't gotten a higher rating on the app.

She's right where we want her. Once she's done crying about it, she'll become obsessed with getting a higher rating, always online, driving up our numbers. She might even pay to check her numerical score and how close she is to gold, multiple times a day.

I finish my smoothie and close my laptop. I've done enough work for today.

"The best thing just happened," I say as I push open the door to Sara's room.

"What?" two voices ask at the same time.

"Oh, hey Robbie." I wave to him and he waves back from his perch on the couch. "Damn, are you guys always here coding?" I set my bag on the empty chair next to Sara's.

"Well, it would help if there weren't just two of us," she says, but with less bite in her voice than usual. She looks at me with soft concern, rather than her usual contempt. I'm not quite sure if I like it.

I squirm and avert my eyes, pushing away all thoughts of that day in the rain.

"So what was it?" Robbie asks.

"Huh?"

"The 'best thing ever,' remember?" Sara says.

"Oh." I feel a smile spread across my face. "I saw two sorority girls talking about the app, and I swear to God I thought one of them was going to cry. How amazing is that?"

"Braden, you can't celebrate a girl crying." Her nose scrunches in a look I'm sure is meant to intimidate me but is way too cute to work.

There's the Sara I know.

Roberto laughs, almost tumbling over the arm of the couch he is sitting on.

"Okay, okay." I take a seat, setting my bag on the ground and flipping my chair so I can sit backward. "That's fair, but she didn't actually shed any tears. Anyway, you're missing the point—people are getting into our app."

"That is kind of cool," Sara says. A smile plays on her lips. And I don't know if it's all in my head, but I think she might be slightly less antagonistic toward me. And not just in that pitying way of before. I smile back and for a moment my gaze lingers on her.

An email alert sounds. We reach for our iPhones simultaneously, but it was me who got the message.

"USC!" I say, standing up as I read the email. "That's ten!"

Perfect. Another big school that ranks high on *US News & World Report.* Not to mention one full of rich kids in the middle of Hollywood, greedy for this sort of status.

I look up from my phone and turn to Sara. "How long will it take you to get things ready for that?"

She looks at Robbie. "We already bought the extra server space. But we need to make sure the algorithm is ready to scale."

Robbie types a few things before looking up. "We are adding a way to sort your general location, so people here won't see profiles of people at, like, USC or wherever."

"All right, nice." I nod. "We also should put out a press release when we do the next launch." The wheels in my head start turning, already trying to perfect the way we present this next move.

"Sure," Sara says.

Robbie shrugs, eyes still locked on his screen.

I wish they understood how important this part is. Otherwise it would just be us three and their CS study group on the damn thing.

"They'll want to know numbers too," I say.

"Two thousand users," Sara says. "As of this morning."

"No," I reply. "That's not how we should say it."

"Why?" Sara asks. "That's what Michael asked us."

I cringe at the mention of the meeting. But I'm glad that she at least used a neutral tone.

"Yeah." I clear my throat. "But we shouldn't say that figure."

"Why?" Sara says.

Robbie is plugged into whatever he is doing, this discussion apparently not even warranting his attention.

"Because we've released it only to Warren students," I say. "So our numbers will be much lower than our competition."

"So say a percentage," Robbie mumbles.

"What?" I turn to him.

I guess he *was* listening. And coding at the same time. I'm impressed.

"There are what, seven thousand undergrads on campus?" he says, like this is obvious. "Can we get information on how many of those people are single?"

"The *Daily* did something about it a month ago," Sara says. "Or at least an estimation, when they wrote that article about dating on campus."

"Perfect," Robbie says. "Then divide our users by that, and bingo, the percentage of single people on campus on our app."

"Yeah but it's been like two weeks," I say. "The number can't be that…"

He spins his computer toward me. I walk toward him so I can read it.

He has the *Daily* article pulled up, along with some sort of fancy CS Engineering Whatever calculator that is definitely overkill for this task.

It's a bit hard to read for a mere mortal social science major like me, but even I can tell where the grand total is.

"That can't be right," I say.

Robbie shakes his head. "Numbers don't lie."

Sara leans toward us. "What is it?"

I smile, feeling the weight lift from my shoulders for the first time since we launched.

"Half of the single people on campus are using our app."

"*What?*"

"Yeah." I nod. "We might just become millionaires after all."

chapter seventeen

Roberto

"What does their company do again?" Sara asks.

Outside the car window, palm trees move past rhythmically. They line the path toward the main quad, all towering and spaced precisely, like Roman columns.

We are in an Uber Black, due to Braden's insistence on not asking an upperclassman to borrow a car, and on our way to seek advice from a Warren upperclassman who went to Braden's boarding school. Or, I guess he really isn't an upperclassman anymore, considering he dropped out in the middle of last year to pursue his start-up idea.

"It's an anonymous message board platform for middle school and high schoolers."

I make a face. "Does the world really need that?"

Braden shrugs. "It got funding."

"Hmmm." Sara flicks a piece of fuzz off her pink tweed skirt. She looks nice, with a white blouse that ties into a bow at her neck and stylish shoes with little buckles.

I feel a bit underdressed myself, in just a button-down and a dark pair of jeans. I wasn't sure if I should dress like I was going to a business meeting, or just to hang out with some other kids around our age. I feel like I chose wrong.

"How much funding?" I ask.

"I don't know. I asked my dad's assistant to look it up, but she couldn't find any numbers." The car turns off campus, heading through the overpriced shops of downtown Palo Alto and toward the residential neighborhood beyond. "The house we're about to visit has got to be worth a few million though, if that tells you anything."

I raise my eyebrows and nod, then settle back in my seat and look out my own window as we zoom past homes with sunny gardens and Teslas parked out front.

I try to wrap my mind around the idea of a kid just a few years older than me with millions. I mean, I've just begun to get used to the ridiculousness that is Braden, a teen who has access to and will one day inherit a butt-load of money.

But someone who has earned it himself? Someone who is done worrying about homework and is instead worried about his company's quarterly report? Someone at an age where a job should mean camp counselor or grocery bagger, who is instead probably running around in thousand-dollar suits as he heads to board meetings? I can't even picture that.

A few minutes later, the car comes to a stop in front of a modest-looking ranch house.

The driver slides a finger across his screen to end the ride and offers us bottled water or mints as we get out. A little bit different than taking the bus or train.

Can I offer you someone's old gum that's been stuck under the seat? might be the BART equivalent.

I close the door behind me and step around the car to take in the house. It's not what I thought a multimillion-dollar house would look like. I always envisioned more Scrooge McDuck levels of elegance. Maybe some big white columns framing a grand entrance. Perhaps someone in uniform who runs to open your door for you and take your coat, before beginning a rendition of "I Think I'm Gonna Like It Here" from *Annie*, complete with a dance break performed by house-keepers in black-and-white uniforms. I was thinking it'd be a house so big there were rooms with no purpose, or maybe one just meant for swimming in money. Okay, maybe that's more what I thought when I was a little kid. But still, the place looks kind of normal. I can't believe they paid so much for it.

Braden punches the doorbell and I can hear it ringing in-side, through a window a few feet from the door, although a curtain masks my view. A few weeds poke out from the cobblestones that make up the front steps, and junk mail and a *Sports Illustrated Swimsuit Issue* poke out from a mailbox with a blue bird painted on it.

The door swings open, and the guy standing in the dark doorway is not what I expected either. He is a little bit taller than I am, although he looks like he could be younger than me. He has shaggy brown hair and wears light-wash jeans with frayed cuffs, a T-shirt that says *Brogrammer* on it and no shoes. He is also holding a bong.

"Heeeyy," he says. "Braden, my man."

Braden laughs as the guy hugs him.

"I'm Brett," he says.

I reach out my hand, but he shakes his head before hug-ging me tight and patting my shoulder like we're old friends. He smells like a concert.

When he finally steps away, he turns to Sara. She stumbles back in surprise at his enthusiastic embrace. "Oh, all right then." A smile breaks across her stunned face and she laughs, and I can't tell if it's out of discomfort or amusement.

We step inside and Brett closes the door behind us. Inside the air is sickly sweet and stale; although plenty of light filters in through the windows, they are all closed.

"So you've really taken to California, I see," Braden says.

"What?" Brett's brow furrows. He follows Braden's gaze down to the bong in his hand. "Oh, yeah, sorry. I forgot I was holding that." He sets the glass object on a tall table lining the hallway. The type of thing you'd usually use to display family pictures or scented candles. "You guys don't mind the smoke, right? I could open a window." He looks to Sara, seeming to have just noticed her business-casual attire.

"Yeah, I'm gonna go ahead and…" His words fade away, but he keeps walking briskly. We follow him into a living room with a large sectional couch and flat screen TV.

He steps over a coffee table littered with beer bottles, lighters and what seems to be a mason jar of weed, making his way to the back wall where huge sliding glass doors reveal a large patio and pool.

He slides the door open, and then walks over to flip a switch on the wall, sending the ceiling fan spinning.

"Is that better?"

I nod.

"Oh, don't worry about it," Sara says, waving her arm in an awkward gesture. "Whatever you usually do is fine." She examines the couch, pursing her lips as she brushes off a spot before sitting down as close to the edge as possible. She folds her hands carefully on her lap.

Braden sprawls out on a large armchair, his expensive leather shoes resting on an ottoman of a different shade of expensive leather.

I sit a few feet away from Sara, leaning back against a throw pillow with a stitched image of a Banksy painting on it, but I'm not much more comfortable than she looks.

I take a deep breath, although it is hard to feel refreshed with this air. Someone tells a joke and the others laugh, but I miss it. I can't stop looking at the jar. I know it sounds stupid, but I usually walk the other way if I enter a room and see drugs. I mean, sure, I've seen them used in school bathrooms or at concerts, and it's not like I can't deal with the idea of it happening around me, but I try not to stick around a party when that's all people are doing. I never made a big deal about it, usually just saying I'm not feeling well or have to get up early and head home.

I just never wanted to be around if something went down. I knew too many kids whose lives were ruined because they were walking around with something in their backpack when the police decided to randomly search them. If a party was busted and I was there… I wouldn't be able to look my parents in the eyes and tell them that, after all their sacrifice, I had messed up my chances to go to college just to stay at a lame party. The state made it legal a few years ago, but only for people over twenty-one, which I am not. And the federal law could still screw everyone over.

I glance behind me at the door. I *am* technically here on official business. It's not like I can just make an excuse and leave. And it's not like I'm just risking my future being here; in fact, I could be helping it quite a bit.

And for some reason I feel like the police aren't about to

break down this million-dollar door with a battering ram. Some bullshit.

I exhale and lean back, trying to make myself look less uncomfortable.

"My roommates and cofounders went out for burritos," Brett says. "But we can just start without them if that's cool with you."

I look to Sara, who shrugs.

"Sure, why not," Braden says.

"Sweet," Brett says. "So what do you want to know?" While he waits for us to respond, he heads back across the room to grab the bong.

"Uh…" I try to think, distracted by the sight of Brett lighting up the bong, and then letting it fill with smoke for a good ten seconds before inhaling. "I guess, do you wanna just walk us through the process, from your initial idea to company?"

He nods as he reaches for a beer and takes a long sip. He wipes his mouth before answering. "So yeah, I usually use a process called ideation. Are you guys familiar with design thinking?"

Sara laughs.

"Yeah," I say. "A little bit. I'm in a class about it now, but it's been my first introduction." I reach for my backpack to pull out my notebook and a pen.

"You want some?" Brett says. I look up to see him holding out the bong to Sara.

Her eyes go wide. I'm about to launch into my speech, that she doesn't have to if she doesn't want to and that she shouldn't feel bad, when a huge smile breaks across her face.

"Sure," she says. "Why not?"

My eyebrows shoot up, but I look away so she doesn't see. I open my notebook to a fresh page and write the date at the top.

I underline it a few times and then write *ideation* below. And now I've officially run out of things to distract me.

I look at Sara, who is balancing the bong on her panty-hosed knees. She holds the lighter in her hand and is looking at it like it's some sort of artifact from an alien civilization.

"I don't, uh, know how to..." She looks to me and then to Brett.

"Oh here," he says, taking the lighter from her. "Watch out for your hair."

She pulls the silky blond curtain away from her face, holding it in a ball behind her head, and Brett sparks the lighter. Curls of white smoke float toward her lips, and then Brett pulls the pin and she breathes it in.

She throws her head back, coughing uncontrollably. Her eyes turn glossy and her face bright red, but she is smiling through her gasps.

"I'll get you some water," Brett says, taking the bong from her.

"You okay?" I ask.

I hear a cabinet open and close and then the sound of a faucet in the kitchen.

Sara continues to cough but nods.

By the time Brett has emerged from the kitchen with a cup, she's caught her breath.

"Thank you," she says, reaching for the glass.

"How do you feel?"

She furrows her brow, considering this. "I don't know." She looks back and forth between us. "A little light-headed, but that might just be because of all the coughing," she laughs.

"Fair enough," Brett says. He offers the bong to Braden, who takes it and needs no help or instruction to smoke.

"Beer?" Brett asks us.

"Sure," I say.

Sara just nods.

"What do you have?" Braden asks Brett. He tries to hand the bong to me, but I shake my head. He sets it on the coffee table without a word.

Brett goes into the kitchen and reemerges with a six-pack. "It's craft," he says, pointing to the logo on the box. "It's made just a few miles from here." He hands me a bottle, which has an illustration of a tree on it. I reach for the bottle opener on the table and pop the top while he continues to pitch it. I'm sure it's fine. "I just really like to know where my stuff is from, you know? With big companies, it's like you don't even know what kind of crap you're putting into your body."

I resist the urge to laugh at the irony as he finishes his statement and reaches for the bong, expertly balancing it in one hand while lighting it with the other; he manages to pull the pin with the same hand that holds the lighter and take a long rip, all while standing up. I get the impression this might be how he spends every evening.

He leans back and blows a stream of smoke toward the ceiling. "Okay, so like I was saying, ideation." He hands the bong to Sara again. Braden moves toward her to help.

I set down my beer and reach for my notebook.

"What you really need to do is approach the creative process in a need-based way. You find a gap in the market that needs filling and bingo."

"So how did you get from that to...your idea?" I ask. With his need-based approach, I picture some sort of medical equipment or a system that helps track the shipment of food so it doesn't spoil, not a chat room for preteens.

"Well, a lot of middle schoolers these days are prevented from accessing the traditional social media sites by their parents, so we thought if we developed a new one that no parent had heard of and made the app appear like a game on their phones, we could fill that market."

"Are you worried though?" I ask. "About bullying and predators and all the reasons middle school parents tried to get their kids off social media in the first place?"

"Nah." He shrugs. "We've got a lawyer on retainer. He says we shouldn't be liable for any of that."

Yeah, but even if they can't sue you, doesn't it bother you that people use what you made for terrible things?

Brett reaches for the bong; he doesn't seem preoccupied with this.

He smiles. "It's honestly ridiculous—" He looks around himself. "Has anyone seen the lighter?"

Sara shakes her head no and then looks down at her lap, where the yellow Zippo is resting. "Oh!" Her head shoots up. "Yeah." She laughs and hands it to him.

"What was I saying?" Brett says.

"It's ridiculous..." I answer.

"Oh yeah, it's ridiculous. You just walk in with a semigood idea and the skills to code it, and you can walk out with more than enough money to live off," he says. "There's really no reason to get a degree or go work for a company anymore, when they're so ready to fund, you know?"

"Yeah," I say, twisting the edge of my notebook. "But what about when it runs out?"

"Yeah, do you ever worry about that?" Sara asks.

"Hmmm?" Brett looks up from joint he is rolling. Apparently he is too impatient to let the bong come back around to him.

"Like with the dot-com bubble," I say. "What if that happens again?"

"I'm really not worried about it." He picks up the Zippo and lights the joint. After a long drag, he continues. "Sure, this could fail. But I also could work my ass off at a Fortune 500 just for another recession to hit. And all of a sudden that good, stable job doesn't look so stable anymore."

Braden hands me the bong again, and I pass it to Sara without a word. No one seems to care that I'm not smoking, but a part of me still feels uncomfortable. I reach for my beer.

Brett continues to talk about the benefits of start-ups and the anachronism that is a college degree while he hooks his computer up to the Apple TV. He doesn't say anything I haven't heard a million times before, about how many dropouts are now millionaires and billionaires. He also carefully doesn't talk about the dropouts that are now living paycheck to paycheck or frantically searching through classified ads for anything that doesn't require a degree.

"Okay, let's see this thing y'all are making then." He hands the computer to Braden. The screen is now in sync with the TV and the app store is pulled up. "Make me an account. Help me find a supermodel or whatever." He wiggles his eyebrows.

Braden downloads the app and accepts the terms and conditions within seconds. "I'm gonna hook it up to your Facebook and use your profile picture," he says. "Makes it quicker."

Braden selects "man interested in women" without pausing to ask Brett how he identifies. I frown.

He then types what Brett dictates for his bio, a few sentences about himself—Brett chooses to highlight his high school alma mater, his status as a start-up founder and his love of all things green, "money and otherwise." And just like that, he's now part of the search to find a perfect 10. Or I guess, to become a perfect 10? I'm honestly not sure what the name is supposed to imply. Maybe I should start reading the marketing materials Braden keeps sharing with me on Google Drive.

The welcome screen of our app loads, featuring a large red button that says: *Find Me a 10.*

Brett leans over to take the laptop back from Braden and click it. The introduction sequence begins.

> Everyone starts at the beginning: for now you are unranked.
> We will show you all singles in your area who allow unranked users to appear in their dating pool.
> As you swipe through users, they will swipe through you.
> Once you get an average "yes" swipe of 6.5/10 you will reach Silver status.
> If you get to an average of 8/10 you will become Gold.
> And if you manage a 9/10 or above, you will be one of the few users who reach Platinum.
> Best of luck!

Another button appears that says: View Singles Near Me. He clicks on it, and a picture of a brunette girl with glasses appears. He swipes yes.

He clicks through the pictures rapidly, making decisions in a split second, based only on the photo, since there's no way he is reading their bios that quickly.

A picture comes up I recognize. Lily, a quiet but kind girl

in my CS class. Her photograph is with her mom on vacation. She is wearing a turtleneck sweater. At the bottom of
the screen it says she is currently Unranked.

Brett swipes left, saying no to her. My chest tightens. I can't
help but feel bad for Lily, thinking about her shy voice when
she asks a question in class. I hate that she's about to get an
alert that her score has dropped.

An alert comes up on Brett's screen: "You have reached
Silver Status!"

"Damn," he says with a shit-eating grin. "People like me."

"Silver's not that hard," I say. I flinch. I don't know why
I said that. I guess I was just mad for Lily. I take a sip of my
beer; it's getting warm. *Whatever.* I'm not really in the mood
to drink.

"So now I can filter out some of these duds, right?" Brett
asks, still clicking through images.

"That's the idea." Braden smiles. "But you might want to
leave unfiltered on," he adds. "That way they can see you
and bump up your score."

"Good point," Brett says. "That's why I can see her then?"
he asks, when a pretty, curly-haired girl comes on the screen,
her information bar reading: Gold. "Because she has silver
settings on?"

"Oh my god." Sara sits up, finally paying attention. "That's
Yaz. I know her."

"She's hot," Braden says.

"She's also *brilliant*." Sara sits up taller in her chair.

"Well yeah, it says right there, former Instafriend intern."

"A definite right swipe," Brett says.

Sara falls back onto the couch cushions. "Can we do something else?" She says. "This feels weird."

"Sure." Brett switches over to Netflix.

He scrolls through Netflix before settling on *Planet Earth*, and I watch as the camera pans over an African landscape, the colors vibrant on the HD, curved screen, all-the-bells-and-whistles machine.

The narrator's voice, a soothing baritone, introduces a family of meerkats and I settle farther back into the couch. I exhale.

I always liked this show. It reminds me of science class, back when it was mapping constellations and playing with baking soda volcanoes. Just a few minutes of sweeping nature imagery paired with quick trivia, and it's like I'm back to that time of building simple circuits that illuminate tiny lightbulbs and planting beans in plastic cups so you can see the roots grow.

Back before science became about complex physics equations, endless problem sets and tedious lab procedures. Not that those aren't important, but they're not what I fell in love with.

Or at least, I thought I fell in love with it. But I don't think I've ever felt quite so passionate as Braden, Brett and Sara seem to right now. They gawk at the screen, and I'm surprised no one is drooling.

The meerkat segment ends and the screen pans over a river of lava, pooling from a volcano. A segment of black lava rock caves from the pressure and starts to flow through the red liquid.

Sara watches with tears in her eyes. "It's just so beautiful." She begins to cry softly.

"I know," Brett says. "And we're destroying it." He shakes his head. "It's a damn shame."

I want to ask—if he really feels so strongly, why he uses

his mind and skills to make a stupid app instead of working on some sort of green technology?

But who am I to talk? I'm here to work on an app that helps people rate each other, not exactly the kind of social problem I dreamed about trying to solve with computer science when I applied to Warren.

By the time we roll into the second episode, Sara's eyes are starting to flutter shut. Her hair is disheveled, strands running like yellow streaks across her face, and there is a slight smile on her lips.

Braden gets up from his chair and takes a seat close to her on the couch.

"How do you feel?" he asks.

"Good." She smiles sleepily.

"Doesn't your skin feel so weird?" he says.

"Whatcha mean?"

"Like...feel." He runs his finger across her arm delicately.

She giggles. "That's bizarre."

I swallow, my stomach in knots, and turn toward the TV.

"The Lion stalks its prey, lying dormant and undetected in the grass until the gazelle is vulnerable."

"Hey!" I say, standing up as I turn back to the group. "How about we listen to some music?"

"That sounds great!" Sara perks up, leaning forward to the edge of her seat, away from the arm Braden had slipped around her.

A half-asleep Brett seems to remember we are here and stands up slowly, then walks toward the speakers in the corner of the room. He fumbles with his phone for a few seconds, and then the first few bars of a sugary pop song by The

Chainsmokers floats through the room. He clicks mute on the TV, and then cranks the dial.

"I love this song!" Sara says, her eyes like shining silver dollars. She stands up and bounces on the couch, holding her sensible shoes in her hand and singing, or more accurately, yelling, along to every word. She makes her way along the couch to me. She points to me as she sings along. I smile and laugh.

She gestures for me to stand up and join her, but I shake my head. I appreciate the pure joy she's exuding, but with only half a beer in my system, I'm not exactly on that level. She realizes I'm not going to budge, and her shoulders fall, just a centimeter. She does one of those jump-to-sitting moves we all used to try when someone in the neighborhood would get a bounce castle for a birthday or First Communion. But because it is a just a couch, she does not bounce right back up, but sinks in the cushion. Right next to me.

"Can you imagine," she says, "if someone wrote a song like that about you?" She grips my shoulders, her eyes bright and urgent. She is millimeters from my face, but her gaze stays on me. She blinks but doesn't look away. "That would be an amazing feeling, don't you think?"

"I—I don't…" I lean away from her, not sure why, but just sort of, overwhelmed with the raw emotionality of the moment.

She looks down for a second, her eyelashes fluttering. But then in half a beat, she is back again, standing up and skipping to the center of the room, where she announces with her chin high in the air that she is going in the pool now.

chapter eighteen

Yaz's phone dings for at least the tenth time in the last minute, interrupting the rose ceremony. I reach for the remote so that I can go back and hear which name he said, although the contestants' reactions did kind of give it away. Dani "with an *i*" is jumping up and down and smiling while Danny "with a *y*" has started to cry mascara-darkened tears.

"Will you stop texting?" I say. "It's supposed to be girls' night."

Yaz sticks her tongue out at me before tapping her screen a few more times. "For your information—" she sets her phone on the coffee table "—I was not *texting*, I happen to be using your app, missy."

"Really?" I set down the remote and scoot forward to look over her shoulder.

"Yeah, it's kind of like, crazy addictive." She quickly types a *hello* to her newest match. She turns and raises her eyebrows. "Guess what level I'm at now?"

"Gold?" I act like I don't know.

"Yeah," she smiles. "I'm like, famous now." Her phone lights up again, the headshot of a guy named Scott popping up. Next to his name, his status: Silver appears.

"Ugh." She shakes her head. "I matched with him early on and he keeps chatting me."

Sorry, watching the bachelor, can't talk! Girls night!

"I have to at least say something." She clicks lock and sets her phone down. "Last night I didn't answer a guy because, like, it was clearly a booty call, and he unmatched with me because of it."

"Oh jeez, really?"

"Yeah," she says. "Only knocked me down 0.3 so it's not a big deal. But if I want to keep my Gold I have to give little bread crumbs of conversation to guys like Steve, or they might knock down my score."

"Oh."

"I like some of my other guys though," she says, as if she can tell I'm upset. "Here. I'll show you my boys."

She walks me through the cast of her own personal, digital version of *The Bachelorette*. There is a cute boy she once had a class with who is only a 5.6, and while she usually doesn't accept requests from people who are unranked, he did offer to take her out to a nice dinner. While, on the other hand, a basketball player who will probably go to the NBA this year with a strong Platinum of 9.7, just keeps sending her group messages inviting her and every other girl he's matched with to parties.

"He knows he can get away with it too, with that ridiculous ranking." She rolls her eyes. "I'm always debating un-matching with him so he'll be taken down a peg. But also, like, what if he becomes a Warrior?"

I nod knowingly, wondering how appropriate it would be for me to go in and "accidentally" cut his total score down to three.

"How about you?" She wiggles her eyebrows. "Any boys?"

I think back to the other day and that... I'm not sure what it was, with Robbie. When I looked in his eyes, I really thought I felt something, some sort of connection. Like maybe he liked me back. Like maybe we could be something.

The memory is kind of fuzzy around the edges, with the image of his face in my mind kind of glowing, and I'm not sure it's only because of the pot.

Ever since, I started to do my dumb Sara thing, picturing cute dates we could go on to get frozen yogurt, or see an old movie. How maybe we could take the train to visit his dad sometime, and I could see where he grew up, maybe his elementary school, or the park where he played soccer. I jumped one hundred steps ahead, like I do with every guy I like.

Which was especially dumb, because just as soon as the moment seemed to happen, it disappeared, like a soap bubble popping in the air. One second, I thought we were about to kiss, and the next he couldn't get away from me fast enough. Proving that, like always, this relationship existed solely in my mind.

"Uh...no." I answer.

She shakes her head. "Kind of ironic, don't you think?"

"What do you mean?"

She doesn't answer at first, instead getting up and walking to the kitchen. She digs through the junk food cabinet. "It's just like, you run the most popular dating app on campus. I can't go anywhere without seeing someone on that damn thing. I've had teachers start class by telling everyone if they are caught on it during lecture, they'll automatically lose points. And—oh!" She pulls a package of Red Vines from the back of the stash. "Sorry," she looks over her shoulder, smiling sheepishly. "Can I have some?"

I nod.

"Did you see the *Daily* story?" She takes the top off the container and pulls out a rope. "That a TA used the app to chat with one of his students, and like, got fired." She bites down on the red candy rope, twisting the end in her hand so it makes a snapping sound.

I sigh. "I did see that." It wasn't my favorite news to come out of something I'd help build, but the way her eyes light up, I can tell she thinks this is a really fun real-life soap opera.

"You should get a profile!" She plops back onto the couch. "It really is fun."

"Well that hardly seems appropriate." I adjust my sweater.

"Why not?" She looks down and inspects the identical red candies, as if weighing which she will eat next.

"Because...that would be weird."

"Mark Zuckerberg has Facebook." She raises her eyebrows and turns her head to the side.

"Yeah, but that's different." I lean back on the couch, moving away from her, but really just trying to get more comfortable.

"Why?"

"Because he's using it to promote his website, not to date people."

"Why can't you do both? Then it's like, download Perfect10, you may get to go out with Sara Jones."

"That sounds an awful lot like prostitution."

She considers this, pausing as she bites into another Red Vine. I click play on the show; I'd much rather focus on these strangers' dysfunctional love lives than my own.

A few minutes later, as the credits are rolling, Yaz's phone goes off again.

"Oh, well this one's cute," she says. "Look at him."

I lean toward her to see. "Nuh-uh." I shake my head. "He literally says 'not tryna date.' I mean, I don't want turn away users, but this is a *dating* app—why would he even want to be on it?" I roll my eyes and stand up, having seen enough of his shirtless beach pics. "You shouldn't talk to him." I head toward the kitchen.

She follows me, gaze still glued on her phone.

"I don't care about that."

I open the refrigerator door and squat down to look for the orange juice, wondering if that counts as my exercise for the day.

"I respect that at least he's up-front about it," she continues. "Most guys here think that, but don't tell you until after they sleep with you."

"What do you mean?" I pop up, looking at her over the fridge door. "*Most* guys are against dating anyone?"

"I mean, yeah… Haven't you talked to a guy at a party and had him give you the whole, you-only-have-four-years-of-college-to-be-a-single-idiot speech?"

I locate the juice carton on the top shelf and close the door with my hip. I skillfully avoid looking her in the eyes as I head to the cabinet for a glass. "Um, sure."

Lie lie lie, you know damn well the only guy you've talked to at a party was Robbie and you both were there out of spite.

I try to keep a good game face as I turn to her, setting my glass on the counter with a clank.

"It's unbelievable." She shakes her head. "Although, to be fair, I definitely know a lot of antirelationship girls here too. That's why everyone is always complaining that there's no dating at Warren."

I consider this as I pour my juice. "I'm not sure if that's true." I set the carton down. "There's a girl who is supposed to live down the hall, but is almost never here because she practically lives with her boyfriend."

"Oh, but that's the thing." Yaz pulls a chair toward her. "I have a theory about this." She sits backward on the chair. "People here are either basically married, or so committed to just hooking up that they act like they hate each other when they're sober or it's like, daylight, which I like to call Vampire Fucking."

I roll my eyes. "That's so stupid."

"Yeah, well, you know." She rests her head on the back of the chair. "They think if you go to dinner with them you're gonna go all *Gone Girl* on their ass, or like start taking sugar pills instead of birth control so you can sue them out of the start-up fortune they plan to make."

"I hate men," I say, before taking a long swig of my juice.

"Tell me about it." She types something on her phone. "But also…" She looks up, clicking lock. "I know more than a few girls who have hooked up with a friend of a guy they started having feelings for, just to prove they're not *that* into him."

"That makes no sense." I lean against the cabinet, suddenly too tired to hold myself up.

"It makes perfect sense…you have a group of super driven, super competitive people. So if they can say, *this person thinks I'm the best person in the world and they have already decided to spend the rest of their life with me*, it's like, check." She makes a squishing movement with her hand. "They accomplished that, and they're happy."

I open my mouth to speak, but she doesn't let me get a word in.

"Or, if they can say, 'Yeah I hooked up with that person but I don't care about them as much as they care about me, in fact I don't care about them at all,' they win that little game—they have proven they are desirable and avoided the embarrassment of possibly pining after someone who doesn't want them.

"But to say," she continues, "'I like them a lot, and will see how it goes, we hopefully will go on a sixth date…'" She clutches her chest. "That is waaaay too much vulnerability for people who are used to winning everything."

"But caring about someone isn't about winning," I say. "Love isn't a competition."

"Sara…" She narrows her eyes, as if trying to tell if I'm joking. "I got an email from your app today basically saying I was in tenth place in the love competition."

chapter nineteen

Roberto

"Hola, mijo, how are you?" My mother's voice rings with warmth. She has more of an accent than me or my father. She speaks almost perfect English now, but her words always sound smoother, in a singsong way, like they are rounded at the edges.

I have this hazy memory from when I was young that almost seems like a dream when I try to remember it now. I am eight years old, wearing cowboy pajamas, and have woken from a dream I cannot remember. My room is quiet and cool and a sort of blue color. A sliver of orange light shines between my door and the floor. Down the hall I could hear my mother's voice, louder than the radio in the kitchen that is playing the Luis Miguel she always put on during three-glasses-of-wine nights, but not loud enough for me to hear what she is talking about. I cuddle my blanket closer and go back to sleep smiling. It sounds safe; it sounds like home.

Sometimes, even now, I wake up to a sound in the house,

or even my dorm, and think it's her. It's hard to get back to sleep after that.

"¡Mamá!" I lean back in my desk chair, tipping back onto two legs. I quickly correct myself, lowering the legs so I am sitting in a way that I won't 'caerme y romperme el cuello,' although it's not as though, from a country away, she can see how I am sitting.

"You sound tired. Have you been getting enough sleep?"

"Sí," I lie. "I've just been very busy lately, with the app launching to more schools and everything. We went to ten more this week."

Back-to-back launches were brutal, but, as I was told by Braden, necessary, to keep our momentum.

"Lo se!" Her voice goes an octave higher. "I read that article you sent me. *The Huffington Post*, very nice, baby, esto es grande."

I smile. "Gracias. My friend Braden has been doing all the press stuff."

"Eh, this boy is your friend now? I thought we hated him."

"We never *hated* him… I just didn't like him that much at first, when it was mostly coding, but he's doing more work now. He's not too bad." I pick up a pencil from my desk. I rub the eraser with my thumb.

"Hmmm." The line is silent for a moment, so I brace myself for what is next. "¿Que tal la chica?"

Oh, great, here we go again. I shake my head. *Dad must have told her.*

"Sara? What about her?"

"How does she feel about this Braden boy? Are they still at each other's throats all the time?"

"Not exactly…"

Actually, it has kind of been the opposite lately. I'd started to notice little things at first—she would bring coffee for us and not "forget" his; he would let it slide when she said something incredibly nerdy. He would tease her, and she would smile and look down instead of scrunching her nose.

I don't know what happened that day, when I got in the car and she went after him. But their relationship changed from tormenting each other to playful teasing. Or not being mean at all.

And then, just the other day… They arrived together at her quad for a meeting, late, laughing and talking loudly about some inside joke as they walked up.

"Sorry, we were just at lunch," Sara said, still trying to catch her breath from laughing.

"We would have invited you but it was so last minute," Braden said.

"Yeah." Sara looked at him, and he looked back at her. "We were actually just texting, and I mentioned this sandwich place."

"And the next thing you know—" he hops into the story "—she was like, 'when did I get so hungry.'"

"And he was like, 'I'm already headed there.' So we just said, why not, and went." She smiles, and her eyes sparkle.

It was like having a conversation with two aliens who had taken over their bodies.

"Que bueno," my mother says.

"What?" I blink, back in the present, in my messy dorm room, with someone making a ton of noise in the courtyard as they attempt to blow away the leaves that have just started to fall. Well, as much as they do fall here in paradise.

"That's good. That your partners aren't driving each other crazy anymore."

"Oh, um." I clear my throat. "Yeah. That's true."

Just then there is a knock at the door. I stand and walk over to open it as my mother starts in on a new subject, talking a mile a minute, something about the flowers she is trying to grow.

I yank open the door to see Braden there, radiating energy.

I raise an eyebrow. But he doesn't explain, he just pushes past me into my room.

"Hold on," I tell him. "I'm talking with my mom."

"I can't hold on." He is moving around, on the balls of his feet, and I am not sure if he is about to dance or fight me.

"Ugh, okay…" I turn away from him for a moment, as if this gives me more privacy. "Mom, I'll have to call you back."

I grumble as I hang up the phone. "What?" I ask. *This better be good.*

He grabs me by the shoulders "We got a meeting with Thatcher Bell!"

This time the lead-up to the meeting is far less hectic. We have a few days', not hours', notice, and are already in a better position, having been live for around a month, not a day. Braden asks me and Sara for a few statistics, but mostly tells us to leave it all to him. I'd feel more comfortable doing so if I hadn't witnessed him crash and burn in the last meeting. But he's the one who's spent every summer since he was in diapers in Martha's Vineyard and Tahoe with guys like this, so I'd have a hard time correcting him even if he was doing something wrong.

I stand outside my dorm, adjusting my tie and wondering if this suit makes me look too much like a kid about to make his First Communion, as I wait for Braden to pick me up in an Uber.

Well, pick *us* up, that is if Sara ever finishes getting ready. I glance at the door behind me, still closed, with no one visible through the glass.

Tires crunch on gravel as a black car pulls up.

"Sorry!" A voice says behind me. I turn to see Sara, her blond hair flying as she races through the door. She shakes her head as she reaches me. "I never budget enough time."

She is wearing more makeup than usual, or at least, than she does when we're up half the night coding. Her eyelids are shimmery and her hair is curled. The ringlets still fall perfectly, so she must have just done them. After all, the last time she curled it she kept telling me how quickly her hair tends to straighten out.

She hugs me, and the sharp smell of hair spray is overwhelming.

"Okay." She leans back, her hands resting on my shoulders for a moment. "Let's do this thing."

I open the car door for her before walking around to climb in the other side. It's a nice car; the inside has all the touches you don't notice are missing in normal cars, but make you feel fancier as soon as you climb into this kind. Leather interior, seat heaters, a glowing touchscreen display in place of a radio with buttons.

"You know, you *can* get an Uber that's not a town car," Sara says, turning to Braden, who is sitting between us in the middle seat.

I pull my door closed. Even that feels different, the door heavier than usual.

"No offense to you, sir," Sara adds to the driver.

"None taken." The driver, a middle-aged man in a suit, laughs.

"Hey," Braden says. "If you're going to get a private car, you may as well really do it."

Sara leans forward and looks over Braden to me, rolling her eyes.

I laugh and turn to him, waiting for another remark filled with elitism and bravado, but he is silent.

He's wearing a black jacket over a crisp white shirt, far from any sort of First Communion, coming closer to a *Vogue* magazine. He looks young though, especially since he's freshly shaven. And actually kind of pale in contrast to his blazer. He looks past the windshield to the road ahead, his eyes unwavering.

The first part of the meeting goes pretty much the exact same way as our previous attempt. We pull up to a rather unassuming building along Sand Hill. We take an elevator up to a modern and airy office. We are told to wait, greeted by a suave but surprisingly causal guy who offers us coffee and water, which we politely turn down.

We are shown to a large office and exchange pleasantries and handshakes with Thatcher Bell, a middle-aged man with salt-and-pepper hair but few wrinkles, perhaps because of medical assistance. He walks with an easy gait. We sit down and thank him for taking the time to meet with us.

And then the question comes.

"So how many users do you have?"

I hold my breath.

"With all due respect, sir," Braden says. "That's not the question you should be asking us."

Mr. Bell raises his eyebrows. He doesn't look offended. Surprised maybe, but not offended. Or at least, not offended yet. I bite my lip. *Braden is playing with fire.*

"You see, the draw of Perfect10 is its exclusivity," Braden says confidently. "We were available only at Warren for our first three weeks. A week ago we launched to ten more schools after reviewing applications from some of the most exclusive institutions in the country."

He sits a little taller. "We are in the process of picking our next ten, but since we've already chosen Oxford and St. Andrews, we're about to be international, while maintaining our selectivity. We could go wider, of course, but we are strategically building a brand, and I think you know that and you were asking me a trick question.

"What you really want to know," Braden says, "is how Perfect10 is doing in the places it's available. You need stats, to which I will say, at the schools where we offer the app, 63 percent of single students are on it. What's more, 75 percent of our users check the app every day, and 25 percent of our users check it more than 5 times a day on average. That is almost unheard-of levels of engagement, as I'm sure you know."

Bell nods and writes something on his notepad.

"And what's more, we've been able to isolate exactly when user engagement skyrockets." He gestures to me and Sara when he says "we," but I didn't know we did that. "We were unsurprised to find that users check their scores far more often when they are nearing a transition point between statuses. We were surprised to find, however, that this effect is much more poignant when users are at risk of falling down a level. It turns out that insecurity, not vanity, fuels our engagement. People become addicted to checking their score when they are afraid they will fall down a level."

I shift my weight. It feels like the room is getting warmer. I wonder if it is too late to ask for water. Probably. But I suddenly feel like my throat is swelling closed.

"We can easily monetize this insecurity," Braden continues. "Perhaps by using a surge pricing model, so the cost of checking your score goes up the more times you check it per day, or by adding video ads before you can see your score if you're within .5 of a change."

"And the ads could be for gym memberships or makeup," Bell says.

A smile spreads across Braden's face. "I like the way you think, sir."

Bell stares at his notepad for a moment, pen still in hand, although he's not writing anything, just tapping the desk so that little pen marks appear on the paper, like tiny blue sprinkles. "I worked in the television business for years, always worrying about ratings. About how many eyes we could get to the show, so they would also see the ads. And I see my kids, with their iPhones, *constantly* on social media—you can barely tear them away. I've always thought that would be a hell of a business to be in."

Braden's eyes light up. "So you're saying..."

Bell smiles but holds up his hand. "I'm just saying you've got me interested, and that I would like to take your idea to the rest of my team, see what the board thinks first. But yes." He stands, and we follow suit. "I'm saying you've made it far-ther than ninety percent of the people who have sat in that chair." He smiles, and I swear to god, his teeth sparkle. Like a cartoon prince. "I guess we sell exclusivity too."

He shakes our hands as we thank him, nodding vigorously at every word he says, even though the adrenaline roaring through my brain is too loud for me to really process what he is saying.

chapter twenty

Oh my god. Oh. My. God.

I cannot believe what I just heard. He wants to take our idea to his board. To his board!

I don't know much about this venture capital stuff, but I've seen enough movies to know that going to the board has *got* to be a good thing.

I shake Mr. Bell's hand and smile so widely that my face would hurt if I weren't high off pure happiness.

It's all I can do to keep my composure as I wave goodbye to the receptionist and wait for the elevator.

"I'm going to run to the bathroom," Robbie says as the doors ding open. "I'll meet you guys downstairs."

I nod and step into the elevator, Braden following close behind.

"Oh my god!" I finally let out the words that have been ricocheting around my head. "I cannot *believe* that just happened. I mean, did you see his face? I was worried at first because, well, you know, that was a bit risky. And after what happened last time—sorry if you don't want me to mention that, but oh my god, who cares now, because that went *so* well and we really only need one firm to like us and oh my *gosh*. Whoa." I stop to catch my breath for a second, putting my hand on my chest.

Braden has just been smiling and nodding along as I've chattered on.

The doors open and I continue as we step off the elevator. "And not to mention, did you hear at the end how he said they were exclusive too and…"

I feel like I have had twenty cups of coffee. I'm practically shaking as I walk a million miles a minute and talk faster. It's like I'm barely registering the words I *am* saying, let alone thinking and then speaking, like my mother is always reminding me to.

"And oh my gosh," I say, holding open the door for Braden as we step into the sunlight. "That was so perfect, the way you pitched it, it was just—" I wave my arms, miming my mind exploding, unable to put my excitement into words anymore.

I expect him to make fun of me for being overexcited, like he did when I danced around my room when my Tory Burch package arrived, or when I cried when I watched that video of panda cubs playing to the sound of "Panda" by Desiigner.

But right now, he is practically as manic as I am. "I know," he says, his eyes shimmering. "I can't believe it."

I practically walk into the big Bell Ventures sign in front of the building, and it becomes real again.

"Yes, yes, yes, yes yes!" I jump up and down, laughing. I pull Braden into a hug and he stumbles back for a second before wrapping his arms around me as well. I fall into him, trying to catch my breath. "I can't believe it," I say into his shirt, before leaning back. His arms don't fall from my waist.

His eyes find mine; they are still shining, fiery and alive. And my breath catches for a different reason.

There is a pause, and the air around us buzzes with electricity. For a moment we just stare at each other. And I wonder if what is running through my mind is running through his. I blink so that my eyelashes flutter and bite my lip.

I look back up, and in a split second we both make the same decision.

We crash into each other. His lips find mine as his hands travel up my body and weave through my hair. He pulls me even tighter against him, and I can't tell if we're so close that I can feel his heartbeat, or if mine is just beating *that fast*. There is a sort of hunger behind this kiss, and the rest of the world becomes a blur. There is just me and him, and the release of this tension that has been building for months first as anger, and now maybe as something else.

And then there's the sound of the door swinging open behind us.

chapter twenty-one

Roberto

With my hand on the door, I stand, frozen. Through the glass, I watch as she laughs and dances and jumps, and my heart is full. I'm full of happiness, not just for what happened upstairs, but to see her this happy.

And then I see them fall together. He wraps his arms around her, and then, as if in slow motion, they kiss.

It feels like my heart is falling out of my body. I want to look away, but I can't.

She leans back and looks at him, smiling the way she does in my dreams.

I won't say I'm watching my life shatter to pieces, although it feels a bit like that at the moment. I know my life is more than this girl.

She might have a laugh that sounds like summer. And maybe it's true that an epic night of partying would pale in comparison to a night spent coding on the couch next to her. That she is the first thing I think about when I wake up in the morning, and the one I think of when I look at the stars at night.

But there is more than that to my life. I was all right before I met her, and I will be all right again, soon enough.

It's not that I think I need her, or whatever bullshit people say. It's just... For a while, I thought we might have been onto something great. I'd started to think of all the places we could go together—I'd hear about a new restaurant opening, or a cool campsite a few hours away that was supposed to be beautiful, and I'd think that, one day, we might go there. She could wear that new dress she was excited about, and we could try foods I didn't know existed before. We could hike until we were exhausted and then cuddle by a campfire. And she would be my best friend, and maybe more.

And maybe, one day, there would be mornings I would wake up next to her, and even though I had coffee to make and classes to get to, I would have five minutes of paradise as I held her and watched her sleep, her head resting on my shoulder.

I know there are ways that I can have a great life without her. I just thought it would be nice to share a life *with* her, at least for a little while. And although I might not be sad forever that we aren't together, I might be missing out on an unparalleled sort of happiness, one I couldn't even fully feel or even understand, without her.

I push the door open, and they step apart. Sara adjusts her blouse and turns, smiling at me. It's different than before though.

"Hey, Robbie," she says. "Ready to go?" I can't shake the feeling that it sounds like she is talking to her little brother.

Before I can answer, her gaze flickers back to him. She blushes and bites her lip as she turns away.

"Yeah." I sigh. "I think I might walk home though. Clear my head."

"Is everything okay?" She is really looking at me now. Giving me her full attention.

"Yeah." I wave a hand, brushing off her concern. I gesture over my shoulder with my thumb. Back toward the building and the meeting a few minutes earlier. "That was just *wow*." I force a smile and try to add some cheer to my voice, to make it seem like the drowning look in my eyes is just a sign of being overwhelmed and unable to process how well our careers are going, and not because my heart is tearing apart.

part three

game changer

chapter twenty-two

"And then he just...kissed me."

"Ahhhh!" Yaz squeals and claps her hands. "I love it." She pretends to faint, falling backward onto my couch. "This is so dreamy."

I laugh. "Yeah, it was..." I try to think, but I can't get this smile off my face, and it makes it hard to produce any sounds that aren't giggles. "It was pretty cool."

"Pretty cool?" She sits back up. "Are you kidding me? You're dating a billionaire."

"He's not a billionaire."

"Yeah." She raises her eyebrows. "But his dad is."

"That." I wave a hand dismissively. "That stuff doesn't matter." I also want to say that Yaz's parents are probably getting close to that *B* word, given that they started the second most popular social media app in Brazil. But I learned that from Google, not from her, so I don't wanna bring it up.

"Of course, of course." She nods. "That's not the only reason you like him, but it's a pretty damn nice perk."

"Dude!"

"Hey, all I'm saying is that in a world full of guys asking
you to come over and smoke before watching an illegally
downloaded movie in a dorm room, I'd die to go on some
dates out of *The Bachelor*."

I roll my eyes. "Speaking of, aren't we supposed to be
watching that?" I reach for the remote. Our usual Friday night
reality TV catch-up and wine-drinking sesh has been completely derailed by Yaz demanding all the details on Braden-
gate.

"Yeah, whatever—this is more interesting anyway."

I shake my head as I scroll through the DVR. "It's not even
like that, okay?"

"All right." She uncrosses her sweatpanted and fuzzy-
socked legs and stands up. "Then tell me what it *is* like." She
walks in front of me, and I lean around her to see the screen.
"But let me get the wine first."

"Okay." Yaz situates herself on the couch, handing me one
of the plastic wineglasses. She unscrews the top of the eight-
dollar wine bottle—and pours some into my glass.

"But what about that other guy?" she asks.

"Hmmm?" I pick up my wine to take a sip.

"Don't act like you don't know what I mean." She stares
me down. "I've proofread too many of your texts to Robbie
to think no feelings are there."

"I don't know." I sigh. "Anything there is definitely one-
sided." I swirl my pink wine, watching tiny bubbles form and
thinking about what a fool I made of myself when I got high.
About Robbie's clear disinterest. "I can't spend my whole life

in unrequited love. Waiting for the perfect boy. I have to give a chance to the one who actually wants me."

"I guess so." She rests her head on the couch. "I just like Robbie. He seems really sweet from the screenshots you've sent me."

He is. But that also doesn't matter. His texts are kind and funny. But they are friendly. And nothing more.

I frown. "Can we focus on what's real for once?" I ask.

"Sure." She sips her wine.

"Where do I start?" Nothing like this has ever happened to me before. I don't know how to girl-talk about anything but boy band fan fic.

"What happened after the kiss?" she asks.

"Well…" I take a sip of wine to stall. "I was kind of nervous and awkward—I wanted to kiss him again but didn't want to invite him upstairs, because I wasn't sure if that was, like, bad to do…"

She rolls her eyes.

"So I kind of just came back here. And I guess he went back to his dorm."

"Dude." Yaz shakes her head before taking a long sip of her wine. "Tell me you at least kissed him goodbye."

"Yes." I look down at my glass. "On the cheek."

"Oh no." She shakes her head. "You ruined it, didn't you? Had a chance with a future *Bachelor* contestant, and you ruined it."

"I did not *ruin* it," I say. "And he would never go on *The Bachelor*, c'mon."

"True." She considers this. "Probably *Millionaire Matchmaker*."

"How many of these shows do you watch?" I narrow my eyes at her. "Are you watching without me?"

"We're not talking about that." She brushes me off. "We're talking about how you *ruined* everything."

I roll my eyes. "I didn't ruin it. That night, he texted me. Even sent a kiss emoji."

"Oooooh." She holds her glass close to her chest. "Things are heating up."

I ignore her mocking tone. "And then on Tuesday we went on a coffee date."

"Oh, very nice." She raises an eyebrow.

"It was nice." I smile. "Like, we've gotten coffee before, as coworkers, and friends and stuff. But this felt different, you know? There was a sort of flirty vibe throughout."

She nods. "Plus you probably didn't make out after the other times you went for coffee."

"Well...we didn't technically make out this time either."

"*Sara.*"

I hold up my hands innocently. "What? It was the middle of the day, okay? What was I supposed to do?"

"Uh, I don't know, tell him your roommate is in class and invite him over. Or for God's sake, just be one of those annoying couples who kiss in the middle of the quad, I don't know."

"Yeah, I guess. I just, I don't know. I don't have much experience in this area. I didn't know what to do."

She shakes her head. "I can't believe, you, of all people, run Perfect10."

I ignore this comment. Unsurprisingly, she's been doing quite well recently, just .4 away from Platinum. I offered to bump her up the last bit, but she said she wants to earn it.

"So," she continues. "What happened the next time y'all hung out?"

"That was kind of it," I say. "We're between launches for

the app, so I haven't really seen him. He came late to class Thursday, and I always sit in front, so it's not like I coulda talked to him then."

"Huh," she says. I can tell she's trying to keep her expression neutral but is thinking that our relationship—or flirtation, or *whatever it is*—is dead in the water.

"But we've been texting, like, *all the time*." I set my glass on the table and reach for my phone. "And really flirty stuff too. Look."

I hand her the phone. I can't believe she's managed to get me invested in this conversation.

"I've been glued to my phone, and we've stayed up until like *two* every night talking."

"Congrats, Sara, you're in a middle school relationship." She laughs. "Let me know if he chats you on AIM, will you? Maybe even puts you in his Myspace top eight." She wiggles her eyebrows.

"Oh shut up," I say. "I'm happy—isn't that what matters?"

"Yeah." She hands back the phone. "And those texts are quite cute, I have to say."

"Thank you." I stare at my open conversation with Braden for a second. I was the last person to respond, writing *lol that's amazing* in response to a Buzzfeed article he'd sent me. There technically wasn't a need for him to respond, but I'm kind of hoping he will. Every time my phone buzzes with his name, it sets off butterflies in my stomach.

And we've been texting so often that I am almost disappointed when I look at my phone and there is no alert from him. Which is insane, because a week ago I was perfectly happy without him.

I exhale and click the lock button on my phone. *"Bachelor?"* I ask her.

She nods excitedly and reaches for the remote. We've caught up on the most recent seasons, so have gone back to old ones we haven't seen. I click on an old first episode, where they introduce the "contestants" searching for love.

We make our way through skinny blonde woman after skinny blonde woman, hearing about their loves of raising ducks, tattooing elderly people or baking erotic cakes.

"People on this show have the weirdest jobs," she says, refilling her glass of wine as a woman with Duck Enthusiast listed as her occupation talks about how hard it may be to choose between love and, well, her love of poultry.

"Hey, at least they're passionate about something." I shrug. "It's kind of refreshing to see people *care* that unironically."

"But about *ducks*?"

"To each their own." I take a sip of my wine as the next girl comes on screen.

Although a lot of these girls look incredibly similar—there are only so many ways a real live human can resemble a Barbie doll—this girl looks *just* like a contestant we saw two before the Duck Enthusiast.

"Is that the girl from earlier?" Yaz asks.

"I don't—"

I am interrupted by Brandy, who informs us in a voice-over that she is actually the twin of the girl we met earlier. As the screen cuts from B roll of her emerging from a limo to her being interviewed, an info bar appears at the bottom of the screen. It informs us that her name is *actually* spelled *B-r-a-n-d-i*, and that her hometown is Los Angeles, California. But it's the final line of her bio that's most interesting.

Occupation: Twin.

"No!" Yaz falls back onto the couch, cackling.

"Oh, c'mon." I shake my head. "That's what they're list-ing as her occupation?"

On screen, Brandi flips her hair and continues her mono-logue. "Yeah, although I haven't met him, I really think Joe could be the one. And at twenty-three, I'm really ready to take that next step in life, you know? I think he'll really like me." She smiles for a beat before adding, "I think I can win this thing."

I roll my eyes and take a sip of wine.

My phone vibrates against the wood coffee table. I set down my glass and pick it up.

I can't help but smile when I see the alert, a text from Braden Hart.

"Your boy?" Yaz asks.

I slide open the text. My eyes go wide as I read the message.

"What? What did he say?" She stands up so quickly that some of her wine splashes out of the glass. "Oh, sorry," she says, looking down at the mess.

"Whatever." I wave a hand. "It's dorm furniture." I am barely focused on my words as I reread the text.

"You don't care about a mess?" she asks. "What the hell does that message say?"

I look up and smile. "He just texted me to put on a fancy dress and heels—we're going on a date."

"Yay!" She squeals. "That's amazing."

"Yeah," I say. "If that's okay with you—it is supposed to be girls' night."

"Are you kidding?" she says. "We hang out every week—this is huge."

"It's not huge." I roll my eyes as I stand and walk toward my room. Although I'm not sure my words are believable, considering I'm blushing and smiling so big that I'm practically giggling.

I pull open my closet door and put my hair up in the ponytail holder that was on my wrist, so that I can concentrate better. I examine my wardrobe.

"Dude!" Yaz yells from the other room. "He sent you another text."

"What does it say?" I lean through the doorway.

Instead of reading it, she walks toward me with the phone in one hand and my wineglass in another.

"Can I have the rest of your wine?" she asks.

"Sure," I say, taking the phone from her. "I don't have a password. You could've just opened it—" I freeze, reading the rest of what he's said to me.

Braden: Don't bother to do your hair though, chopper will mess it up in seconds

"What?" Yaz asks.

I look up at her, speechless. I shove the phone in her general direction.

"Oh my god, a helicopter, dude this is just like Season 7 with Grace and Chad omigod omigod!" She paces up and down my room and rambles on about how much this resembles The Bachelor and her favorite rom-com and every glamorous romance she's ever read or watched.

I nod along and head back to my closet to see if I have anything that even vaguely resembles what you're supposed to wear on a date with the heir to a multibillion-dollar fortune. I flip through my dresses from H&M and Forever 21, and start to think there's nothing of that particular description in my closet.

chapter twenty-three

Braden

Fuck, I think I really like this girl.

I take a deep breath to calm my nerves. All it does is make me realize how shaky I am, my exhale rattling. I look at the flowers I got. Lilies, per the hipster shopkeeper's recommendations.

Stupid, so stupid. Should've gone with roses. Long-stem red roses would have been perfect. Nothing beats classic elegance.

I could've gotten the Paris of flowers, and what did I get her? The San Francisco of flowers? The Austin of flowers? Hipster BS. What was I doing?

I check my watch. It's ten to eight. Too late to go back for a different bouquet. All I can do is hope for the best and knock.

I raise my hand to do so, but the door swings open before I can make contact. A striking brunette with wide eyes almost runs into me.

"Oh!" she says, breaking into a big smile. "Hi, I'm

Yazmine." She extends her hand, staring me down. "You must be Braden."

She steps back to allow me in, seemingly forgetting she was about to leave. "So, tell me about yourself," she says, closing the door behind me.

"Yaz!" Sara's voice emerges from the other room. She stumbles into the doorway, hopping on one heeled foot as she attempts to slide her other one into the matching shoe. "Weren't you *leaving*?"

"Yeah, yeah." Yaz shakes her head as she slinks off toward the door, her nosy-friend opportunity spoiled for today.

Sara looks at me, and her eyes soften. "Lilies!" She lights up. "My favorite." She finally gets the shoe on and crosses the room in two graceful seconds, taking the flowers and pulling me into an embrace. "They're amazing."

"I'm glad you like them," I say. I mentally take back all the curses I just sent the hipster florist's way.

"I love them." She crosses over to the kitchen, pulling a plastic vase from the cabinet. Only she would bring a vase to college. I watch her as she fills it with water and expertly unwraps and trims the flowers before placing them in the vase. All while keeping her dress pristine.

Damn, that *dress*. I try to keep my eyes on her hands as she works with the flowers, or her lips as she rambles on about Yaz and Perfect10 being like *The Bachelor* or something.

But it's hard not to look at that dress. It's tight and black with a plunging but classy neckline, cut in a way that makes it clear she couldn't possibly be wearing a bra underneath. It is longer than most dresses you'd see around campus, but it hugs her body perfectly, showing off the way her hips curve into her long legs, especially in those heels, which must be at least five inches.

"Which is ridiculous, don't you think?" She concludes her story.

I clear my throat. "Uh, yes, totally."

She smiles. "I cannot say how relieved I am that you feel the same way. Like of course our business model is completely different than some sort of love competition show." She adjusts a few of the flowers. "Okay, there." She sets the flowers in the middle of the table and stands back to admire them. "Beautiful."

"I was just thinking the same thing."

She smiles innocently as she slides on her coat. "Shall we?"

We step into the cool night, and I think about taking her hand, but I'm not sure how to without being awkward. I'm not sure I've ever done that sober. Actually, I don't think I've ever really held a girl's hand, except as a way to lead her in the direction I want to walk, which is really more like leading someone by their wrist than holding their hand.

I have never strolled with someone, hand in hand. I've never wanted to take someone's hand just because I want to feel what it's like, to have her fingers laced with mine.

Not to sound too much like a douche bag, but I kind of know the playbook forward and backward when it comes to the random, often drunken, hookups. But it's been a while since I've *dated* a girl. Since eighth grade, I think. Catharine Grimes. We kissed at my best friends bar mitzvah, and then "dated" for the rest of the summer. Which basically meant we texted on Sidekicks constantly and would awkwardly avoid each other while hanging out with a group of twenty or more of our friends. She was my first and last girlfriend. And then

I went to an all-boy boarding school and girls became conquests you would go out and find and exaggerate about to
your friends when you got back.

Nowadays, when it comes to the club and bar and dating
app scene, I know exactly how to play the game, and I know
how to win. I'm not thrown off by a girl who is hot or rich
or cool. I know how to act like I don't care, so they will.

It's easy, because, honestly, I really don't care. There's always a new set of Laker Girls. New aspiring dancers and actresses land at LaGuardia and LAX every day. Hell, they even
crown a new Miss America every year.

But a girl I care about—I have no idea how to deal with
this.

Sara is a few feet ahead of me, her pace faster than mine
even though she's wearing those ridiculous heels. She waits,
so I can catch up. The wind blows as she turns to look back
at me, and she tucks a stray hair behind her ear, which is
adorned with a little silver teardrop earing.

"So you were just joking, right?" she says when I meet her.
"With that thing about the helicopter?" She laughs. "Because
Yaz thought you were serious."

"No." I smile. "I wasn't joking. We just have to walk to
Main Quad since that's the only place it can land."

"What?" She stops walking and just stares at me.

"Yeah," I laugh. "C'mon." I take her hand to show her the
way. She adjusts so that our fingers weave together.

I haven't used the chopper here before, and when it used
to pick me up in high school, my father would always have
me take a car to a nearby airport or helipad.

Our pilot charges him more to land at remote locations,
not to mention the fines you can get from the city, or in this

case, my school, for landing somewhere you don't have permission to be.

But I think my father will forgive me this time, if I tell him it was in the interest of wooing a girl who would actually be able to carry on a conversation with my parents over dinner. An actual possible, respectable match for me. Tonight, I need to go for wow factor, not practicality.

It is unusually quiet as we walk through Main Quad, with only the sound of Sara's heels clicking against the stone disrupting the California night. Lamps burn along our path, creating circles of light among the shadows. The sandstone arches of the arcades that line the quad look regal in the quiet, blue night. A bit different than during the day when this place is filled with tourists snapping pictures and hundreds of athletic-wear-clad students, biking through the quad and dodging between arches as they race to class.

We make it to the oval, the circle of road just beyond Main Quad, filled with about a football field's length of grass. This is where I told Jeffery to land.

Above us, the wind rustles the leaves of palm trees, but there is no chopper in sight yet.

I look to Sara. She smiles easily; I manage to smile back before looking down, embarrassed. I want to say something, but suddenly small talk seems so hard.

I clear my throat. "I don't know why he's not here yet." I reach into my pocket and pull out my phone.

I had a text from Jeffery ten minutes ago saying he's on his way.

"It's okay." She smiles. "I got nowhere else to be."

I nod and smile back, feeling the weight melt off my shoulders.

After an awkward few minutes that feels like a century, I can see the light of Jeffery on approach.

We stand back as the chopper lands, kicking up the few leaves on the meticulously kept lawn. Once he makes contact with the earth, the propellers begin to slow toward a stop.

"I usually get on with them still going," I say. "But I thought you'd want it this way. Since it's your first time."

"Yeah," she says, making a face. "It would not have been cute if you'd told me to get on with those things going." She laughs. "You'd probably have seen me cry."

I smile politely. Although it was probably the furthest thing from her mind, I can't help but think how odd it is that she's the girl and she's seen me, the guy, break down crying.

"Okay, ready?" I ask, when the propellers completely stop.

She laughs nervously. "I'm not really sure."

"Here, I'll help you." I rest my hand on the small of her back.

She nods gratefully, stepping forward.

I open the sleek back door of the helicopter and wave hello to Jeffery. I take Sara's hand and help her step up, carefully, in those crazy heels. She moves slowly, and I am rewarded with quite a view for my help.

She slides into the cabin and I follow her, pulling the door closed.

"How's your night, sir?" Jeffery asks.

"Going well so far," I say. "This pretty girl agreed to have dinner with me. What more could I want?"

Jeffery laughs as he turns around to hand us two pairs of headphones. "Nice to meet you, ma'am," he greets Sara.

"Hi!" she says, clearly nervous just being in the helicopter, although we haven't gotten off the ground yet.

I hand her a pair of headphones as I talk to Jeffery. "It's getting a little late for dinner already, so I—" I watch Sara as she tangles and untangles her harnesses. "Babe, like this." I click mine into place, slowing down my motions so she can watch.

"Ooooh." She clicks hers into place. The straps stretch across her chest in that low-cut dress. "Thanks."

I bite my lip. Although I'd called her names like *babe* and *sweetheart* many times, I was being sarcastic and mocking. Just now, I'd done it sweetly and as if it were second nature, and she responded like it was totally normal.

"Ready?" Jeffery asks from the cockpit.

I look at Sara, whose eyes are wide in anticipation.

"Yeah," I say.

chapter twenty-four

The ocean below is dark and stormy, at once both beautiful and terrifying. I am leaning as much toward the window as I dare.

When we started out there were so many lights below, some twinkling and pretty, others the harsh beam of streetlights on the highway. But as we reached the ocean, there were fewer and fewer bright spots.

The coast is dotted with a few large houses with their lights on and a big resort every once in a while. But often there are sleepy towns with just a few twinkling lights. And now there are whole sections where there is just the shadowed outline of trees and the reflection of the moon on the water. From the air, it is sometimes easy to imagine that this part of the earth is untouched by man.

I turn back into the cabin, toward Braden. "This is amazing!" I yell over the sound of the propeller.

He laughs. "You've said that twelve times already."

"Well, it's *that* cool!"

He shakes his head as if he is frustrated, but a smile plays at the edge of his lips, and I bet he's happy with how much I like his surprise.

After about thirty minutes, we land in a grassy field near the water. Part of me wishes we were going somewhere farther, because I want to see more—I want to see the entire world from that perspective.

But I must admit, I am also very grateful to be back on solid ground, literally.

"Get out on my side," Braden says as he unclicks his harness. "That way you're going downhill."

I nod as I undo my own seat belt with shaking hands. I try not to think about the propellers above that are still spinning, if slower than before, and what would happen if I walked uphill instead.

Braden hops out first and extends an arm toward me. I slide across the seat and take his hand. I probably squeeze it a little too hard as I step down, my heels balancing precariously on the grated metal step.

I make it to the ground and sigh in relief. My shoes sink into the soft grass as I step forward, my hand still in his. Rolling hills of dark grass lie before us and sprinklers water the grounds, the water shimmery and silver in the moonlight. Luckily the ones near us seem to be off, although damp wisps of grass brush my open-toe shoes. The bright smell of the grass mixes with the cool scent of salt water drifting off the ocean waves.

In the distance there is a large house with many lights on, shining into the dark, quiet night. It is the only man-made light visible, and although it seems to be trying its darndest, it doesn't manage to block out the stars the way the lights in the city do. Thousands of them sparkle in the sky above.

I look from the sky down to Braden and our intertwined hands.

"This is beautiful," I say.

He laughs. "You ain't seen nothin' yet," he says as we walk toward what looks like a small car, parked nearby.

I look over my shoulder and wave goodbye to the helicopter pilot. He seems surprised at first, but then waves back. As we get closer to the little car, I realize it is actually a golf cart.

"The house is too close to the water to land by it," Braden says. "I had someone bring the cart out though, since I thought you might wear heels."

"Oh, thanks," I say. "You didn't have to do that." I wonder how that person got back to the house. I mean, they probably weren't wearing heels, but still it seems silly for them to drive out and walk back just so I don't have to make that same walk.

"Honestly," he admits, "I'd do that even if it was just me wearing gym shoes." He shrugs. "Guess I'm lazy that way."

He drives the golf cart across the field like it is a go-kart, making big drifting turns and keeping the accelerator flat against the floor. I grip the handle beside me, the only thing that separates me from the outside world, since the cart has no doors.

My knuckles are probably white from my grip, but at some point during the drive, my heart stops racing from panic and starts racing from the thrill. I let out a screech that turns to laughter as he narrowly misses one of the blaring sprinklers.

He is still speeding as we pull up at the side of the house, flying up a sweeping cobblestone drive that leads to a garage with four doors the size of cars and one mini, golf-cart-size door.

I lurch forward as he comes to a halt, breathing heavily as I clutch my chest. "You're insane," I say.

He just shrugs as he pushes a button that makes the little door open and we pull in. The garage has that weird distinct smell that all garages seem to have. A staleness of the air, combined with the slight smell of gasoline, the leathery smell of sports equipment and the fresh smell of various gardening products.

But that's where the similarity ends to every other garage I've been in. There is not just a Tesla, but *two* Teslas, alongside a Porsche crossover and a shiny red, convertible Porsche.

I try not to stare as we walk past cars that look more like works of art than automobiles on our way to the door leading to the rest of the house.

I follow Braden through a mudroom with no shoes in it and into a large living room.

The whole back wall of the room, and maybe the entire house, is glass, opening to a dark view. I make my way across the hardwood floor. Up close to the window, you can see that the house rests on a cliff overlooking the ocean. The darkness of the water is hard to distinguish against the darkness of the sky, but just below, white foam makes the crashing waves visible. I can only imagine how this view must look when the sun is out.

I turn at the sound of movement behind me. "Welcome," Braden says, extending his arms.

"Whose house is this?" I ask breathlessly.

"Mine." He smiles. "Well, I mean, my parents'."

I look down at my dress. Definitely not meet-your-boyfriend's—or not-boyfriend-but-something's—parents attire.

"They're not here," he adds, as if he knows what I'm thinking. "In Paris this week, I think." He checks his watch, as if they move countries by the hour; although from what he's said before, it seems close to that.

"This is our beach house," he says. "Welcome to Big Sur, Sara." He smiles. "Or, I guess, Big Sur adjacent—they won't let you build on the national park."

He shakes his head, and I nod like I understand. *Ah yes, I encountered the same problem when I tried to build my hunting lodge in Yellowstone*, I think.

"Are you hungry?" He checks his watch. "I guess it's a little late—sorry about that."

"No problem." Now that he mentions it, my stomach does ache a little bit, but it wasn't like I noticed while I was in a freakin' helicopter. "Do you wanna order pizza or something?" I ask. I doubt there's much food here, since no one's been living in the house. "Does anyone deliver this far out?"

He laughs. "I had something else in mind."

We walk through the house, past a grand dining room and another large sitting room that opens onto a big back porch. Or maybe *porch* is the wrong word. It's more like a giant balcony overlooking the ocean. On it is a table, set with clean white linens and tall candles.

"This is amazing," I say as I step onto the balcony. I shiver a bit but don't mind; the air smells of the ocean, crisp and fresh like salt and citrus fruit. "How did you set this up?"

"Our housekeeper did before she went home." He picks up a set of matches from the table and lights a candle. It flickers from the wind off the sea.

"That's so nice."

"It's her job." He shrugs. "Shall we have some wine?"

Inside the house is an industrial-sized kitchen and a large

pantry that seems to be solely for wine. I pick out a bottle based mostly on the picture on the label.

"A nice choice," Braden says, when I hand it to him. "I think this wine is older than us." He uncorks the bottle and pours me a glass. "My parents offered to have a chef come over, like they do when they're here. But I thought it might be more romantic if I cooked for you. So I had some groceries delivered."

I take a sip, and it doesn't burn like I was expecting. It tastes heady and warm, like the heat of summer or when you are cuddled up by the fireplace in the winter. It is the kind of flavor that overwhelms your senses.

Braden opens a large stainless steel fridge and pulls out a plastic-wrapped tray of cheese and meats and sets it on the counter. "In case you're hungry while I cook."

The wrapper crinkles as I peel it back. I don't know anything about cheese. I mean, I love mozzarella sticks of course, and Parmesan on my pasta. But I don't know *fancy* cheese any more than I know *fancy* wine. Although, I guess I like the latter now.

I pick a piece that isn't too smelly and nibble it. It tastes sharp and poignant and a little nutty. Not bad.

"This one's yummy," I say.

Braden smiles. "A little better than dorm food, right?"

He opens the fridge again and pulls out two giant, blood-red strip steaks. "So I was thinking—" he says as he opens cabinet after cabinet, obviously not familiar with where anything is "—we could do New Year's Day for the next big launch." He pulls a large frying pan from one of the cabinets and sets it on the stove, turns on the Brunner, then drizzles the pan with olive oil.

He throws the steaks into the pan, and they immediately start to sizzle.

"It'll be after the holidays when everyone is sad they didn't have people to bring home, and with Valentine's Day looming in the near future." He is pulling spices off the rack and throwing them on the steaks, seemingly without rhyme or reason.

"So I'm thinking people will be really desperate and prime targets for the app."

I frown. "It sounds so bad when you say it like that."

"It's true though." He leans against the counter and picks up his wineglass.

I give in to the game of it. "Plus, there's the whole no-one-to-kiss-at-midnight thing with New Year's Eve."

"Exactly!" He raises his glass. "See, I knew you were a little evil genius too."

I roll my eyes but take the compliment.

He puts a lid on the food. "Let's go take a picture," he says. "While it cooks."

"Uh, okay," I say. I set down my glass and follow him out the door to the balcony.

"Over here," he says, pointing to the railing. I walk over the slats, hoping the wine or my shoes won't make me fall.

"Stand like this, against the edge... Okay, put your arm on it like this." He positions my left arm so that it's resting against the railing, as if I was just chilling here casually, for some reason facing away from the beautiful view. Nothing about this feels casual though. "Okay, good. And then turn like three-quarters toward me—perfect." He backs up and snaps a few pictures on his phone.

"Pretend like you are laughing," he says. I do so and feel super awkward. "Yeah like that, act happy."

I thought I was.

"Yeah, one of these should work," he says without looking up from the screen.

"How do I look?" I try to catch a glimpse of the picture, but he doesn't turn the screen toward me.

He swipes and taps at the screen, gaze glued to his phone.

I clear my throat and try again. "Can I see?"

"Yeah..." He clicks a few more buttons. "Here." He smiles and hands me the phone.

It's open to his Instagram account. The girl in his most recent post—me—stares back at me.

I almost don't recognize myself. He's done a great job editing me, changing the light and shadows in the right places to highlight my curves and hide my flaws. And my skin looks radiant... Did he *airbrush* me?

A perfect place with a perfect girl, the caption below reads. It was posted a few seconds ago but already has forty-two likes. I scroll to the top of his account and gasp.

"You have twenty–two *thousand* Instagram followers?"

He nods. "Actually it's twenty-two thousand seven hundred and fifty...nine," he says, looking up. "Or at least it was this morning. You have to use another app to get the exact amount when you have this many."

I laugh. "Are you, like, famous or something?"

"Nah." He brushes this off. "Just popular."

A repetitive beeping alarm sounds behind us.

"Oh *shit*." Braden turns and runs into the house. I follow him into the kitchen, now filled with gray smoke and a burning smell.

Eyes burning, I blink through the smoke to see that a small fire has engulfed the frying pan and half the stove with it.

"What do I do?" I yell over the beeping alarm.

Braden is opening and closing cabinets again, this time aggressively, the door making a snap each time. "I know there's a fire extinguisher somewhere."

Oh my god there's no time, I grab the nearest liquid, my wine, and throw it on the fire.

The flame bursts upward. "Ahhh!" I flinch away.

"Alcohol is *flammable*," Braden says through gritted teeth. He steps forward, fire extinguisher now in hand, and doses our dinner with puffy white foam.

When the fire wanes to nothing, he sets it down and turns back to me. "How do you feel about cereal?" he asks. He looks at me with puppy dog eyes, his hair askew and a little bit of black soot on cheek.

"Right now, it's my favorite food." I smile.

We pour bowls of sugary cereal and new glasses of wine and head outside to our overdressed table.

"Breakfast for dinner was always my favorite as a kid," I say, scooping a spoonful that has the perfect ratio of marshmallows and oat pieces.

"Mother would never let one of us do that," Braden says. "But sometimes our nanny, Marie, would, when my parents were out of town. We'd make pancakes with chocolate chips." He smiles at the memory. "She knew she might get in trouble if they found out, but she always said kids should get to be kids." He pauses to take a bite, then says with food in his mouth, "She was like a second mom to me."

I nod like I know, even though I don't. Braden is so confusing to me—a moment ago it was *just her job* and not nice for his housekeeper to set this special table for us. But now he's saying his nanny was like his second mom. How can someone be so spoiled and so sweet all at once?

I turn to look at the water. We are close enough to hear the waves crashing against the cliff below.

"God, it must have been amazing coming here when you were a kid," I say, changing the subject.

"Yeah," he says. "But we only came a few days a year, if that. It's mostly an investment."

I study his face while I take another sip of wine and try to imagine the sort of life where you own a house you use only a few days a year.

I shake my head and reach for my water, thinking maybe I should ease off the alcohol for a little bit.

"I love the ocean." I set down my glass. "I just feel…right, when I'm by it." I close my eyes for a second, taking it in. "It's so easy to get caught up in the little stresses of life. But the ocean is *so big*. You know? It doesn't know who you are. It doesn't care about your college apps or what internship you get next summer."

"It's pretty great," he says. "Although I must say, I think I like the Mediterranean Sea better than the Pacific."

"Really?"

Braden nods.

"I don't know—I think this is pretty great." I gaze over the water again. "But I've never seen the Mediterranean, so I have no point of comparison."

"Well, I'll have to take you sometime," he says.

I laugh, but uneasily. I'm not quite sure he's kidding. For

the hundredth time tonight, I wonder how the heck this is my life.

Only a few cornflakes float in my milk, now sweet from the sugary cereal.

"So, uh…" I swirl my spoon around my bowl. "Are we going back to campus tonight or…?"

"Oh." His eyes widen. "We can if you want to. But I, um, was thinking we'd stay here."

I press my lips together and stare at the water. I was afraid he was assuming that. I look back up at him, my stomach in knots. "I mean, I don't—I don't want to create any sort of expectations for—" I struggle to find the words.

Braden's brow furrows. He seems confused by how upset I'm getting. "Hey," he says softly, reaching for my hand across the table. "What's going on?"

"I, um, I've never uh, *been* with a guy, you know, and I don't want to tonight."

"That's all?" He laughs, sounding relieved. "I didn't kidnap you. You don't have to stay here. But if you do, we can also just like, make out, and then crash."

I just smile, and after a pause, he adds. "Or not that either, if you don't want to." He holds up his hands innocently.

I scooch my chair closer to him. "No, that sounds good." I kiss him on the cheek.

A smile begins to form on the edge of his lips, and his eyes sparkle. I lean forward again and kiss him. His lips are soft and he kisses me back lightly, like he's not sure that I'm sure. I wrap an arm around him and lace my fingers through his hair, then pull him toward me. He takes the hint, and his lips press harder, more eagerly against mine.

It is my second kiss ever. And it is remarkably, amazingly, like the ones I've seen in movies.

I pull away. "Yeah, let's keep doing that," I whisper.

He laughs against my lips and kisses me again, the scent of the sea around us and the taste of wine and sugary cereal on his lips.

I feel like I'm in a dream.

chapter twenty-five

Roberto

"Is it thirty-five?" Mateo looks at me hopefully.

I spin the paper toward me to double-check the question. "Yeah."

"Yes!" He pumps his fist. "I'm a genius."

I laugh. "All right, but let's see if you can do this next problem." I hand him back the paper. I used to tutor him every week when I lived at home, and since I am in town this week for Thanksgiving, I am checking in to see how he is doing.

He insisted he was "too old" for me to do the problems with him, and I could check his work only when he was done. So I brought my laptop with me, and we've been sitting at his kitchen table doing our homework—multiplication and linear algebra, respectively.

"Want me to check yours?" he asks, leaning out of his seat as he peers over at my screen.

"Sure," I say, turning it toward him.

I hear muffled laughter from the kitchen, where Mateo's mom is putting away groceries and starting dinner.

"Nope." He shakes his head. "All wrong." A smile missing a front tooth spreads across his face as he sits back down and starts on the next problem.

The savory aroma of onions sautéing in oil wafts from the kitchen. My stomach pangs. Dining hall food is truly not the same as the real deal.

Mateo scribbles quickly before dropping his pencil and tossing the sheet back at me. "Forty-five!"

I shake my head before handing the sheet back to him.

"Ugh." He sets his head down on the table. "I'm sick of math.

"Mom!" he yells toward the kitchen "When is dinner?"

"No sé." Mrs. Rodriguez peeks her head through the doorway. "When are you going to finish your math?"

His eyes go wide and he sits up properly, looking around for his pencil.

"That's what I thought." She laughs as she steps into the living room, picking up extra notebooks from the table and setting down place mats. "Focus on the problems in front of you. Don't be trying to create more for yourself." She shakes her head.

He nods, copying the next problem into his notebook.

I have barely read my next question when a pencil is jabbed into my shoulder. *"Psst,"* Mateo whispers. "Is this right?"

I look. "No."

He slumps back into his chair. "I hate math. It *sucks*."

"Hey, hey," I say. "We'll figure it out." I reach under the table for my bag. "And here." I unzip the front pocket and pull out the brochure. "I was going to give this to you later, but not if you give up on math."

He grabs the pamphlet.

"It's a camp, for kids your age to learn about computers."

"Cool!" Mateo starts to flip through it.

"It's over spring break so you won't have to miss school," I say, but he doesn't seem to be listening, his gaze glued to the page.

Mrs. Rodriguez stops to read over his shoulder, place mats in her arms. "Déjame ver, mijo." She picks up the pamphlet.

"And it's fully funded," I say.

She raises her eyebrows.

"Well," I say. "I mean, the tuition is covered, but you'd have to get him there, and it's near LA." I know that would mean either her or Mr. Rodriguez taking off work, maybe even twice in two weeks, which might not be possible.

"Can I go, Mom?" Mateo looks up at her.

"If you get in, we'll make it happen." She hands the pamphlet back to him. "But you have to fill out your own application. I'm not going to do it for you."

He nods eagerly and reexamines the cover of the brochure, which features kids playing with remote control robots in a sunny park.

The lock turns with a click and Mr. Rodriguez walks into the house.

"*Dad!*" Mateo loses his shit, like nearly every kid does when Dad gets home.

Mr. Rodriguez walks over and ruffles Mateo's hair before shaking my hand. "Home again, Robbie? Shouldn't you be out partying?"

"*Ale,*" Mrs. Rodriguez says sternly, although he was clearly just messing around. "It's very good of him to come home to his father." She looks at Mateo as if to say, *You better do the same when you go to college*, even though that's, like, a decade away.

"All I'm saying is that when I was his age, I was going to plenty of college parties." Mr. Rodriguez puffs out his chest.

Mateo laughs and sits taller, mimicking his dad's body language.

"Mmmm," she says. "Were there a lot of parties at Weller Community?"

"You know, there weren't before my time, but I brought the party. Really put the *community* in community college."

Mrs. Rodriguez side-eyes him. "Do you mean the trivia nights you used to have?" She turns to us. "He was a total nerd," she whispers, not very quietly.

"Hey Robbie, are you staying for dinner?" He expertly changes the subject.

I try not to laugh.

"Yes! Stay!" Mateo says.

"No, thank you," I say. "I would be happy to, but I should be getting home to eat with my dad." I click my phone to check the time—6:53 p.m. *Shit.*

"I'm actually already late." I start to pack my things.

Mateo nods knowingly. If there's anything a little kid gets, it's not to piss off your parents when it comes to being on time for dinner.

"Hola," I say as I push open the door. Dad is sitting at the table, which is already set. It smells great, even though the food has probably been sitting for fifteen minutes. "I am so sorry." I set down my bag and begin to explain.

"It's okay."

I freeze. "What's wrong?" I ask. Nothing says *something's off* more than when your parents aren't mad at you when they usually would be.

"Let's talk about it with your mother," he says. Always insisting on coparenting, even across the miles.

We fill plates with tortillas and beans and chicken, cooked slowly in the recipe of spices my maternal grandmother left us. He makes it pretty much perfectly now, and I barely remember how it tasted during the first few months after Mom was gone, when my father struggled to re-create the meals he'd eaten for years without ever considering how they were made.

My father grabs a real sugar Coke for me and beer for him from the fridge while I call my mother, propping the phone against the kitchen wall.

"¡Mi amor!" she says as soon as her face appears on the screen. She waves at me, the motion pixilated because the connection is poor.

My father hands me my soda and takes a seat at the table. We fold our hands and bow our heads and my mother says grace, her words traveling up to a satellite floating above Earth and then back down to us in our cramped Oakland kitchen.

"Amén," we say in unison, and I reach for my food. Like Pavlov's dog, nothing makes me hungrier than this signal that it is all right for me to eat.

The food has the same effect as hugging my dad, or hearing my mom's favorite song. Home.

After a few bites, I summon the courage to ask. "So what is this thing you wanted to tell me?"

"Well." My dad exhales. "I don't think we will be able to go to Mexico this Christmas."

"¿Qué?" I look from him to my mother on my phone and

back. But of course, she does not look shocked at the news. They've talked about this already, before telling me. This is the start of my school break, and I assumed we'd be driving down soon. I packed accordingly before I came from school.

"¿Por que?" I ask. "And why didn't you tell me about this earlier?"

"We wanted to tell you earlier," my mom says. "But we kept hoping we could work something out."

"Work's been slow," my father says. "They've been cutting down on how many shifts we can take a week, to get rid of overtime. I've been calling every day to see if I can pick up an extra one, but haven't been very successful. But, of course, they need people to work the holidays. And they made it clear that if you do, you are more likely to make it through the next round of layoffs." His eyes are sad, apologetic.

My head falls. Of course my dad is the first one to try to figure out a way to keep his job, even with his company downsizing. He's the hardest-working person I know. While I've been tinkering away with a dumb app, he does real work, every single day.

"Is there anything I can do?" I say. "Maybe I could get a job at school, at the library or something, and that way things will be less stressful?" But even as I say it, I know it's no use. No part-time work I do could make up for my dad working every day.

"Thank you, mijo," he says. "But you shouldn't have to worry about this. ¡Concentrate en tus estudios! We will make it to Mexico soon—Christmas just isn't possible this year."

I shake my head and look at my food, suddenly losing my appetite. *This is such bullshit. It shouldn't take an expensive, international trip just to see my mom.*

"And this way," she says, "we can put money toward a lawyer. The quicker we are able to save up for that, the sooner I can apply. Hopefully as soon as the bar is lifted I will be ready to go," she says.

"And if I lose my job," my dad adds, "who knows how long it would take to save that."

"We just have to wait a little longer, mijo," my mom says.

It seems like we are always waiting. For the money to apply for the waiver. To hear back about the waiver. And then, when we didn't get it, for the rest of the bar to pass. And it seems like the whole time, or at least when they are talking to me, my parents are eternally hopeful. They always talk about the things we will do and how it will be *when Mom gets back*. Lately, it's becoming harder and harder to feel like that day will ever actually come.

Even when I've thought it might be better to just pay someone to get her across the border, they refused to hear it, worried that getting caught trying to cross could set her case back even further. They have so much faith in the system.

"I know you want to be together now," my mom says. "But it is much better for your father to keep his job. To save this money, to get a lawyer. I've looked it up, and people online say it's like night and day, if you have a lawyer. If I have one, I could be living with your father by Christmas next year. We just have to be patient."

My father is silent, sipping his beer and listening to her talk. I wonder if he believes as much as she does.

"I know you are frustrated, mijo—"

"We've been at this for years, Mom." I interrupt her, in my frustration doing something I normally would never dream of.

"Yes, so we should be able to make it a few more months,"

she says. "Plus it doesn't seem so bad when you consider that I am only forty-two and I want to live until ninety, and do that in the US."

"Supongo que sí." I pick at my food.

"It's not that much time, mijo. Lo prometo. I will be there soon." She shakes her head, as if she can dismiss any worries just like that, and smiles warmly. "Now tell me, how is school?"

I tell her about the project and how well the meeting went with Thatcher Bell. I avoid talking about Sara. Complaining about not being with the girl I have a crush on seems petty, if not cruel, when talking to people who can't be with the one they married because of me.

It seems so crazy that an invisible line, almost arbitrarily drawn, could have this power to separate people who love each other for years at a time. It doesn't seem fair or just.

We talk late into the night, and at the end of the call I wave goodbye to my mother, wishing more than anything that she was here so I could hug her and she could kiss me good-night on the forehead. I would tease her for needing to go on her tiptoes, since I'm taller than her now, and tell her it embarrasses me. But secretly, I'd be happy to have her fussing over me, ecstatically happy to have her back.

I fall asleep dreaming about money. About fancy lawyers who specialize in immigration. About plane tickets to Mexico. About a house for my parents in the suburbs.

I wake up and email Braden and Sara ten more schools where I think we might be able to launch the app.

chapter twenty-six

Braden

I wave to Robbie and Sara through the crowd.

"Yes, that's right," I say into my cell phone. "I'm trying to inquire about the status of a bus I ordered—it should be heading from Warren to Berkeley. And no I will not hold. I've been on hold for the last fifteen minutes."

I cover the receiver with my hand as Sara walks up. "This is ridiculous."

Over her shoulder, a large black coach bus pulls up to the curb. "Just kidding, bye," I yap into my phone before ending the call.

"What's going on?" Robbie asks.

The doors open and the girls pile off, most of them in short skirts and tank tops, or football jerseys and short shorts, as I detailed in my email.

"Yeah, *Braden*," Sara says. "What is going on?"

"I sent you guys an email about this, didn't I?" I say. The first girl off the bus, a beautiful blonde with a Victoria's Secret—

type body, walks up and shows me her phone and Platinum status. I hand her a ticket to the game, a ticket to our tailgate and fifty dollars, as promised.

"The first seventy-five girls with Platinum status to RSVP get a free trip to the bowl game, an invite to our tailgate and a small payment."

"I thought the point was to invite University of California students to the tailgate," Sara says, "so they'll join the app. What's the point of inviting people who already use Perfect10?"

I keep handing out tickets and cash, not looking at Sara. "It shows the Berkeley people that the people on the app are hot."

She scoffs. "You definitely did *not* email us about this."

"Huh, must have forgot to send it," I say. More like decided not to, thinking it would be easier to deal with her reaction in public, and when it was already too late to cancel. "A pleasant surprise then." I smile as a Rihanna look-alike steps off the bus. "Happy New Year's to us all," I say.

Once all the girls are off the bus, we head to our tailgate. I rented out the nearby lot using my own money, like I am for this whole event, since we don't have investment yet.

"This is awesome," Robbie says as soon as we are in view.

There are large banners adverting Perfect10 as well as cute pop-up posters that say "Valentine's Day is around the corner. Who wants to be your date?" and "No midnight kiss? No way that happens next year!" and a few football themed ones like "Score with Perfect10." There is also a DJ stand, open bar and piles of free T-shirts, buttons and stickers with our logo. And, of course, a tent for Sara, Robbie and I to post up at, and try to pitch the app to as many suckers as possible.

"Thanks," I say.

"Hmph," Sara says.

My temporary employees are milling about, clinking long-neck bottles of beer and wearing Perfect10 T-shirts a size too small. I must say, our logo stretched across their chests is a beautiful sight.

"Was this really necessary?" Sara asks. She doesn't specify what, but she is staring daggers at two girls spraying bottles of cheap champagne at each other, so I can make a guess.

"It's not like we're the first brand to use models to sell our product."

"They aren't *models*—they're Warren students." We get to the founders tent and I walk around the back, but she doesn't follow, instead standing in front of the folding table and staring me down.

"They're here to be pretty—they're models."

She just looks at me.

"Hey." I reach out and lift her chin with my finger. We texted nonstop all winter break, and I didn't search for solid Wi-Fi all over the French Alps just to mess things up now. "You're the most beautiful woman here. And you're not a model, you're a freaking founder."

A smile curls edge of her lips. She walks around to my side of the table.

Our first potential customer is a Cal freshman boy who weighs about 110 pounds. He walks up to Sara immediately.

I sit down to let her take a stab at the business side for a change, and it turns out she isn't half-bad. It doesn't hurt that the freshman is half paying attention to what she is saying and half drooling over her.

She points to her phone, but he's looking at her chest. "Well

I have mine on demo mode, but it would normally be your own picture here…"

The boy nods, still in a trancelike state. I stifle a laugh.

"…do you wanna download it? Okay, great! Use this code to start at Silver! Bye!"

Sara turns to me as he walks away. "I think that went well!" she says.

"I'd say so."

She wiggles her shoulders, sitting up a little taller. "I bet I get more people to download it today than you do."

"I doubt it…" I say, but my attention is across the yard, where a Very Drunk Girl is trying to climb the DJ stand with a red cup in her hand, presumably to request a song. *Jesus.* Is this what The Chainsmokers have brought us to?

A phone starts to ring, and I look away from the girl. It's odd to hear a phone on full sound nowadays.

"Sorry, I have to take this," Robbie says. He takes a few steps behind the tent and starts speaking in Spanish.

I half listen, and am happy to know I am not too rusty. But then I get distracted once again by the girl, who I think has a Cal Bear temporary tattoo upside down on her face, as she verbally assaults our DJ. I'm debating getting up and saying something when she loses her balance and spills her full beer on the DJ, or, more precisely, on his MacBook.

The music fades with a zapping sound.

"Oh *shit*!" I stand up.

"I'm on it!" Sara pops up and runs across the yard.

What the hell was I thinking, watching this build in slow motion—I should've kicked that chick out as soon as she stumbled into our area. Sara has reached the DJ stand and is talking with him. I don't know what she's saying, but there are a lot of hand motions involved.

"Sorry about that," Robbie says, falling back into his chair. "What's going on?"

His face is flushed, and I can't help but think about the tidbit of information I learned at the beginning of his call. "Your mom lives in Mexico?" I ask. I peel the edge of a Perfect10 sticker off the plastic table with my thumbnail. When he doesn't reply, I look up.

The color has drained from his face. "You speak Spanish?"

Across the yard the music starts back up.

"I speak three languages," I say. "You guys think I'm dumb just because I'm bad with computers."

"Just don't tell anyone, please?" He rakes a hand through his hair. "I...I don't want people to make a deal about it. Pretend you didn't hear, okay?"

"Whatever, man. My parents barely live in this country either."

"That's different." He glares at me.

I open my mouth to respond when Sara bounds up. "I had to give him my phone to play on, but we are back in action. I told him we would cover a new MacBook."

"Awesome," I say.

A few feet away from the table, a cluster of girls hover, holding Bud Light Lime-A-Ritas and eyeing us.

"I think they're too shy." I nod toward them.

"Mine!" Sara whispers. "I call them." She continues this competition against only herself.

"Knock yourself out," I say.

"Hey, guys!" She waves the girls over. "Do you wanna hear about the app?"

She reaches over and picks up my phone from the table.

Oh no. I reach forward, but she's already holding it and turning back to them. I realize just a second too late what is about to happen.

"So it's pretty easy to use, but I'll show you," she says. She is super bubbly and energetic, a great salesgirl. "Oh perfect, it's even in the recently used." She taps the phone. "So this version will look a bit different because…" She cringes and tilts her head away from the screen like she's seen a ghost. She quickly recovers, flashing the girls a sweet smile, ever the professional.

"Actually it's not in demo mode. How cool!" She smiles too big. "You guys will get to see the real thing."

Fuuuuuuuuuck. This is not great. This is really, really not great.

She finishes the presentation and gets two of the three girls to download the app. "Make sure to grab a T-shirt, and tell your friends!" She waves after them.

When they're just far enough away, she turns on her heels and stares me down. I'm surprised her glare doesn't burn a hole in the ground below me. I'd fall straight through to the center of the earth.

"You have an account."

"Yeah." I lift my shoulder, attempting a natural shrug. "But like…from before we were a thing." My voice is really high. Why is it so high?

"I can see your chats." She holds up the phone. "You talked to someone two days ago."

"About the business of the app. I was telling her about the event."

She tilts her head, keeping her eyes on me. "Do you wanna

read through the messages together and see if they're professional?"

Beyond her, Robbie leans back as far in his chair as hu-
manly possible, clearly not wanting to be around for this conversation. It reminds me of my reaction around my parents.

I sigh. "Okay, fine. Maybe I shouldn't have still been flirting, but we never actually said we were exclusive." I grab the
phone from her before she spikes it at the ground, or worse,
reads more. "But here, I will delete it."

I hold up the phone, and show her that I really am delet-
ing the app. "There."

"So, then, are we now?" She puts her hands on her hips.
"Exclusive?"

"Yeah," I say. "If you want. Do you wanna be?"

"I do." Her tone does not soften.

"Well then cool, I guess you're my girlfriend."

"I guess so." She narrows her eyes at me. "You really know
how to ruin even the nice moments."

"I'm rough around the edges," I say. "But that's why you
like me, right? You're the one who redeems the bad boy."

I hold my breath. She shakes her head again, but this time
she's smiling.

chapter twenty-seven

Greek Row looks strange in the daylight. I'm headed back from class and decided to take the long way around so that I can think. I'm not even sure what I need to think about. But something's been making it hard to sleep, making my skin itch, and I can't pinpoint what.

I take a deep breath. *Calm down, Sara.* It's probably just new semester jitters.

I make my way down the sunny street. There are a few guys playing beer games on the lawns, unsurprising because it's not like anyone has much homework yet, and a few sorority girls tanning themselves while reading large chemistry and math textbooks.

Ahead on the sidewalk, a couple is talking. It's clearly not a pleasant conversation. There's a lot of arm waving and tense body language. As I get closer, I can hear bits of what they're saying. "It's over—get it through your head," the meathead, gelled-hair type guy yells. I wonder if it's too late to cross the street and walk on the other side.

His new ex begins to cry. *Poor girl.*

She turns her head, and I recognize her. *Oh no, poor girl that I know.*

Colleen sobs as the guy walks away, gets in a Jeep Wrangler and peels away down the street, speakers blaring. She folds into herself and crumples down to the sidewalk. The Greek Row sidewalk, where people spill beer, vomit and pee each weekend.

No, no, no. This will not do.

"Hey there," I say as I approach.

Colleen glances up before letting out another sob and hanging her head. She sounds like a small animal caught in a trap.

"Are you okay?"

"Do I look okay?" She raises her head, and there is fire in her eyes.

Uh, not really. "What happened?" I say instead.

"I was just *dumped.*" She gestures down the street. "What does it look like?"

"I'm sorry." I squat down so I'm at her level.

"He was my most stable hookup, Sara." She whips a hand across her now-red face. "And now he's done with me."

"There will be other guys," I say.

"There will not be other *nine point eights*, Sara. Do you know how few of those exist?" Her gaze bears down on me. "I haven't slept in two days, my status is slipping, and I've been up half the night on that dumb app, trying to get my score to stabilize."

I recoil. I didn't even know she was on Perfect10.

"You of all people know that the algorithm rewards you

when a high-ranked person says yes to you. What do you think is going to happen when he logs in and unmatches with me?"

I swallow, my throat suddenly tight.

"This is going to cost me my Gold," she says. "No one in my sorority is a Silver, Sara. My life is *ruined*."

Oh gosh.

"Your life is not ruined," I say, as nicely as possible. I reach out to pat her on the head.

She just lets out another sob in reply.

"Let's get you up." I take her hand, but she doesn't budge. "Maybe we could get some coffee? Or I could walk you home?"

"What's the point?" She buries her face in her hands and continues to cry.

I look around, but no one else on the street has budged. Some girls are watching us from across the street, but don't seem like they're gonna help anytime soon.

A black Escalade stops at the curb in front of us. The back window rolls down and Braden peeks out. "Need a ride?" he asks.

I pause for a second. To be honest, I'm still kind of mad at him about the app thing. Since we became official boyfriend-girlfriend, we've barely talked.

I mean, *I've* barely talked. He texts me, and I send one-word replies. I just can't get one of the messages I saw out of my head. A few days before the game, while I was home with my family and my mom was joking about how smitten I seemed with this boy I was texting, when I thought something real was forming between us, he was chatting with her. And he wrote, **I heard that Smiths song again today, thought of you.**

Like first of all, please. Braden doesn't listen to The Smiths, he listens to Drake. Trying to be Fake Deep by saying he listens to old music—classic fuckboi.

And second… It was so emotional. I guess I would have expected something more purely physical. Knowing him, I would have guessed that before we were together, he'd been sending sleazy texts to girls. It's seeing him send sweet things that hurts the most.

Also, he sent her a heart emoji. And not even the two small pink hearts that are more friendly. The red heart. The *love* heart.

From the sidewalk, Colleen lets out another sob.

"Yes." I turn to Braden. "Yes, we would."

Braden gets out to help get Colleen into the car and hands her a bottle of water. She cries during the entire ride, but we manage to get her back to the dorm and into her room.

"You should sleep," Braden says.

Colleen sniffles and nods as she climbs into her twin extra long. Her room is neat, not as clean as mine, but good for a dorm. And she has all these prints of poems on her walls. I don't know why I expected posters of pop songs or celebrities.

"Here." Braden tucks her in. "I'm Postmating food for you, and Sara and I will wake you up when it comes. Just sleep for now."

Colleen nods.

"And drink water." He picks up a S'well bottle from her desk and lays it beside her on the bed. "You'd be surprised how dehydrated crying will make you."

Colleen laughs and pulls the water bottle toward her, cuddling it as she closes her eyes to sleep.

I shut Colleen's door behind us quietly. "Thank you," I say. "That was really kind."

"No problem," Braden says. "I saw you guys, and figured I would help."

I nod. We head down the hall to my room.

"It's strange though. Girls crying on the ground is usually a drunk thing." He laughs. "Sober at noon is a new one."

"I think she was pretty out of it," I say. "Maybe not drunk, but she said she hadn't really slept in days."

"That'll do it."

We step into my room. The common room is empty, but someone left an empty yogurt container on the table. I cringe as I pick it up and throw it away.

"It was so freaky," I say. I pull a Vitaminwater from the fridge and unscrew the cap. "She kept talking about Perfect10. Like it was...ruling her life or something. I've never seen anything... I didn't think people would get that upset because of something we made." My voice is thick and my eyes burn. Oh great, I'm gonna cry now too.

Braden seems to notice. He steps closer. "Hey, hey," he says. "It's okay." He brushes his hand against my cheek. "That was not our fault, okay?"

I don't say anything, afraid that if I speak my voice will crack.

"I'm sure the guy was a dick, but it sounded like he was just as much of a dick in person as he was online, okay?"

I nod.

He leans in and brushes his lips against mine. A sigh escapes me and I kiss him back, letting my body melt into his.

He trails a hand from the small of my back into my hair. I put my arms around him. I slip my hand under the hem of his shirt and feel the warm, bare skin of his back.

His lips press on mine, and this kiss turns from comforting to exhilarating. My body starts to overtake my mind, and thoughts of anything besides his lips and his skin and the bulge pressing against my hip disappear.

He leads me by my wrist into the bedroom, where thankfully, Tiffany is nowhere to be found.

We fall onto my twin extra long together, and there is no room for us to not be touching. Not that we would want that.

We do the same thing, but horizontal. When he reaches around to my bra clasp and looks at me, a question in his eyes, I nod.

And so I make it to second base. And not just over the bra.

His hands are kind of cold, but it feels nice.

When he moves his hand to the button of my jeans and I shake my head, he groans, but doesn't push me further. Instead, we stop and watch Netflix, and I start to get cramps like I'm on my period, even though I'm not. I guess my body is frustrated we had to stop too.

I try not to feel dumb for taking it so slow. True, it's not like any of this is new to him, but everything is new to me. I mean, he was my first kiss.

And I know, *I know*, that some people have that in middle school. And that many people do *a lot* more before they get to college. But I don't want to rush it. I want to enjoy each small step and new first, even though I'm starting later in the game.

Eventually Colleen's food arrives, and it turns out that Braden ordered some for us too. We eat takeout and talk about new classes we're in and how happy we are to be back in the sun after a break in the snow. We watch more Net-flix and cuddle, and every once in a while he kisses the top of my head.

Overall, it's a really nice afternoon.

But I am distracted the whole time. I lie there and run Colleen's words through my head. Because Braden is right, that guy was an a-hole both online and off. But I can't stop thinking: Colleen *barely* talked about the guy.

Mostly, she talked about our app.

chapter twenty-eight

Never before have I been in the curious position where the boy I like, likes me back.

Sure, there were boys who liked me. But they we all either super creepy or okay, but not the guy I would've picked if I had my choice. And I spent hours wondering if maybe I should give them a chance.

And then there were the boys I liked. Some—hell, *most*—never even noticed me, never saw me. And the ones who I thought might, like Chris, were always so close but not quite there. For every sweet moment there were hours of reading through texts, talking with friends and analyzing "how things were going."

They never told me they liked me back, just sprinkled bread crumbs of affection. Enough to keep me hungry for more, but never enough to fill me up. It kept me from moving on, but also from ever feeling secure.

It was "that dress looks cool on you" instead of "you look

beautiful tonight" and "are you going to the bonfire tonight?" instead of "I hope to see you there."

I was always sort of dragging both of us along, trying to turn a boy who just wanted to hook up into a boyfriend, or one who was unavailable into a future possibility. Convincing myself I was somehow building it into something swoonworthy, something I didn't have to try so hard to keep together.

But to have someone texting me back before I even have time to stress about whether they've read the message? To have someone who shows me off in pictures rather than telling everyone we're just good friends? To have someone planning dates instead of texting me at 2:00 a.m.?

To have the stars align and luck fall on my side and the universe smile and somehow the guy I *like* like is actually the same one who *like* likes me—it's remarkable.

It makes me wonder how I was so confused about situations in the past. Of *course* those "relationships" weren't going anywhere. Those guys clearly were not into me. When someone is into you, you can tell. It's not like that. It's like *this*.

A few days ago, Braden announced that he wanted to have me meet his friends. I kind of thought it was one of those vague, nice things you say in a relationship that never really happens, but sure enough, this morning he texted me about dinner tonight with a group.

He picks me up at my dorm in an Uber Black. I'm wearing dark jeans, a black blouse and the short, fat kind of heels that dress up an outfit while remaining wearable.

"Do you like sushi?" he asks as we speed off campus toward town.

"Yeah," I say. "I've missed it a ton since I came to school." Raw fish isn't usually served in a dining hall, and I've been daydreaming about the California rolls at my family's favorite takeout place.

The driver pulls to the curb in front of a low-slung building made of light wood and sleek black marble.

"This is some of the best stuff I've had on this side of the Pacific," Braden says as he opens the door of the restaurant for me.

A hostess in a black cocktail dress greets us and asks for the name on our reservation. The wall behind her is a waterfall, cascading over marble.

"Hart," Braden answers and she smiles as she types with red lacquered fingernails.

I peek around the waterfall at the interior of the restaurant. The dining room is dimly lit by fixtures made of tiny lanterns that look like they're floating above each table.

Men in hoodies and women in bodycon dresses sit in black leather chairs, drinking from tiny ceramic glasses and picking up food so tiny that I can barely see it across the room. Robbie would think it was hilarious. We always joke about how strange the dress code is in Silicon Valley.

"Your party is already here," the hostess says.

She tosses a curtain of sleek black hair over her shoulder and turns on her not-so-sensible heels.

We make our way to the other side of the dining room, where she pulls back a bamboo divider to reveal another room with a table that seats ten. Seven are taken by a group of laughing and talking people who are apparently my age but seem much older. They are like a scene straight off my Instagram "Discover Page." You know the kind, the strangers with mind-blowing lives and four thousand likes per selfie. They're somehow all ridiculously beautiful, with polished outfits, blown-out hair and dazzling smiles.

We step into the room, and half the table turns to look at us.

"Sara, this is Heather, Ava, Brian, Myra, Jason, Christine and Bennet," Braden says, gesturing toward the table. "Everyone, this is Sara."

They all greet us at once, rendering individual words indistinguishable.

I half raise a hand and smile as Braden and I take the two remaining seats.

The napkin on my plate is folded so intricately that I almost feel bad undoing it. I am gently pulling on the corner of mine when Braden yanks his open. I blush and quickly undo mine and place it on my lap.

I open my menu and scan for a word I recognize or a price under forty dollars, to no avail.

Looking up, I open my mouth to speak to Braden, but he is deep in conversation about prep school crew team with the guy next to him. He is twisted so far that I can't see much except the back of his suit jacket. Part of me misses Robbie. Braden can be great and all, when you are the center of his attention. But Robbie is good at making sure everyone in the room feels comfortable. I could use that right now.

"So." Across the table a girl with olive skin and striking green eyes sets down her drink. "Henry messaged me last night, on the PT—that's what I'm calling Perfect10 now." She turns to Braden. "B, if you start to use that, you owe me money, by the way."

He laughs. I am very aware that he does not turn to me, and

that she was clearly addressing him alone. I wonder if he has mentioned that I am his cofounder, as well as his girlfriend.

"Ava, are you kidding me? Henry?" the girl sitting across from her, Christine, I believe, says. "Boooo," she adds.

Ava rolls her eyes and takes another sip of her drink. "I don't know, I was drunk and I answered, okay?" She shrugs and her friend places her head in her hands.

A waiter in an all-black ensemble and white apron parts the bamboo divider and Ava flags him down.

"We'll start with four orders of these and these, and maybe two of the live octopus, just to try," she says, looking down at her menu. "Oh, and they need drinks." She gestures down the table toward us.

I flip the menu over but the waiter is standing behind my chair before I locate the drinks.

"Umm..." I feel my face grow hot. "Water is fine," I say.

"I was going to go with the sake..." Braden says, turning toward me for the first time since we sat down, but really he's turned toward the waiter. "Which would you recommend?" Braden holds up the menu.

"Either of these." The waiter points to two items.

"All right, let's go with the Premium then, thanks." He picks up his menu and then my own. "And she'll have some too."

The waiter nods and takes both menus. I guess I didn't need to attempt to decipher it after all. I wait for him to ask for the ID that I don't have, but he walks away without a word.

"Okay," Ava says, sitting up taller. "Where was I?"

"You were making a huge mistake, again," Christine says.

"Right." Ava nods as she swings her purse from the back of her chair onto her lap, the metal Gucci logo catching the

light. "So I go over to 'watch a movie.'" She lowers her voice
and makes it sound dopier, clearly doing her boy voice. Pulling a pack of cigarettes out of her purse, she taps the pack
against her wrist. She pulls one out and puts it between her
lips, then sparks a bedazzled lighter with expert technique.

I look around to see if anyone else is shocked. Surely you
can't smoke in here?

She takes a drag before continuing her story. "So we watch
all five minutes of some dumb robot fighting movie before
we're very much *not* watching the movie anymore."

The waiter parts the bamboo and steps into the room with
a tray of ceramic carafes and tiny cups. "You can't smoke in
here," he says as he sets down the glasses.

Ava puts out the cigarette on a ceramic plate, smearing
black ash over the intricate flower design. "Anyway, so there
we are, half-naked, with Transformers like, battling each other
or whatever in the background, when his phone goes off."

The waiter sets a tiny glass in front of me, and Braden
reaches to fill it with a clear liquid from the carafe.

"And he literally takes his hand off my..." She looks around
the restaurant. "Well, you know, and goes and checks his
phone. And then, I kid you not, he tells me he has to go, because a girl who is Platinum just asked to meet him at Joe's
Bar. He says it like, of course I'll understand that he has no
choice." She throws back a shot of sake.

"Jesus," Christine says. "Well at least now will you believe
me when I say he's not worth your time?"

"Eh." Ava shrugs. "Well see."

Christine looks defeated.

"Do you have your Juul?" Ava asks, changing the subject.

The second girl reaches into a small leather purse and pulls out what looks like a flash drive.

"Can I get some tea?" Ava asks the waiter with a winning smile as he leaves the room.

"I don't know," Braden says, looking at Ava. "The guy has a point—how can you pass up a 9 or above?"

About half the table laughs, and the other just looks at him. It is pretty much divided according to gender.

I elbow him in the side.

"What, it was a joke," he says.

"It's a rude joke," I quip back.

"Thank you, new girl," Ava says. "Braden, I like this one."

The waiter sets her tea in front of her and she nods briefly. "The girls he typically brings around just kiss his ass, if they speak at all."

The other girl laughs. "Yeah, sometimes they just stare into space."

"Or at their reflection in every shiny surface," Ava adds.

I smile at the compliment, although I feel a bit sick to my stomach about the context.

The waiter returns and sets down tiny plates of raw fish perfectly arranged with spices and sauces.

I wait for a few other people to take food before I pick up my chopsticks and carefully take a small piece of bright pink fish that I'm guessing is tuna.

"Hey." I nudge Braden with my elbow. "Do you know what—"

"One second," he tells me, before turning away and yelling down the table, "Hey, will you pass the lobster?"

I shrug and turn back to my food. The piece of fish is so tiny that I eat it in one bite. It is tuna, garnished with a sort of spicy ginger sauce. It's really good, but I couldn't tell you what made this *this*, and the sushi from the place at home cheap.

I reach for another one, but Braden places his hand on mine. "You don't want that," he says. "It's fattening."

"Sure I do," I say, shoving a piece in my mouth.

"Sara, be a lady," he says.

My shoulders inch up toward my ears, and heat builds in my stomach. My natural response to a rude comment by a douchey guy. Or I guess, in this case, my boyfriend.

I sit up straighter and look right at him. "I *am*," I say with food in my mouth. He glares at me, and I am debating how far I want to take this showdown when something across the table catches my eye.

Ava puts the flash-drive-looking item to her lips. She lowers one hand and raises the other, holding her tea.

As soon as it reaches her lips, vapor billows around the glass. She lowers the cup and sets it on the table. "It's very hot tea," she says.

"Is that how you try to hide it?" Christine asks.

"Is it working?" Ava says.

I reach forward and pick up the little cup in front of me. I look around to see if the waiter is nearby, even though he didn't ask me for ID. Still, High School Me is panicking inside my brain. I raise the cup to my lips and sip the hot liquid. It is surprisingly easy to drink, or maybe not surprising given the price tag.

I continue to sip my drink and nibble at the food. Ava and Braden continue to flag down the waiter and order more bottles of sake, and more colorful, strange, tiny plates of food.

The conversation grows louder and my body warmer, and although Braden barely talks to me, I start to not really mind.

Because, after each sip of sake, I feel more and more like I am good friends with all of these intimidating strangers.

"Oh, I almost forgot," Christine says, as she pours herself more sake. A bit spills on the table and she dabs it with a finger and then licks it off. "My parents said we could have the ski house for spring break."

"Oh, fabulous," Ava says. "I'll cancel the hotel tomorrow."

"Everyone's invited," Christine says. "There are plenty of bedrooms."

"There are plenty of guest suites," Ava says.

Christine rolls her eyes. "There're only two apartments in the guesthouse."

"Dibs!" Ava says, raising her hand and knocking over a glass of water in the process. "Oops." She tosses her napkin over the spill, but water continues to snake down the table.

"Sara," Christine says, turning to me. She puts her hand on mine. "You should come too. You would love it. Have you ever been skiing in Aspen?"

"Nope. I've never been skiing ever." I tuck a loose hair behind my ear.

"Well then you *have* to come," she says. She leans closer, "And I'll let you and Braden have the guesthouse. Ava can get over it."

"That's so nice of you to invite me," I say. In my mind I picture my calendar. I mean… I guess I could probably see if I could leave the camp early… But still, I'm not sure if I should miss any of the week.

On the other hand, a mansion in the mountains? My mind swims in sake, and I can't help but daydream about the majestic scenery, and spending time curled up by the fire, no stress or worries for almost an entire week. A break from it all.

"So you'll come?" Her eyes are bright.

"Yeah." I let myself smile. "I'll make it work. Wouldn't miss it."

We close out the restaurant, and as we stand on the curb waiting for our cars, I wedge my phone out of my tiny purse.

I open iMessage and click on the top name—Robbie.

Me: Hey, please don't be mad

He responds immediately, before I can send the second text.

Roberto: why would I be mad?

I continue typing as Braden opens the door for me and I slide into the Uber.

chapter twenty-nine

Roberto

"You're really gonna flake on the camp?" I ask. I was in bed when she texted me last night, and I woke up hoping it was a dream. But alas, no, Sara really is considering dipping on the coding camp she helped organize to do rich kid spring break. I asked her to come over, thinking I'd have a better chance of changing her mind in person.

"Like I said, I'm not sure what I'm going to do." She paces around my kitchenette, picking up an old mug of tea from the table and putting it in the sink.

"But you're considering it?" I say.

She grabs a paper towel to wipe the liquid ring left on the table. Classic Sara stress-cleaning behavior. "It's a free stay in a *mansion*, so, yeah, I'm considering it."

I exhale and look out the common room window. When she got here this morning, she had what looked like a large bruise on her collarbone. It took me a second to realize it was a hickie. That he gave her.

I tried not to let the frustration, the nausea I felt thinking about him with her, affect my judgment. Not to confuse those feelings with the matter at hand, about which I have a right to be mad.

"You were the one who pulled me into this in the first place," I say, turning back to her. "I asked my neighbor to sign up and everything. You can't just bail."

"I'm not bailing," she says. She paces across the room, the rubber bottoms of her fuzzy slippers squeaking. "Most of the administrative stuff I can handle before, and then I'm sure I can get someone to cover my shift."

"That's not the point," I say. "You recruited everyone to do this. It is basically your camp this year. How will it be for morale if you don't even show up?"

"Maybe that's not my problem," she says, her eyes darting from me and back away frantically. "You're right. So far I have carried this thing, done way more work than everyone else. Maybe it's someone else's turn. I don't want to be the girl who always does the work for someone else. Why can't I, just once, be the slacker, the one who skips class to do something fun?"

I cross my arms. "I can't believe you'd ditch these little kids for a bunch of people you don't even know."

"I do know them." She flinches. "They're my friends."

"They're *his* friends," I say.

"Yeah, and I'm his girlfriend, Robbie. Why can't you understand that?"

The awkward silence hangs between us. I feel like she's punched me. "I don't know. You're the one who always hated him," I sputter. "I've been indifferent to him."

"Well, I like him now," she says.

"Honestly, Sara, I don't even know who you are anymore."

"Really, because I'm dating Braden? That's just dramatic."

"No." I run a hand through my hair. "It's not about him, although, frankly I think that if someone seems shitty for the first ninety-nine impressions and then gives one good one, then maybe they are still, you know, a shitty person." I let myself make the dig, even though I know it distracts from my broader point. I can't help it. "Whatever, date him if you want. But really? First with this app that helps people objectify each other, and now you're ditching the outreach that was your heart? I thought you were in this to change the world. I thought you wanted to be a female pioneer in the next wave of technology. I thought you wanted to build something useful, something helpful. Is this what you really pictured doing? Hawking a morally bankrupt app so it'll pay for your spring break trip with the cast of Keeping Up with the Kardashians Junior?"

"Oh, fuck off," Sara says. The words sting. It might be the first time I've ever heard her swear. "Don't act like you didn't build half the app too."

"Then we're both guilty." I open my arms. "But at least I've started to feel bad about it. At least I've started to think about getting out. You're not even fighting it—you're letting it change what is *you*."

She stares at me in silence, before mumbling, "I need to go now. I have brunch plans." She stalks toward the door.

"I'm sure you do," I say.

But she is already walking away. On her way out, she realigns my roommate's framed *Animal House* poster on the wall so that it is level. Then she leaves and slams the door, sending it back askew.

chapter thirty

I've never been nervous going after school to get extra help from teachers. Or chatting with them during recess, or speaking up during class. Honestly, for a good part of my childhood, I was friendlier with the teachers than the other kids.

But today is different. Because today I'm going to Professor Dustin Thomas's office hours. Which are by appointment only. And have a wait-list.

Even though we did well in his class, I'm still scared of him.

I wipe my palms on my pencil skirt and listen to his assistant type.

Suddenly, the large mahogany door opens. "Sara, come on in." Professor Thomas smiles.

I smile back, but it feels mechanical. Am I supposed to show this much teeth?

"Thank you for meeting with me, sir." I stand in front of a visitor's chair, waiting for him to sit first.

"No need for the formality," he says. "I like to be tough

in class to teach you guys something. But the students who pass get to call me Dustin. And considering you all were my first A-plus, you can probably call me Dusty or something."

"Okay…"

"But don't." His expression turns serious. "Don't call me Dusty."

"Noted." I nod.

"So what brings you here, Sara?"

"I was wondering…what your thoughts were regarding… the market regulating itself? I mean, shouldn't companies fill whatever demand there is for a product, and then consumers have the responsibility to, you know, take it or leave it? Because it's not like it's on the company to decide what a right or wrong product is—they're just supplying the option, giving people the choice. And frankly, isn't that just more freedom, having more choice?" I realize I'm bouncing my knee rapidly up and down. I stop and fold my hands over my lap.

He studies me. "I'm not going to lie, darling. It sounds a bit like you ate the collective works of Ayn Rand last night and are now vomiting bits and pieces onto my desk."

I recoil.

He continues. "But my inclination would be…no. I think that enough companies have literally poisoned unknowing consumers for us to wonder if regulation is obsolete."

"Right." I nod.

"I don't like abstractions though. Or analogy. What are you really worried about? I doubt you came here just to discuss theory."

I exhale. "Robbie thinks that Perfect10 is bad for people. That it lowers the level of discourse in the dating pool. That it encourages people to degrade each other."

Okay, maybe that's not exactly what he said. Maybe I filled in the blanks a bit with my own worries. But Robbie is the one who put this in my head, so he will be the one to tell Dustin Thomas that the first A-plus ever in his class was for an evil product.

To my surprise, he nods. "Yeah, I could see that." He rests a hand on his chin. "You did the assignment correctly. I said to build a product and pitch it to me like I was a VC. You built a product and pitched it to me, and I could see how it would make money. So I gave you an A-plus, because it's the first product in the years I've been teaching the class that I could see one of my colleagues investing in. I could see how it would grow, how it would make money. You did it. You completed the challenge. You did not, however, build a company I would have invested in. Preying on human insecurity to make a buck is a viable strategy for a company, but not something I want in my portfolio."

My heart sinks. Part of the reason I ran with the idea, pursued it beyond the class, was that I thought we had a stamp of approval from him.

"No shame in what you're doing," he says. "I'd just rather invest in something that appeals to our better natures."

"Like what? A dating app that helps people find a real connection? Like, one that gives you points for hanging out together and having meaningful conversations?"

"Yes, maybe."

"But that wouldn't be profitable," I say. "As soon as someone finds love, they leave the app and you lose a customer. Two customers! It's basic math."

"You'd be surprised, Miss Jones. People are willing to pay more for good things than to avoid bad things."

What he's saying completely contradicts our business model. But I smile and don't say that, because he is, after all, a genius.

"Now, if you ever build something like that, you should give me a call."

I thank him and stand up to leave.

"And one more thing, Miss Jones," he says as I reach the door. "I wouldn't worry too much about the state of love. Well, at least what your app can do to it. I don't think it'll be going anywhere, since Hart pissed off Mike Williams."

"How do you know about that?" I blurt out without thinking.

"Hart called me before the meeting," he says, as if I should know. "I told him not to go. But of course, just like his father, he's hardheaded as the devil."

What? I knew Braden was being led by his ego when he took that meeting, but I didn't know his ego had led him straight past the advice of another VC.

"Um, right. Okay, thank you," I turn to leave but stop myself. "We do have other interest. From Thatcher Bell."

"Bell would want something like this." A wry smile crosses his face. "Well, if he does offer, I just hope he doesn't run into Williams at the Rosewood or golf club before you close."

When I step out of the building, I check my phone to see I have five missed calls. Two from Robbie, and three from Braden. *What the heck?*

I debate who to call back first and determine I probably have some obligation to my boyfriend, even though I've been aching to patch things up with Robbie.

It rings exactly once before he picks up. "Hel—"

Braden cuts me off. "Thatcher Bell just emailed. They want us to call them right now to talk numbers," he says.

"What?"

"Sara, they're making an offer."

chapter thirty-one

Roberto

"Hoooly crap!" Sara says as soon as she walks in the door. "Are we about to become millionaires?"

Braden smirks. "I mean technically since I was born—"

She swats his arm. He smiles mischievously and puts his arm around her waist. It feels like an invisible hand is squeezing my chest. One with claws too.

"But yes, I think we just might be," he says.

I don't want to assume anything before we hear it from the horse's mouth. We have no idea how much or how little it could be.

Sara leans her head on Braden's shoulder, and my stomach turns. The time before she got here was weird enough when it was just me and Braden sitting in his professionally decorated room.

But it turns out this is worse. I should have kept my mouth shut about my opinions about him, about the company. What good did it do? Now I've lost Sara as a best friend, and there she is, literally in his arms.

I shake my head. I need to keep my eyes on the prize. The potentially giant dollar sign that would be a lottery ticket for my family, and my ticket out of this godforsaken company.

They can have all my shares. Hell, they could have them for five hundred dollars, just to make up for the time I spent coding. But a few million doesn't sound bad.

"What are we waiting for?" I say. "We're all here. We should call."

"All right, let's do it," Braden says.

Sara is grinning like a madwoman.

We huddle around Braden's phone as it rings over speaker. It feels like there is no other sound in the world but that drawn-out beeping, and then pausing and then beeping. Every syllable buzzing with anticipation.

"Hello." Bell's voice interrupts the ringtone. A wave of excitement washes over me. I feel like I might jump out of my own skin, I'm so amped. By contrast, Bell's voice sounds so normal, so *casual*.

"Hi, it's Braden from Perfect10."

"Oh, hey man, sorry, it's hard to hear you, I'm on the golf course and the cell service is shit."

"Oh, well we can call you back later if…"

"No it's fine." He laughs. "I didn't pay half a mil to buy in for them to rush me. Now is good."

Braden looks over the phone at Sara and me.

I raise my eyebrows and shrug. *I have no idea how to do this. Don't ask me.*

"We were, uh, really happy to hear you guys are interested in, uh, angel investing," Braden settles on saying.

"Well, that's actually what I needed to speak with you about," he says.

My stomach plummets.

"We're definitely interested in the product," he says.

My spirits rise again.

"And my partners love the idea and what you've done so far, but they aren't...totally comfortable with the idea of putting so much money into a company run by teenagers."

We all look at each other. There's a bit of static on the line.

I lean toward the phone. "So what does that mean?" I ask cautiously.

"It means that we're willing to make an offer, but not a seed investment. We're willing to offer five million for ninety percent of the shares. You will retain the rest, but operations will be put in the hands of Instafriend, another company in our portfolio. We've been invested in them for years, and they have the experience to run this sort of thing."

Oh my god. *Five million dollars. Holy shit.*

Sara's eyes meet mine and she lets out a squeal.

Braden shoots a look at us and takes the phone off speaker before pressing it to his ear.

"I see," he says a few times, in response to words I cannot hear. I don't really mind though. I'm deciding which tropical island to take my parents to first.

"Well, we'll consider this and get back to you," Braden says.

My attention snaps back to him. Part of me wants to say, *Are you kidding me? Take the money now.* But I know we need to at least have a lawyer check out the deal first. Which is probably why it's good that I'm not the one on the phone.

He hangs up and Sara lets out a louder version of her earlier squeal, this time with the accompanying dance. "Yes! Yes, yes, yes, yes!"

And hey, I'm not usually a happy dance kind of guy, but I almost feel like joining her. Or at least, I would, if I wasn't looking at Braden and trying to figure out why he is frowning.

Sara is jumping up and down when Braden clears his throat. Her feet land on the floor hard, her mood sinking. "Wait, what's wrong?"

"Didn't you hear what they said?"

"Yeah, five million dollars, Braden." She looks at me. I shrug. I feel the same way she does.

"They want us to give up the company."

"So? We still get to keep some, and we also get *five million dollars*."

"*So*, they're being ridiculous," he says. "Not totally comfortable with college kids running their company? What BS is that? How old do they think f-ing Mark Zuckerberg was?"

I look back and forth between Sara and him. "I mean, I think Zuckerberg is more the exception than the rule—"

"We've handled everything *quite* well so far." He talks over me and steps over Sara's foot as he paces the room. "For God's sake, we've built a five-million-dollar company already."

"But it's only a five-million-dollar company because they value it that way," I say. I lean against his roommate's bed, my energy fading. "Without them, we don't have anything."

"We have our users," he says, "Our momentum..."

"I'm sorry." I laugh. "But I can't exactly pay my dad's electric bill or my tuition on momentum, Braden."

Braden shakes his head. "You need to think bigger than that. This could be a billion-dollar app."

"At which point we'd make a ton more off our shares," I respond. "But this way we know we get paid, even if the thing fails."

Braden stumbles back like I slapped him. "Why do you think it will fail?"

"Why are you so sure it won't?" I ask. "This was a class project we were hoping for a C on, and now you're acting like we're sitting on the goddamn Google algorithm."

"How do you know we're not?" Braden's voice is louder now.

I push off the bed and move forward a few steps. "Because people are always going to want to search for things on the internet. We invented a fad, and we might as well cash out now."

"It's not a *fad*, it's—"

"Braden." I grit my teeth. "At a certain point, people are going to grow the fuck up and realize that rating people like prize livestock is not love, and that status from strangers is the not the same as having people who care about you. And I'd rather be on a beach somewhere enjoying my one and a half mil when that happens than going down with the ship."

"*God.*" Braden turns to Sara, as if just remembering there's a third cofounder. "You don't agree with him, do you?"

"I, uh… I don't know," she says.

I don't wait around to see what she decides.

chapter thirty-two

Braden

I reach out my hand to help Sara down the steps, running my gaze up and down her figure. She steps forward and her right leg is almost entirely visible through the slit in the floor-length dress. It fits her perfectly, tight everywhere it should be and elegantly draped over the rest. With her every move, the silky fabric shimmers. It looks almost like molten silver has been poured over her body.

"I knew you'd look great." I wink as I slide an arm around her. The designer dress was worth every penny. And trust me, there were *a lot* of pennies.

"Thank you." She blushes and tilts her head down as she tucks a stray blond curl behind her ear. "And thanks for the dress. That really wasn't necessary."

"Of course it was." I had the dress and a note telling her when to be ready delivered to her room this morning. I thought it would be romantic, plus I wanted to avoid a conversation about how nothing she owned would do for this event.

I open the door of the waiting car and watch her while she slides in. I follow her and pull the door shut.

"So where are we going?" she asks as the car turns around, heading away from the dorm and toward the street.

I laugh. "Not a fan of mystery, eh?"

She shrugs and smooths her dress over her knees. "I like plans."

I shake my head. I can feel a smile on my lips, despite my best effort to prevent it. "Well then, here." I pull the invitation out of my breast pocket and hand it to her.

"It's a gala thrown by the Browns. For some charity, about…kids or animals or something, I don't know. But he's one of the first employees of Apple, and she's—"

"Our congressional representative. I know who they are." She flips the invitation over, although there's nothing on the back. "And their charity is for pediatric cancer research. It says it on here."

"Yeah, yeah. Right."

She studies the invitation. "Will they be there?" She looks at me through perfectly painted eyes.

"Yeah, I assume so." I undo one of the buttons on my coat and adjust the way I'm sitting.

"Oh my gosh." She holds the invitation to her chest. "She's one of my favorite people."

"Really?" I try not to laugh. I can't think of anyone I'd get that excited to share some overpriced chicken in a hotel ballroom with. I don't think I've looked up to someone that much since I was five, and that was Batman.

These sorts of events are kind of work for me now. Smile and shake hands with my parents' friends, who I'm counting on to get me a job or secure an investment for me one day.

It's not that I don't get that these people are important, it's just that I know they're important in a *you show up and act like they're a big deal so they give you a tax break* way, and not in an actual *I'm humbled to meet one of the leaders of my country* way. I've seen enough to know that the real leaders in this country are on my side of the campaign donation.

I adjust my tie in the reflection of the window. Outside, the darkness is interrupted only by a few ambient yellow lampposts among the palm trees.

I hate how quiet it is here sometimes.

"Can you put on some music?" I ask the driver. He nods and reaches for the radio dial. We listen to the repetitive bass of Top 40 hits the entire way there.

The car pulls onto the still relatively quiet drive of the country club, toward the large stone building nestled among the dark green hills of the golf course. I watch out the window as the people in the limo a few cars in front of us step out. The next guest has driven himself to the fundraiser, albeit in a Tesla. As he leans over to shake the valet's hand and give him the keys, I just barely catch his profile. He looks familiar, but I can't place whether I know those features from a past Forbes's list or some party my parents threw years ago. Maybe both.

We step into the night, but it's basically the same temperature as the air-conditioned car. Later the temperature will drop just enough to prove the seasons change, at least somewhat, here. But with the sun having set only an hour ago, the heat still clings to the earth.

I hold out my arm to help Sara out of the car. I smile as we step into the light of the doorway and the white noise of other people's conversations. The uneasiness in the pit of my stomach dissipates. It may not be as easy or seamless as I'd like to sit in a car alone with Sara, but walking in here with a girl like this on my arm—and knowing that, when my parents' friends ask, they will be pleasantly surprised to learn she also brings a brain and, soon enough, a world-class degree to the table—makes it all worth it.

"It's so pretty," Sara leans in and says to me.

I just nod. Honestly, I've been so busy watching the other guests watching her I haven't noticed much about the room. I glance around now. The ceiling of exposed wood beams coupled with the glittering candles that make up most of the light in the room give it a warm feel. Throw in the choice of lilies as centerpieces, and it's a little bit Pinterest wedding for my taste. But these sorts of events are always a bit like that on this coast. I would prefer to be at the Plaza anytime.

"Let's get a drink," I say.

I flag down a waiter walking around with half-filled flutes of champagne and swipe two off his tray with confidence.

"Is that okay?" Sara asks, taking hers reluctantly. "Like, half these people work for the government," she says out of the side of her mouth.

"Yeah, which means it's even less likely the police are gonna come in here trying to bust people."

She raises her eyebrows. "That's one way to look at it." She tosses back half her glass in one go.

"Braden Hart, is that you?"

I turn at the sound of my name. Representative Brown, standing nearby in a small group, greets us with a warm politician's smile. She touches the arm of the man she was talking to and shakes his hand, and then walks toward us. After a few steps, she looks over her shoulder to make sure her husband has also gracefully exited the previous conversation and is following her.

"No way," Sara whispers. "She knows who you are."

I turn to her and laugh. "Yeah, my family went skiing with them two Christmases ago," I say.

"What?"

"Try to pick your jaw up off the floor. She's going to want to talk to you."

Sara doesn't get a chance to answer me before they are standing in front of us, Representative Brown in a classic blue pantsuit and her husband, in classic Palo Alto fashion, sporting dark jeans and no tie, although his hair is more gray than not.

"Mr. Brown," I say, reaching for his hand. "Congresswoman Brown, how are you?"

"Well, you know." She shakes her head. "You plan and plan these things and then it's always something you didn't anticipate that goes wrong. This time, it's the caterer."

"Let's hope no one wanted the vegetarian option," Mr. Brown says gruffly.

She nods, making a face.

"At a meeting of Democrats near San Francisco? I'm sure that won't be an issue," I say.

They both laugh.

"I have the best staff around, though—they'll sort it out. I'm not too worried," Rep Brown says, ever the diplomat. "But I'm sorry, here I am going on about catering and being rude…" She looks at Sara. "Why don't you introduce us, Braden?"

"Oh, right, this is my girlfriend." I rest a hand on the small of her back.

"Sara Jones," she says, reaching out her hand.

"Ah, that's very sweet," she says, shaking Sara's hand. "I'm glad you brought her—young love is such a beautiful thing."

She looks back and forth between us, glowing. I just smile awkwardly and avoid looking at Sara. *Love is a bit of a strong word*.

"You know, we were your age when we met." She looks at her husband and smiles.

Sara coughs and covers her mouth so as not to do a spit take with her champagne. "Really?"

"Yes." She turns back to us, nodding. "I was one of the first girls allowed into our university."

"And she was the smartest in our class, boy or girl," Mr. Brown interjects.

She pats him on the arm.

"No, really," he says. "You'd hear guys say all the time, 'You know that Mary is probably one of the prettiest girls here, but no one can ever talk to her during class. She's always sitting in the front, asking all those questions.' But I loved that. I thought she was the most magnificent *person* I had ever seen."

"Oh." She blushes.

"Really." He nods. "But I was too afraid to talk to her."

"That's right." She looks at him. "Until the election."

He smiles. "I was the fifth generation in my family to go there, and three of them had been class presidents."

"And the one was later on *the board*," she says, raising her eyebrows conspiratorially. As if there weren't a handful of people in this room on the board at an Ivy.

"So naturally, everyone thought I would run," he said. "The only problem was, I was an engineering major who wanted to spend his off time drinking beer, not in long meetings about budgets for student clubs."

A smile breaks across my face. I can't help but laugh at that; I love when old people talk about their days partying.

"So," he continues, "I went to Mary with a proposition. I'd be her campaign manager."

"I hadn't even thought about running at that point," she says. "But he had all these ideas from his uncles' campaigns and was so sure I could win." She shrugs. "So I said 'why not?'"

I nod and take a sip of champagne.

"Well naturally, I lost *terribly*." She laughs. "What would you expect—a year before, they were split down the middle about whether to let women in at all. They weren't going to make me their *president*." She grimaces at the mere thought. "But I'll tell you this…" She leans in, like she is going to tell us a secret. "We shook up that campus. We campaigned hard, and had debates on real issues, about feminism and the war protests—none of the stupid popularity contest stuff that usually dominated. And we won most of the girls and a good chunk of the boys. That wasn't enough, of course, because there were only, what, a thousand girls on campus at the time. I still have some of the letters people wrote to the school newspaper, supporting me, hanging in my office on the Hill. So then—" she points a finger at her husband "—the day after they announced the results, he asked me out. Only took him four months of seeing me every day."

"Well it would've been unprofessional to ask in the middle of a campaign," he says.

"That's…" Sara clears her throat. "That's really lovely."

I turn to her, but her glassy eyes avoid mine.

"We better stop boring you kids with our stories." Rep Brown leans forward to shake my hand and kiss me on the cheek. "Looking forward to seeing your parents at the next fundraiser," she whispers in my ear, before leaning back seamlessly with a brilliant smile.

"Certainly." I nod. "Have a nice evening." They head off to the next group they need to schmooze, and I turn around, tilting my champagne flute to examine the few drops left, unsure if there's enough for another sip.

"Want to sit down?" I ask Sara. "They'll probably start soon."

"Hmmm?" She looks at me blankly.

"Do you want to find our seats?" I ask again.

"Oh yeah, sure." She shakes her head, as if trying to snap out of some sort of trance.

"Are you okay?" I ask. I place my hand on the small of her back as I guide her toward the ballroom. "You seem unusually quiet."

"Yeah, I'm fine." She smiles, but her eyes are flat. "It's just..." She makes a face. "You know."

I actually do not know.

We find the place cards for "Mr. Braden Hart" and "Guest" and take our seats. I unfold my napkin and drape it over my lap. I flip open the program resting on top of my plate and skim it. The main speeches are before the meal. Which would be disappointing considering my growling stomach, but I'm not looking forward to this dry chicken as much as I am to the drinks.

"Do you think they'll bring wine around before this?" I point to the first speech. "I'll try to find a waiter," I add before she can answer.

I search the room, half rising out of my chair.

"What do you think we should do?" Sara says.

I turn back to her. "What, like white or red? I think it's chicken so…"

"No, about Perfect10."

"Oh." I narrow my eyes. "I think it's obvious, right? It's our company. We're not just going to let them take it from us."

"They're not exactly *taking* it," she says. "I mean, I wouldn't exactly call paying millions for the work of college freshmen a hostile takeover."

"Hey, don't sell us short like that," I say. "Picasso was thirteen when he started painting. Page and Brin created Google from a Stanford dorm room."

As PhD students, not freshman, but maybe she doesn't know that.

"Zuckerberg started Facebook during sophomore year."

She laughs. "I don't think comparing ourselves to them is necessarily productive."

"Who else would I compare myself to?" I catch the eye of a waiter across the room and wave him over.

He fills our glasses, and I assume we're done with that conversation for now.

"I just don't know." Sara takes a sip of her wine, then stares at the glass. "It's a lot of money to turn down. It could change everything for me. For my family. And for Robbie."

"Yeah, but think about how much more we could do, how much more we could make, if we build this thing? Cashing out now is something that we might really regret."

"I really don't think I'll regret making a *million* dollars, Braden. We could end up with nothing if we don't take this. And I get that it's different for you, that you…have the comfort to take the risk for the big payout. But for some of us, this means not stressing about college anymore, it means helping my parents retire someday. And hell, for Roberto, it could mean helping his parents reunite." She pushes the wineglass farther away from her. "I just don't think you understand the ridiculousness of debating five million or one million dollars when to some people, money stress means not being sure how to budget for both utilities and food this month. It's different for him, and I think it's something we need to respect."

"I'm sorry." I shake my head, reaching for my wineglass. "I'm not compromising the future of our company because his family hasn't worked as hard as mine."

"*Excuse* me?"

"It's not my fault he's poor."

"Did you really just say that?" Her voice is at least an octave higher than it was before.

I shrug, my glass still at my lips. *What?* "What did I say?" I set down my wineglass.

She just looks at me as if she's disgusted. God, *women*—it's not enough to constantly try to please them and apologize for everything. We have to guess what they're mad about too.

"You're unbelievable," she says. "Are you really so self-centered, so narrow-minded, that you can really think that? That you don't see that his family has sacrificed so much for their son? And worked *so* hard? That it is just luck and privilege and...geography that separates his situation from yours?"

"Sara, you're making a scene." I put my hand over hers.

She pulls her hand away like I've burned her. She reaches for the clutch I bought for her.

"Where are you going?"

"Home," she says. "I'll just call an Uber."

She takes off toward the door, heels clicking, as the

Congresswoman takes the stage. Everyone stands to clap, and I weave through the crowd after Sara.

I push through the door, and the roar of the room is replaced by the sound of her footsteps echoing down the hallway.

"Sara!" I yell.

She stops and looks over her shoulder but doesn't walk toward me.

"You can't just leave me." In just a few strides I close the distance between us. "Do you know how embarrassing it is to be at an event like this without a date? You can't leave right as it's starting."

"I'm sure you'll make friends," she says. "Hell, you know half of these people already and I know none. I doubt I'd be any help."

"That's not the point, Sara, and you know it."

She turns away again.

"Sara," I say through gritted teeth. "If you walk out that door, that's it—we're breaking up."

She spins around, the bottom of her floor-length dress twirling. She extends her arms to the side, her purse sparkling in her hand. "I guess we're broken up."

chapter thirty-three

The room is quiet when I get back. My roommates are nowhere to be found, beds left behind unmade, with various considered and rejected shirts and dresses strung about between the crumpled sheets. They're probably getting drunk at a frat party, or high and watching movies with friends. Normal college stuff.

I let my keys slip out of my hand; they clatter against the table, breaking the silence. In my room I slip out of the stupid five-hundred-dollar dress he had no business buying me. Couldn't he have just bought me a beer or a Domino's Pizza, like a normal college boyfriend?

It's funny how quickly "put this on and be ready at 8" can go from looking like a cute surprise to like being summoned as arm candy, when you scratch back the pretty facade and catch a glimpse of the person writing the note.

I slide on baggy Warren sweatpants and my old high school track-and-field T-shirt. I'm pulling my hair, still crunchy from hair spray, into a messy bun when my phone lights up.

Yaz: So what exactly happened?

I texted her when I left the benefit, but she was slow responding. This is her second message, following a bunch of frowny emojis she sent over an hour ago.

Me: Nothing.

I send the first message and keep typing.

Me: I mean like nothing new. it wasn't a big fight. It wasn't really anything... I just realized I spent so much of my time trying to rationalize his behavior, trying to remember he's done more good than bad. Trying to convince myself and other people he wasn't a total dickhead and it was just like why? You know. Shouldn't it be easier than that?

I think of my parents. They aren't dramatically "your eyes light up the room, I can't live a moment without you" in love. They might have been when they first got together, but it isn't like that now.

They don't go on fancy vacations, and the gifts they get each other are always nice, but useful, like a sweater or new kitchen mixer. And when my mom would find out my dad had to work late, she wouldn't cry that she couldn't spend a night without him, she'd mumble "well that sucks" before asking me if I wanted to go for a gals' dinner.

But, when we watch TV, she always sits next to him, leaning her head on his shoulder. When he leaves for work, she'll run down the stairs, hair half-dry, to kiss him before he goes. And when she's sick, he brings her tea and her favorite fuzzy blanket.

I also have a number of distinct memories of leaving a restaurant or movie theater when the weather was cold. He'd
offer her his coat and make the same joke about how funny it
is that she's always cold when she "looks pretty hot to him."
And it just seems so sweet and easy.

My dad always told me not to judge a guy by how he treats
me, but by how he treats the waiter. Because he might be trying to impress me now, but it's how he treats people he's not
trying to win over that shows you his true character. And that
after the initial flirtation fades, that is the person you'll be in
the relationship with. He would give me this speech when
I was heading off to homecoming or another school event,
even though I was always going with a group of friends, so
it wasn't too terribly relevant.

But now that I think about it, he has a point. Maybe a
mean person who happens to be nice to you is still a mean
person. And maybe you are the exception, but that doesn't
mean you're special. It just means that they want something
from you.

My phone buzzes.

Yaz: Have you made it home?

I stare at the words. I guess, I type, still not really sure I
can say this dorm room is my home. I pause and click back-
space. There's no need to be melodramatic; she meant it quite
literally.

Me: Yep

I slide the phone into my sweatpants pocket and pad into
the living room, not bothering to click on the light, the shine

of the streetlight outside the window making it easy enough
to see.

I stare at the hulking flower arrangement that seems to
take up most of the room. I think of the helicopters, the Instagram posts about me *being the most beautiful girl in the world,
the only one who could make me settle down.* I reach out and touch
one of the roses, and the edges of the petal crumple in my
hand. No longer silky soft, the flowers are dry and fragile.
They're dying.

I look at the pieces in my hand, then sigh and dust them
off as I make my way to the couch. I flop down and pull
the throw blanket off the back, cuddling up with me, myself and I.

It starts to rain outside and I wonder if I should make tea.
I'm not sure if it would help. I'm not really cold, not really sad.
There's just a kind of a dull, vague pain throughout my body.

It's different this time, to see the sky open up over California. It's not a one day of gloom in an always-sunny place,
but needed replenishment in a time of drought. Funny how
easily your perspective can change like that.

I am deep in my melodramatic thoughts about metaphors
and karma and am seriously considering turning on some
Adele or Lorde when someone knocks aggressively on the
door.

"Hello!" Yaz says as soon as I open it. She looks almost
manic with her soaking wet hair, makeup smeared down her
face and giant smile. She shoves the large cardboard box in
her arms toward me and pushes past me into the room.

"What are you doing here? It's pouring rain."

"Are you kidding? One of my girlfriends is going through
a breakup. My bat signal went off." She slides off her rain-

coat and folds it over the back of a chair. "Neither snow nor rain nor heat nor gloom of night could keep me away. I'm like a Marine."

I laugh. "I'm pretty sure that's the Post Office, not the Marine Corps."

She wrinkles her nose, which is slightly pink from the cold. "God, that seems a bit over-the-top for people delivering letters."

I shrug as I shut the front door. "You gotta think about a time before Snapchat or texting."

She considers this, bobbing her head back and forth as she leans down to peel off her clunky Hunter boots. They make a loud squeaky sound every time she moves. It's so funny how people here pull all sorts of rain clothes out of nowhere as soon as a cloud appears.

It rains in Minnesota, and people just wear whatever they were gonna wear that day. But in California, rain is An Occasion.

"Okay!" She runs her hands through her dripping hair and exhales. "Where was I?" She takes the box back from me. "Right, so we have wine, chocolate, ice cream, Chinese menus—because ordering it to my room and then getting it soaked as I walked across campus seemed stupid. Figure out what you want, and I'll cue up a rom-com for while we wait, or maybe something less romantic and more girl power? How about *Chicago*, or do you think it's too murder-y?"

She blinks at me, waiting for a response, but I just smile, thinking that maybe some of the grandest, most romantic gestures don't come from boys after all.

part four
exit strategy

chapter thirty-four

Roberto

"Should I get hot wings?" Sara asks. She looks at me over her menu, biting her lip as she considers this important quandary. "Like, I'm not hungry at all. But at the same time, they're just one of the best foods invented, so how do you not?"

I laugh. "It's up to you."

We're sitting in a sports bar near campus. It's one of the few places that actually resembles a college bar. Only a few places in town cater to students—most establishments are wine bars and swanky restaurants courting tech employees.

She flips the page of the menu, her freshly painted nails sparkling in the dim light of the pub.

Sara told me about the breakup as soon as I opened my door. The words sort of tumbled out of her mouth, "Braden-and-I-broke-up-and-I-know-we-are-not-talking-but-I-need-my-best-friend-and-can-we-just-skip-the-drama-and-go-get-a-beer?"

So I said, "Okay, let me get my keys." So far, we've talked

a lot about sports games neither of us saw but we heard happened, the weather being nice again, a dog she saw from across the street, and now, Buffalo wings. Which is fine with me.

"Are you guys ready to order?"

I look up to see our waitress, a thirtysomething woman in a black minidress and high ponytail. Her name tag says Natalie.

"Uh…" I glance at the menu. I realize I've spent the last four minutes studying Sara instead of the beer selections. "I'll take a Guinness."

That seems like the type of thing they probably have everywhere. Natalie nods and scratches a few words onto her notepad. I close my menu.

"Do you have a recommendation for wine?" Sara looks up from her menu.

Natalie narrows her eyes. "You look pretty young. Can I see some ID?"

"Oh." Sara pulls her purse onto the table. "Sure." She hands her the card quickly and turns back to her menu.

"This is expired, *Lauren*." Claire taps her notepad with her pen.

"Yeah, I know." Sara crinkles her nose. "I'm here for school. Doing my fifth year, and haven't been back to Ohio to renew it."

The waitress nods knowingly. "I'm from the Midwest too, small town in Iowa." She winks. "I'll get you a beer."

Natalie sets down Sara's fake ID and scoops up the menus.

Once she's over by the bar, I hold up my hand to block the side of my mouth and whisper, "Did I miss something? You didn't ask for a beer, right?"

Sara shakes her head, a huge smile spreading across her face.

"Nope. I was gonna get a rosé." She laughs. "But I wasn't gonna argue after that."

"Yeah, that was smooth," I say.

Sara reaches for a pretzel from the bowl in the middle of the table. She examines it before taking a nibble.

I chuckle.

"What?" she asks, her eyes wide.

"I was just thinking about that first party we went to, and how nervous you were, trying to order and everything. Look at you now." I gesture in her direction. "You have a whole backstory. You, Sara Jones, a fifth year. I would never have seen that coming."

She snorts but a smile plays on the edge of her lips. "My name is Lauren."

Over by the bar, Natalie pushes the tap back into place and loads two full pints onto her tray.

"Shhh shhh," Sara says, although I wasn't saying anything. "She's coming. Don't talk about it anymore." She transitions from a full panic mode to a gracious smile as Natalie slides up to the table with our drinks.

The opening bars of a song I used to really love and forgot about starts to play in the background as I take the first sip of my beer and Sara asks me another small-talk question.

There are two empties, one half-full beer, a half-eaten bowl of pretzels and one napkin ripped to shreds in front of Sara when she says, "Do you think there is a point to heartbreak?"

She doesn't look away. Her hands are still fiddling with napkin bits, but she looks me in the eye as she asks a question that most people would step around, even with those who know them best.

"What do you mean?"

"Like everyone says everything happens for a reason and you learn about yourself and all that. But it seems so scary. To give so much of yourself away."

She looks down at her half-empty beer.

"Even just dating Braden for a few months, I could feel myself becoming more like him." She shakes her head. "I hate feeling like who I am is being muddled by getting involved with someone if they aren't *it*, you know?"

I consider this. "I think that if you love someone, you probably like the things that make them *them*, you know? Like their little quirks and sayings as well as the way they look at the world and live their lives. There's a reason you're drawn to their spirit, right?" I swallow and look at my hands. I'm trying to keep the vision in my mind a generic one. To not think of her, and the way she gets over-the-top excited about color coding or her inexhaustible energy or even just her smile as I say these things.

"So when you start to notice that you're picking up these little habits, or maybe that even when you think about the bigger questions in life, you can't help but have things they said pop into your mind…that's not a bad thing, right? Because you're becoming more like that quality that drew you to them. Which is not to say loss doesn't hurt, or that having that person leave that place in your life won't suck for a while. But I think that if you walk away having become more like the one you admired, who was able to light up any room— and make a boring trip running errands something you'd look forward to all day, then how could it have been a bad choice?"

Sara sweeps up the napkin bits, piling them high on the dark wood table that is slightly sticky in a way that bar tables always seem to be. "But what if you don't like the way you're changing? What if you find yourself becoming more selfish, more negative, more angry?"

I consider this. There is a polite answer, and a true one. I go for true. "If you don't like them, maybe you shouldn't be with them."

We both laugh about that.

"Ugh." She places her head in her hands. "I am so stupid." She looks back up at me. "How is it that I could be so *romanced* by someone, have a crush on him, think maybe even I might one day love him and not even *like* him as a human?"

"I don't think that makes you stupid," I say. "I think a lot of us are drawn to people who are—" I try to ease the feeling in the pit of my stomach while I think of Braden and Sara together "—charming. Even if that charm is manipulation. Even if they're bad people, they're tempting when they say the right things."

She presses her lips together and nods. She looks down at the napkin bits. "I'm sorry, you know, about…" She looks me in the eyes. "Questioning doing the camp. And how I reacted when you called me out on it. And just…for being a shitty friend recently."

Sometimes this weird thing happens, where someone hurts you, and you end up comforting them. Reassuring someone that you're not that mad about the bad thing that they did. It's almost like you end up apologizing to them, when you did nothing wrong.

Sara looks at me, her long eyelashes blinking over her doe-like eyes.

I'm not going to pretend that her ditching me and the organization that is so important to her wasn't wrong. And I don't want to say, "it's okay" because it wasn't. But I know Sara isn't her worst moments. There's a reason I am still her friend, that I am still here now.

"Just, you know, next time, do better," I say.

She nods.

As night creeps closer to early morning, the bar fills up with more and more people. The crowd gets younger and less dressed. The vibe turns from people sitting in booths and nibbling on food to people crowding together so close that you can barely get to the bar or the bathroom without stepping on toes.

"Do you wanna take a shot?" Sara yells over the music, which has doubled in volume in our time here.

"Sure!" I yell.

We shimmy our way to the bar. There is no room to stand against the bar, so we hover behind a guy and girl who already have their drinks. Hopefully they'll move soon.

They don't seem to notice us though, and I'm scared to say excuse me. I can't hear what they're saying over the bass radiating from the speaker, but given their body language, it does not seem pleasant.

The guy reaches into his back pocket and pulls out an iPhone. He opens an app I recognize far too well and pulls up the profile of the girl. She has Silver status. He holds out the phone and makes a show of unmatching with her.

Rage grows in the girl's eyes. She picks up her full beer and throws it on him.

"Oh shit." I stumble back to avoid being sprayed, bumping into Sara in the process.

"What the fuck?" he yells.

"You hurt someone's rating just because they won't sleep with you on the first freaking date!" the girl yells. "It's against the rules!"

"There are no rules!" He wipes beer off his face. "And please, don't act so innocent—I know you've been giving head for upvotes for months."

"What did you just say?"

"Lizzy, what's going on?" Another guy has pushed through the crowd.

"This asshole just called me a whore." She crosses her arms.

He shoves past us, closing the distance between them. "What'd you call my sister?" He grabs a fistful of the guy's shirt.

"Get your hands off me." The douchey guy coils his arm, and I realize what is about to happen.

I turn and grab Sara's shoulders. "Move."

We're pushing through the crowd when the first punch lands square in the brother's jaw. He must fight back, because I hear people yelling "Stop!" and a few chanting "Fight, fight!"

I do not look back. I've heard too many stories to want to stick around to see if someone uses a broken bottle or something worse.

Despite the pandemonium of what might be Palo Alto's first bar fight, we're able to make it out the front door. I breathe in the fresh air of the quiet street and let out a long exhale.

"That was wild," I say.

When Sara doesn't reply, I turn to make sure she's okay. She doesn't look injured, but her face is chalk white. "What the hell have we done?"

chapter thirty-five

Sara

"Dude, it started a legit fight." I set down a tray on one of the long industrial tables.

Yaz sets hers across from me and slides into her seat.

"That's bonkers," she says.

I nod and take a bite of my tacos. Not bad for dining hall food. I finish chewing and dab my face with a paper napkin. "I'm seriously starting to be embarrassed that people know I made it," I say.

"About that…" Yaz moves her fork around her salad. "I've been meaning to tell you. I deleted the app from my phone."

My chest tightens. "For real?"

Yaz was one of the biggest fans of Perfect10 I know.

"Yeah." She nods. "It is messing with my psyche too much. I know I'm awesome, and I don't need random dudes to weigh in about whether or not that's true."

"Fair enough." I sip my lemonade, the processed soda-like

kind they stock the dining hall with. The sugar coats my teeth immediately.

"I felt bad about it," she says. "Since I wanted to support you, but if you're questioning it too…"

"Don't feel bad for quitting that dumb thing," I say. "Trust me, I've been wishing I could quit making it."

I pick at my food. "This isn't what I thought I'd be doing at all," I say. "It was our last resort idea to not fail the project, and then everyone was so excited about it. I'd never experienced something like that. So many people looking to me, telling me to do something. But it was like all of a sudden I was running full force on a treadmill I don't remember getting on.

"I didn't question it enough." I sigh. "Robbie did. But I didn't listen. People were just so hyped about it. And it felt like my chance, you know? This idea that everyone loved. And I couldn't be sure that if I made something else, I'd stand half the chance."

"Well that's just ridiculous," Yaz says. "You don't need *this* thing to be successful. You built it. You and Robbie, and he-who-shall-not-be-named too, I guess. If you build something else, something that lifts your heart, I think it could be just as successful. If not more." She takes a bite of her salad.

"You really think so?"

She nods as she swallows her food. "I know so. You are a code-blooded bitch too."

I text Robbie that I have an idea to run past him, but that I want to do some research first. I head straight from dinner to the library, and stay there until 10:00 p.m., pulling articles about couples married for seventy-five years and that *New*

York Times thing about the thirty-six questions to make you fall in love. I find anthologies of the greatest fictional love stories, and philosophy and sociology writings about human connection.

I check out so many books that the librarian asks if I am working on a thesis before giving me a hand trolley to transport them.

Robbie bursts out laughing as soon as he opens the door. He holds the door as I wheel my books into his room.

"Are there any left in the library?" he asks.

"Ha-ha. Funny." I start to stack the books on his table.

"Do you have your laptop?" I ask. I didn't bring mine to dinner, and I'd been doing most of my research on library desktops.

"Yeah." He pulls his Mac out of his backpack.

I lay the books on the table and open them to pages I marked.

"What is all this?" He starts to turn a page.

I swat his hand away out of reflex. He yelps.

"Sorry." I turn to face him and put my hands on my hips. "I was thinking. Maybe we can reinvent the app, make it about real human connection, not about status. About bringing more love into the world, not...whatever it is this thing is doing now."

"Have you talked to Braden about this?"

I shake my head and turn back to my books. "He'll likely shoot it down, because every time we help someone find someone—"

"We lose two customers. Right," Robbie says.

"Plus he's probably plastered by now." I try to picture where he might be. At some party? Some bar? I don't know how he deals with heartache, but I doubt it's with ice cream and a rom-com marathon. I keep getting texts with dubious spelling from him at 2:00 and 3:00 a.m. It's an interesting rotation between *I miss you, let's get back together* and *screw you, never talk to me again.*

I had to put his texts on Do Not Disturb to get some mental clarity and distance.

"Look…" I fall into a chair. "It probably won't go anywhere. But I wanna see if I can do it," I say. "Working on something so exciting I don't even know if I can pull it off is why I used to make things, and I don't know, I guess I feel alive again thinking about it."

Robbie pulls up a chair. "Let's do it."

A few hours later, Robbie is knee-deep in the books, and I am typing up some preliminary notes on his laptop when his phone rings.

"One second." He stands up. "I gotta take this." He steps into his bedroom, shutting the door behind him.

I just nod and don't look up. I am plugged in, typing rapidly as I hit flow state, new ideas coming to me every second. My hands fly over the keyboard and—

Wait, what just happened?

The page I was working on disappears and an error message replaces it.

No, no, no, no, no.

Luckily, I know how to recover documents like the back of my hand, thanks to my parents' confusion that because I know Java, I must also be well versed in tech support.

I make my way to the deleted documents on Robbie's computer, and sure enough, there is the one I was working on. But something else catches my eye.

To Sara, it is titled. It was created in November. Which is weird, because he gave me a candle for Christmas, and my birthday isn't until June.

My cursor hovers above the file I am supposed to click on. I pause and look around. His bedroom door is still closed.

I know I shouldn't. But it's *my own name.* I think I have a right to...

I slide the cursor down and click on *To Sara.*

The program takes up the whole window. The screen goes dark and then a question appears. Like a trivia game.

What is the best Beatles song?

Below the question is a small answer box. It's funny, because that seems way too subjective of a question for a Trivia game. Hell, fifty Beatles fans might give you fifty different answers. Well, I mean, let's be real, a good third of them are gonna pick "Let It Be," and for good reason, but still. You can't design a Trivia password with a subjective question unless you want only one person to get into it.

My fingers hover over the keys. *I mean it did say my name, might as well try.*

I type "Hey Jude" and click Enter.

The screen flashes green, and another question pops up. I am too excited about my correct answer to consider how weird this is.

When color coding binders, what color should the Urgent Tasks section be?

I type, *Blue because it is calming and red sets off stress hormones in your brain. The last thing you need when facing a deadline is more stress.*

This comes back with a flashing red screen so I try just

blue and it works. I guess my first answer was *too* correct. Whatever.

I am asked about my dogs' names, my favorite types of doughnuts and my favorite movies.

I am typing quickly, the competitive part of my brain taking over, so caught up in getting answers right and getting to the next level that I forget that questions like this are usually passwords. Leading somewhere, unlocking a message.

So I am taken aback when the screen flashes green after I correctly answer that Dani was the contestant who should've been chosen but was totally robbed last season on *The Bachelor* and another question doesn't pop up.

Instead, this message appears.

Dear Sara,

Caring about you means I want you to be the happiest you can be. I want the best for you. I want more laughs that make your eyes sparkle. More of that joy that rolls off you when you're dancing to your favorite song. I want the coziest feeling of warm blankets and tea to find you every time you are sick or sad.

And I don't know if I'm the one who can make that happen. But I hope I can be.

I know this is foolish and dorky, but I mean, when you have a crush on someone, isn't that the time to be foolish and dorky? To risk looking like a complete idiot for the chance to be endlessly happy?

So after all these questions there's one I'm still afraid to ask.

But I thought I'd let you know. Just in case I maybe could make you happier.

I wanted to tell you that I think I am falling for you.

And I wanted to ask, if maybe you might feel the same way too?

I stare at the message for a long time. It's so cheesy and ridiculous, and so I'm not really sure why I'm crying.

Maybe it's because fancy dinners and helicopters are great, but a bad temper and fighting are sad replacements for passion.

Maybe because I didn't realize that the person I wanted to go everywhere with and talk with about everything that happened to me, who made late nights studying less brutal and good news worth celebrating, that maybe… That was the person I was in love with.

In a sort of trance, I stand and walk to Robbie's bedroom door. I am not even sure what I'm going to do, what I'm going to say, as I raise my hand to knock.

The door swings open. Robbie stands in the doorway, holding his phone to his ear.

"I…" I gesture behind me toward the table.

His gaze goes to the screen. "Te llamo luego," he says into the phone before hanging up.

There is panic in his eyes. "Sara, I can explain—"

But I don't let him. I step forward, grab him by his T-shirt and pull him in. I kiss him, and at first he sort of gasps in surprise.

But then his lips soften against mine and we sort of settle into the kiss. His hands find my waist and I weave my fingers into his hair.

When we break apart I say, "I think I am falling for you too."

chapter thirty-six

My phone blares. I jolt awake. I pick it up from my nightstand, catching the time off the clock: 3:30 am.

I tap Ignore.

Next to me, Robbie mumbles, but doesn't wake up. Since Tiffany is out of town visiting her boyfriend, I invited him to sleep over. Nothing happened, I mean, we kissed more of course, and cuddled. But nothing else physical. And we didn't even talk about what we were, what this meant.

I snuggle back up next to him. Maybe I will just enjoy this moment, and figure out all those questions tomorrow. How very unlike me.

It is silent for a moment, and then my phone starts ringing again. *I swear to God.*

I tap the green button and hop down from my bed. "Braden, it is *three o'clock in the morning.* Stop calling me."

"Saaaaara," he whines. "Why don't you answer my texts? What if it was about the app?"

"Is it?" I ask.

"No," he says. "But—"

"Braden, I will talk to you tomorrow."

"No, we have to talk now. C'mon, I'm right outside."

"You're *what?*"

"Just let me in, and we can talk it out."

"Go home, Braden."

"I'm not leaving until you come out." He pounds on the door, and I think I can hear him both on the phone and in real life.

"Sara!" he yells. And yes, I can definitely hear that without the phone. He is not outside, like downstairs, he is right outside my suite door. He must've walked into the building behind someone.

Jesus. I throw on my robe and head outside.

The front door is practically shaking from his incessant knocking.

I yank it open. *"Go home."*

Braden is wearing a suit. Or at least the remains of it. His tie is undone, and his shirt is half-buttoned.

"I've been thinking," he says, leaning against the door frame for balance. "And I have decided we should get back together."

"We should what?" I recoil, my muscles tightening. Fight or flight.

"You and me." He gestures sloppily. "We should start dating again."

"No, I heard what you said… What do you mean, you *decided?*"

"Well…" He looks around, as if trying to figure out how else to explain what's happening. "I decided I can forgive you for embarrassing me at the fundraiser. I still think the benefits of our relationship outweigh the negatives."

"Oh my," I say. My anger is replaced with a wave of exhaustion. He does not understand, does he? "This is just... unbelievable."

"What is unbelievable?"

I don't know how to explain how bizarre his words are. "This is not how relationships work."

He narrows his eyes.

"We shouldn't be weighing the costs and benefits," I continue. "We should just be hanging out with each other. We should be *friends* with each other. And not in a social climb-y networking way. But just, you know, genuinely like spending time with each other. It should be easy. We should have fun when we're together. Trust each other more than any other person in the world.

"Do you feel that with me?" I ask. "Honestly?"

He shakes his head. "Stop being ridiculous, Sara. This isn't some soap opera. We're not on *Gilmore Girls*.

"This is real life," he continues. "You don't pick partners because they want to sit around and cuddle or bake cookies. You pick people who will advance your standing in the world. We're staring down a multimillion-dollar empire. This match isn't about being...normal, dumb and happy. You have the potential to be much more than that. To be great."

"I'd rather be happy," I say, reaching to close the door.

He pushes his arm into its path. "You don't understand," he pleads. "I need you, Sara. You make me better."

I cross my arms, closing my robe tighter. "That is not my job."

My bedroom door opens behind me, and my stomach

drops. I turn to see Robbie stumbling out, rubbing the sleep from his eyes. "Is everything okay?"

Fire builds in Braden's eyes. "What the hell is he doing here?"

I am at a loss for words. "Oh, I—"

"You slut, what the *hell* is he doing here?" Braden yells at me. I flinch as he steps forward, closing the distance between us.

"Hey!" Robbie rushes up to push him back.

Braden regains his balance, and his head bobs back and forth.

"You wanna go?"

I try not to laugh hysterically, because Robbie has broad shoulders and works out every day, and Braden smokes and has the sort of metabolism where he doesn't have to work out and takes advantage of that. A fight between them won't be much of a contest.

But that doesn't mean they won't hurt each other in the process.

"Hey." I step forward and place my hands on Braden's shoulders. "Just go home, okay? Sleep it off."

"Don't touch me." He pushes my hand away.

"Braden, I'm sorry," I say, and I mean it. Although I know I shouldn't be with him, I can't imagine seeing an ex with someone new so soon after a breakup.

"Yeah, *you will be*," he says.

chapter thirty-seven

Braden

I wake up to a hangover, no texts from Sara and an email about a grade update for Math 190. I shimmy down to the foot of my bed and pull my laptop off my desk, then type in my password, still lying down with my arm at a weird angle.

Grade results posted! the message bubble on the website says. I roll my eyes. Really? An exclamation point? When is this ever an exciting moment?

I click on the alert.

Hart, Braden, Assignment Four Grade: 73.

Damn it. I slam the computer closed. The test was two days after Sara and I broke up, and I wasn't exactly in the best state of mind to take it. That, plus my lousy attendance record due to hangovers like this, and I am now looking at a solid C in the class. A nice parting gift from her, I guess.

I lie back and close my eyes. Maybe I will just sleep for the rest of the day.

My phone vibrates against my desk.

Arrrgh. I flip it over.

Call from: Father

Great. I have to answer. I tap the green button.

"Hey, Dad," I say, putting the phone to my ear.

"How's my favorite son?"

I roll my eyes. "I'm your only child."

"That I know of," he says.

I laugh, but given my parents' complicated relationship, it might not be that far off the truth. Which makes it a little less funny.

"How goes it with the company?" he asks.

Of course, he never likes to spend too long talking about personal lives, even thinly fictionalized ones.

"Good," I say. "I told you we have an offer."

"Right, right," he says. "From whom again?"

I bet I'm the only kid in the world to have this much success and still be forgettable to my parents.

"Bell Ventures."

"Oh," he scoffs. "They run a half-assed shop. You'd do much better elsewhere."

"Yeah." I scrub a hand across my face. "I mean, they want to buy it almost outright."

"Then that settles it. A flattering but useless offer—brush it off and get back to initial meetings."

"It's not quite that simple," I say.

"What do you mean?"

The door opens, and Jesse, my roommate, walks in, wearing a backward baseball cap, pastel shorts and no shirt.

I wave and point to the phone. He nods and turns to place his longboard on top of his desk.

"I mean we have to vote," I tell my father. "And my partners are not the easiest people to convince."

"These are your employees," my dad says. "If they're your friends too, that doesn't mean—"

"They're not though," I say. "My employees." They're not my friends anymore either, but that's another point entirely.

Jesse climbs onto his bed, puts his giant headphones on and plugs them into the turntable on his nightstand.

"They code and you run the business?" he asks.

"Yeah, but—"

"They implement your ideas. You control the big picture."

"Yes, I mean, but they're not my employees. We all have equal votes for this."

"Why is that? What do these people bring to the table when it comes to business?"

I open my mouth to answer him, but he keeps steamrolling, uninterested in my reply.

"Are the share distributions formalized anywhere? Because if not, you have no obligation to divide the business equally."

I didn't think it was possible for my headache to get worse. "I don't really think that would be fair," I say.

"This is not *camp*, Braden—not everyone gets a participation trophy." He pauses. "Is this attitude due to your involvement with that girl? Are you thinking with parts of your body that are not your brain?"

"What? Dad, *no*."

"Do not let your woman tell you what to do. At home, maybe, but not in your business."

"She's not my—"

"I know, I know," he says, like I've accused him of something. "She's your partner, and capable herself. I get it. In this day and age, you can't just have a cute blonde on your arm anymore. You need a cute blonde with a good résumé. Can't bring a Silicon yoga instructor to a society function, Braden. You need a beautiful woman with a beautiful pedigree."

I groan softly. I've been subjected to this speech before. I don't know how to tell him that the first time I tried to date a chick who is more than good looks and a huge Instagram following, she stomped on my heart.

He continues, "But that doesn't mean she gets to be the alpha. She's still the woman. *You* are the alpha."

I know he's probably right about the business stuff, but have seen enough terrible fights between him and my mom to disregard his messed-up relationship advice. But I don't say anything. I'm too tired to attempt changing the mind of someone who thinks a phone is a one-way device.

"Do whatever it takes to get control," he says. "Whatever it takes."

I exhale and look at the computer on my desk. "I think I might know how to handle it." One idea keeps coming back to me in my most heated moments, when I'm most pissed at Sara. But I've been too uncertain to act on it.

But if I need to do *whatever it takes.*

"I, um, would need some help from you though, Dad."

"Just tell my secretary whatever it is," he says. "Listen, I've got to go. I'm pulling up to the restaurant. Nice talking to you, though."

"Oh, okay," I say. "Bye."

But he is already gone.

chapter thirty-eight

Roberto

I pull off the sweater I'm wearing and toss it on the floor before rummaging through the pile of clothes on my bed. I pick up a few hangers and move them aside, not sure what I'm looking for but sure it's not that loud-ass pattern.

Tonight is the night. My first real date with Sara. I've fantasized about this moment so many times.

And, no, I don't mean like that.

I mean, I've thought about what restaurants I would take her to. What stories I would tell to make myself seem both thoughtful and fun. I've thought about how, when we were walking side by side down the sidewalk, I would just sort of brush the back of her hand with mine. So lightly that it could have been an accident. And that maybe, if she wanted to, she would look over at me as she laced her hand with mine. She'd roll her eyes, letting me know that I wasn't as slick as I thought, but then she would smile.

I thought of how I would minimize the awkwardness of a

first kiss at her doorway at the end of the evening, although I guess that's already taken care of.

But never once did I think about what I would wear.

I grab a red pullover and tug it over my head, then check myself out in the mirror.

Oh no. That doesn't work at all. I look like I'm headed to Christmas mass or something. I pull off the sweater and reach for the navy blue one crumpled on the floor. I guess I had it right originally.

I check the time. About ten minutes until I told Sara I would "pick her up" at the other side of the building. I wipe my hands, which keep collecting sweat, off on my jeans.

I turn my attention to my hair, heading back to the mirror. It's sort of standing up on one side and doing a weird swoopy thing, which might look cool if it was a few inches longer and I was still in the Bieber-obsessed middle school days, but is definitely not working right now.

I reach for the gel on my shelf, making sure to use exactly a pea-sized amount. The worst possible scenario would be having to rewash my hair. I take a deep breath, and try to calm my pulse—which is at two shots of espresso in a row levels.

There's a knock at the front door.

"One second," I call out. I run my hand through my hair a few more times. It still looks pretty weird.

Sara, I'm assuming, knocks again, louder this time.

"Sorry!" I say, turning away from the mirror.

Fuck, this will have to do. I rush from my bedroom and across the common area. "Sorrysorrysorr—"

I pull open the door, but it's not Sara waiting there for me. It's Braden. His gaze falls on me but shows no emotion.

"Oh." My hand drops from the doorknob and I take a step

back, my brain firing a million miles a minute but my words and actions slowing down.

He pushes past me and crosses the room, his movements fluid and graceful. Like a snake.

"Were you expecting someone else?" he says. His voice is cold.

The hairs on the back of my neck stand up. "I…ugh." I glance from him to my bed, visible through the doorway, still covered in half my closet. "No." I shake my head.

He doesn't seem angry. At least, not in a way that makes me think he's about to throw a punch, but there is still something setting off the flight-or-fight response in my brain. Something that warns me not to poke the sleeping bear.

Don't bring up Sara! Don't bring up Sara! The message is like a flashing neon sign floating through my brain.

Braden crosses the room and takes a seat on the couch, setting his feet on the coffee table so the shiny red soles of his shoes are facing me.

I am very aware that I did not invite him in. I don't usually think about stuff like that—I'm a pretty welcoming person. Having grown up in a community that calls neighbors aunts and uncles, I might even be welcoming to a fault. It's always come naturally to me. When I'm working or hanging out in my room, I'll leave the door open so that people feel welcome to join.

But right now, I am painfully aware that this is my room, my space, and that I don't like having Braden in it. He is an intruder of negative energy in my happy, messy dorm room home, and I don't like it at all.

He turns his head toward me. "I have an offer for you."

He waits while I take the seat across from him. I sit on the very edge of the chair. "What's up?"

"I talked to my dad," he says. He takes his feet off the table and sits up properly, folding his hands over his knees. "And he is willing to loan me two hundred thousand dollars out of my trust fund. I would like to offer it to you as a buyout."

"Wha—?" I start to speak but my mind goes blank. I snap my mouth shut. My first thought is how ridiculous it is that he just *called up* and asked his dad for that level of money. Like it's change for a gumball machine.

But at this point, I expect the ridiculous from this kid. I shake my head. *Focus.* "Why would I take that if I can get way more from Bell?"

"Because..." He leans back and smiles. "Their offer is contingent on primary control. They won't just buy out your part. And I'm not gonna take that deal, *ever*," he says. "That's over."

"I thought we were still discussing what we're gonna do," I say. The world starts to spin. We weren't done talking about the offer—how could it just be over?

He shakes his head. "I won't sell. I decided in the last few days. Not just to him, but to anyone. I want to build this thing, and I'm not giving it up. If you want out, it's this money or nothing." He stares me down. "You can stay and keep working on this for the next few years hoping to build something big. And when we eventually monetize, maybe a few years after graduation, you might start to make an income." He pauses, as if letting me picture the time passing. Three plus more years of bills and budgets and international call limits and pain. "But I have a feeling you're already sick of this app, and I do not want people with that sort of mind-set on my team. So while I won't let us sell the shares to a third party, I would be happy to buy your portion from you. If you want, if you *need* money now, this is the only shot you got."

Part of me is furious at the way he says *need*. Like I'm some sort of addict and he knows he can control me by waving my fix, a thing that controls me and not him, in front of my face. Something he knows limits my choices and options for action. A worry he's always been free of.

It's infuriating that not only is money *so* different for him than it is for me, but that he *knows* it, and knows he can use it to make me do what I might not want to.

But is leaving this company really something I don't want to do?

I think of my parents, of electric bills and medical bills and plane tickets and immigration attorney fees that have never really even been an option. I think about how long it would take to make this much money.

It's kind of a perfect deal for me. I get to walk away with a life-changing amount of money for a class project I spent a couple of extra months perfecting. Sure, it's less than Thatcher Bell offered. But if that's really off the table, this deal might be the most pragmatic thing for me.

But why would *he* want to pay me?

"So you're gonna pay me almost a quarter of a million dollars just to stop coding for you?" I narrow my eyes.

He shifts in his seat. "Well...that's not all," he says. "The money would come to you in monthly payments and would be based on a gentleman's agreement of sorts, since we've never formalized our ownership shares," he says. "And part of that agreement would be that you wouldn't contact or spend time with the other founders of the company. Either of them." His gaze bears down on me. "Ever."

It feels like the floor drops out from under my feet.

"You want me to stop seeing Sara?" I ask breathlessly. "Is *that* what this is about?" Is he really that mean, that insecure? That he would do all this just to keep someone else from dating his ex?

He doesn't say anything but instead reaches down for his backpack. He pulls out a manila envelope and sets it on the coffee table before standing up and walking out the door.

I reach for the envelope and pull out a sheet of thick white paper. It shows a law firm's header at the top, I flip through it. A contract surrendering my equity in Perfect10.

There is still something bulky at the bottom of the envelope. I peek inside and see green. I pull out what seems like $1,000 in cash.

There is also a business card for an immigration lawyer, with a hand-scrawled note on the back that reads: "Here's a small advance. Think about it."

Shit.

"Hey!" Sara's eyes light up as she peeks her head through the door, and my heart warms, despite everything. I still can't believe I get to be the reason she smiles like that. "Wait—" Her happy face drops. "You can't see me yet. I'm not ready." She reaches out and covers my eyes.

I laugh. "You're being ridiculous."

She leans forward and gives me a quick peck on the lips, but doesn't move her hands. I can smell her perfume. It's different than what she usually wears, new, but still sweet and fresh. Both are like flowers. Maybe one is roses and the other daisies?

Let's be real, I don't know anything about flowers or perfume. I like it though.

For a second I smile, standing there in the darkness like an idiot. Not wanting this moment to end.

I raise my hand to move hers.

"Uh-uh, no way," she says. "Here, I'll lead you." She pulls me forward.

I shake my head but take a step forward.

"Sara, you realize I've seen you up coding at 4:00 a.m. with no makeup, right?"

"Yeah, but—"

"And you looked gorgeous then and I'm sure you look beautiful now. Will you please just let me—ow—" I bang my knee into something.

"Watch out for the chair," her quiet voice says.

"Let me see," I say through gritted teeth.

"Sorry." She lowers her hand, and I see the mischievous grin on her face. "I just wanted to look cute for our first date."

"You look great," I say, taking her hand in mine.

She steps forward and stretches onto her tiptoes to kiss me again.

"Sara," I say when she settles back onto her feet. I trace circles on the back of her hand with my thumb. "I need to talk to you about something."

"Oh no." She takes another step back. "What's wrong?"

"Nothing," I say, my voice high. "Or—I mean—I don't know." I run my free hand through my hair. "Let's sit down."

"Yeah, yeah, okay." She nods and leads me to the couch. She sits down and pulls her feet onto the seat. Her socks are fuzzy and have little hearts and computers on them. I kind of want to ask her where the heck she even bought something like that, but it's not the right time.

"Listen." I take a deep breath. "I need to tell you something."

chapter thirty-nine

Sara

"He tried to *buy me*?" I yell. White-hot rage flashes in front of my eyes. I stand up on the couch, because I can't just stay sitting down. I try to take a deep breath, but I can feel my heart beating, racing. Hear the blood rushing past my ears, making it sound like there's static in the air.

I look at my feet, sinking into the couch cushions, and step down onto the rug.

Just because I'm the most insulted I've been in my entire life doesn't mean civility and consideration for the wear on fabric has to go to hell.

Plus, on the floor there is more room to pace.

And that's exactly what I do, circling the coffee table, stepping over the edge of the rug, passing the window, then the TV. One foot crossing in front of the other as I make my way past the kitchen, and then picking up speed as I move past the couch again, beginning my second lap. All the while making little noises of frustration. Unstrung syllables that don't form words.

Roberto's voice quietly emerges. "Um, that's not *exactly* what I said…"

"Oh, I heard what you said." I spin in one swift movement to face him, brandishing my finger to point right at his heart. "He offered you *two hundred thousand dollars* to stop dating me." I say each word with a punch. I know the gravity of my sentiment is probably undercut by how bright red my face is and by the cuteness of my socks, but I want to be heard. "*What?* What does he expect? That I will just…go back to him after he blackmails you away?"

"No." Roberto sighs, folding his hands together. "I think he knows he can't have you. He just doesn't want to lose you to someone else. Me, in particular."

The spinning world slows down and a cold blue sort of feeling mixes in with the red heat of anger.

A sort of sickness. That I could be seen as such an object. A prize to be won. Or for a sore loser to break in half.

A sort of sadness. That Braden could really feel that way about another person. *Do* that to me. To Robbie.

"There's more…" Robbie says. "He told me if I don't leave, he would never sell. And he gave me this card."

He holds out a business card. I take it.

"What.?"

"It's for an immigration lawyer." He rubs the back of his neck. "He knows about my mom. Heard me talking to her on the phone at Berkeley. The implication is—if I want to help with my mom's legal fees, this is the only way."

The words hit me like a truck. "He's trying to hold your mom's case over your head?"

Robbie nods.

My heart beats against my chest, panic rising. Going after someone's family, their ability to reunite, and using that to leverage ownership in a start-up. That is not just college douche bag behavior. That is like real evil. "Well fuck that," I say.

Robbie cracks half a smile at my swearing, but his eyes remain sad.

"If you are being pushed out then I am going too," I say. "Then his no-contact clause only applies to him."

"But he won't buy you out," Robbie says. "And if you leave for nothing, what kind of justice is that? He gets to win because he's a bully?" He pushes a hand through his hair. "What we really need is a way to kick him out. But I don't see how we can. He seems content to keep doing this forever."

It sounds terrible. Forever. Meeting with Braden almost daily, refreshing my in-box to make sure he hasn't emailed me, fighting with him round after round about what to do about the company.

A company that appeals to the Braden in people. We can pitch Perfect10 however we want, but the truth is, we don't sell people a way to find love; we sell them vanity. Real love—it's not about being the hottest, or smartest or coolest or whatever. It's not a goddamn competition, and people aren't a prize to be won. Real love is about two people fitting. Like how Robbie and I do. I'd rather help people find that.

Of course, Braden would never transition to the sort of app Robbie and I have been toying with. Even if Professor Thomas thought a different approach could be viable.

An idea prickles the back of my mind, and the weight on my shoulders starts to lighten. "Robbie," I say, sitting up. "I know someone who can help us."

chapter forty

Sara

"Why are we meeting here?" Braden makes his way down the hallway, his posture slumped. He has deep purple circles under his eyes.

This morning I finally texted him back, after about a hundred unanswered messages. I told him I was willing to talk, but wanted to meet in a public space, and suggested the water fountains on the second floor of Business School Building One.

"It's away from the freshman dorms," I say. "Plus I just got out of class near here," I lie.

"What's going on?" he asks.

I may have also implied that it was an urgent matter.

"I...um..." I had not thought of a plan to stall him. Luckily, before I have to, Robbie rounds the corner.

"What's he doing here?" Braden asks.

Robbie walks up next to me, and although we do not touch, I feel more relaxed just being in his presence.

"I thought I was clear on the terms of our deal," Braden tells him.

"I haven't accepted it yet," Robbie says.

"What choice do you have?" Braden asks. "You've had a week to consider. I'm getting impatient. I don't think you want to test me."

Just then, the door behind me opens.

"He's ready for you," Professor Thomas's assistant says.

"Okay, thanks," I say.

"What the hell is going on?" Braden asks.

"Why don't you come into my office and I can tell you," Professor Thomas says, stepping into the hallway.

Braden snaps his mouth shut, his face turning a pale shade of green. He follows us into the office. Even as cocky as he is, throwing a fit in front of a venture capitalist is not something he'll make the mistake of doing again.

We sit three across in front of Professor Thomas's desk. He places a piece of paper in front of us.

"I have been discussing your company at length with your colleagues over the past week," Professor Thomas tells Braden. "And have decided to make a substantial investment." He points to the paper. "Under this agreement, I would invest in the company with the understanding that it will pivot direction. Perfect10 will shut down immediately, with plans to relaunch a reimagined project to the same users in a matter of months, while recruiting new users in the meantime."

"I... What?" Braden looks completely confused.

But Professor Thomas continues, unfazed. "I would purchase ten percent of the company for five hundred thousand dollars. Which would leave Roberto Diaz and Sara Jones with forty-five percent equity each."

Braden laughs and looks at me. I stare back, unblinking. "Don't you mean thirty percent each?" he asks. But he must already know what's happening, because he grabs the contract off the table. "Why isn't my name on this?" He holds up the paper, crumpling it with his grip.

"Because..." Professor Thomas reaches into his drawer and pulls out another piece of paper. "You will sign this and surrender your shares in the company for a payment of ten thousand dollars."

Braden scoffs. "Why in God's name would I do that?"

"Because if you don't," I jump in, quoting Professor Thomas's wording from our previous conversation, "Then Robbie and I will sue you."

"For what?" he says. But his tone sounds more like he is saying *screw you.*

"Breach of fiduciary duty," I say. "For when you knowingly went against expert advice and pitched to Michael Williams when you knew it would likely be detrimental to your company and the holdings of your partners."

"And then you lied to us," Robbie says. "Which also opens you up to charges of fraud."

"And before you use your trust fund to assemble the best team of lawyers you can afford," Professor Thomas says, "remember that my net worth is double your father's, and that I will be paying all of Sara's and Roberto's legal fees."

Braden suddenly looks small in his chair, his shoulders slumping and body folding in.

"So I suggest you take your ten grand now and get out. Before I take much more from you. Including your reputation in this industry." He places a contract in front of Braden. "You burned an awfully important bridge earlier this year, and I'm willing to forgive and forget. But not if you stand in the way of me acquiring this company, and taking it in the direction I want, which does *not* include you. If you don't, then you'll know what it's like to have me as an enemy, and I'll wish you luck trying to find work in this town."

Braden and Professor Thomas stare each other down. I hold my breath. My heart pounds against my chest.

Braden exhales, a low rumble from his chest. "Do you have a pen?" he asks.

Yes! My heart soars. Suddenly I feel more awake, like someone shot adrenaline straight into my heart. It's all I can do to not stand up and happy dance.

Braden signs the paper in an aggressive scrawl as Professor Thomas cuts him a check. He leaves the room without even glancing at Robbie or me.

"All right." Professor Thomas places Braden's contract in a drawer and shuts it with a snap. "Let's get down to business."

chapter forty-one

Roberto

"Dad, check your email," I say into the phone. I'm walking back to my dorm but I couldn't wait until I got there to tell him. Plus, I was hoping to catch him during his twenty-minute lunch break.

Sara went immediately from the meeting to her afternoon class, because, of course she did.

"No veo nada. What am I looking for?" he asks. I picture him in front of his computer at home, wearing his reading glasses, as he always does, although he is checking on his phone. "I only have Target coupons."

I try not to laugh. "Refresh the page, Dad."

"Oh, okay."

I wait for the reaction.

"Oh!" he says. "Is this a plane ticket?"

"It's a ticket voucher," I say. "So we can work around your work schedule, but it's enough to go to Mexico at any time of the year, even last minute. And because you don't have to drive, you can go even if you just have a weekend. Dad, my professor just invested half a million dollars in our company."

He is quiet for a moment, and I wonder if I've lost cell service. Or if he didn't hear me.

He clears his throat, and I realize that he may have not been speaking because he did not want me to know he was choked up. "Mijo, I am so proud of you," he says. "And not just because of all your success," he says. "But because the first thing you thought to do was for family."

"You and Mom have done so much for me," I say. "And I wanted to do something, even just something small, to thank you guys," I say. "And trust me, this is just the beginning. I plan on buying you and Mom a giant house one day."

"Okay, but make sure you are still keeping your grades up, even while you have all this app stuff happening. No olvides tus prioridades."

I smile at the ground. I guess old habits do die hard. I don't know how much I'll have to achieve before my parents don't check in to make sure I'm taking my studies seriously. It annoyed me when I was in middle school, but now, it sounds like home.

"Of course, Dad."

That night, Sara and I finally have our first real date. I wear a new button-down shirt, spritz on cologne I haven't used since prom and knock on her door at exactly 6:30 p.m.

She's wearing a floral sundress and shiny gold flats. We head into town and get burgers and milkshakes at a '50s-style diner. And it's like a first date and a fiftieth date all at once. We talk about me surprising my parents with the tickets and our classes and the company and what's happening on our favorite TV shows, and it's like nothing has changed and everything has changed.

We arrive back at our dorm just as it becomes fully dark outside. "What should we do now?" Sara says, as we approach my room.

I unlock the door and step inside. It is quiet, which makes sense for a Friday night, when most of my suitemates are out somewhere. I peek into my room, but my roommate is nowhere to be found.

"Whatever you want to do," I say.

She steps toward me, toward my bedroom. She peeks in the door, toward the two beds, both lofted into the air.

"There's been something I've really been wanting to do…" Sara says, a mischievous smile on her face.

And so, we build a blanket fort.

"I feel like the loft beds create a perfect opportunity," Sara says, as she reaches up to tuck my blanket into one of the slats.

I set down two cups of Baileys and hot chocolate on the desk and wait for further instructions, since she is clearly the one art directing this adventure.

She turns around. "Can you tie that there?" she asks, holding a blanket corner. "I can't reach."

I nod and we switch places. She takes a sip from her hot chocolate. I reach up and tie the blanket to the slat of my bed.

With a *poof*, a pillow smacks me in the butt. I turn around to see Sara, my throw pillow in her hand and a sparkle in her eyes.

"What was that for?" I ask.

She shrugs. "You have a cute butt."

I roll my eyes. Gesturing toward the makeshift tent that

now connects the two beds, I ask, "Is this what you had in mind?"

She nods and bends down to step inside the fort, mug in hand.

I follow her. Inside, some of the florescent light from my overhead fixture filters in, but mostly it is shadowy and dark blue. Sara has laid my comforter across the floor and added a few pillows we had stolen from her room as well.

We both sit down. I take a sip of my drink, the sweetness of the hot chocolate mixing with the slight burn of the alcohol, and then set it down carefully on the blanket.

"This is exactly what I needed," she says, leaning back onto the pillows. "I feel like a kid again."

"Hopefully you didn't have Baileys in your hot chocolate as a kid."

She rolls her eyes, but a smile plays at the edge of her lips. "You know what I mean."

"Yeah," I say. "The blanket fort is definitely a throwback. A small break from being baby CEOs."

"Oh," she says. "That reminds me. We never officially laid out what our jobs would be, besides Braden as CFO I guess, which doesn't even matter now."

I had just assumed Sara would be CEO as we move forward, since she's been the de facto leader from the beginning. I thought maybe I would head up app development or something.

"I was thinking I could be COO," she says. "I really like all the organizational and operations efficiency stuff."

"But you've always been the leader..."

"I've been the organizer," she says. "I'm good at that. The planning and execution of stuff. But you've been the real

leader. The moral leader. You were the one who first realized we were going astray, so you should be the one to lead
us forward. You have the vision for it."

Her eyes on me, unblinking, I feel truly seen. Sara doesn't
just have a crush on me, she understands and appreciates the
beliefs I hold at my core.

"Alright," I say. "I'll take the job. As long as you're by my
side."

"Always," she says.

Sara leans toward me until her lips are just centimeters from
mine. My heart pounds against my chest. She leans forward
and brushes her lips against mine, and I am flooded with excitement and relief somehow at the same time. I kiss her back,
and it's like letting out a breath I didn't know I was holding.

epilogue

Roberto

"That'll be $4.65," the barista says. I don't think I'll ever get used to five-dollar coffee.

I scan my phone and thank her as she hands me my cup. They are super busy today, as students caffeinate and cram for their last finals before heading home for the summer. I make sure to add a good tip.

Across the room, a familiar face catches my eye. Braden is sitting at one of the tables near the milk and sugar station with a laptop in front of him. But he is not typing. Instead, he is looking at me. I decide I don't need Splenda that badly, and head for the door.

"Robbie!" he yells after me. "Wait!"

I glance over my shoulder. He is hurrying toward me, backpack in one hand and laptop tucked under his other arm. And for some reason, I do wait. I guess I'm bad at looking someone in the eyes and then turning away. Even someone like Braden.

He is breathing heavily when he reaches me.

"I'm on my way somewhere," I say. Because it's true, but also because I don't want anything to do with whatever he thinks is about to happen. "I need to keep moving, but you can walk with me for a minute."

He nods. "How are you?" he asks.

"Pretty good… You chased me out of a coffeehouse to ask me how I am?"

He looks down at the pavement. "I, um." He clears his throat. "Also wanted to see how your mom was doing."

"Not that it's any of your business," I say. "But she's good. She's going to appeal her case in court soon." I stare him down. The entire time we were kind of friends, when we saw each other every day, he never asked about my family. Why the sudden interest?

He nods. "Listen, man, what I did…when I offered to, um…"

"Buy my girlfriend away from me? And in the process insult me? Try to manipulate me through my socioeconomic status and my mom's immigration status?"

He winces. "I thought of it more as a way to…create a bearable working environment for myself. But yeah, sure, what you said." His voice is shaky. "It was wrong, okay? I know that now."

Impressive deduction. I resist the urge to roll my eyes.

"Anyway," he continues. "I want to do something to make it up to you. And I know you have money now, but I'm sure you could also invest it back into building the company or something…so, I want to offer you my family lawyer, free of charge, for the remainder of your mom's case. He's done immigration work for us before, since my mom's family is from France. Anyway he's good—really good."

He holds out a business card. Which I assume doesn't include a threatening note this time. I look down at his hand and pause for a long moment before taking it.

"I know it doesn't undo what I did," Braden says. "But it's the least I could do to say I'm sorry."

"Yeah, it is," I say. "The least you could do." I clear my throat. "But, uh, thank you, Braden." I gesture to Business School Building One, on our right. "This is my stop, I've got to go."

"Oh, okay," he says. "I'll see you around."

I reply with a slight nod as I push open the door and power walk my way to the second-floor conference room, taking the stairs two at a time. Through the glass wall, I can see that Sara and Yaz are already here, along with the camera crew. Sara suggested bringing her friend in soon after we closed the deal with Thomas. Yaz knows more about the business side of things, because of her experience at Instafriend. But unlike our previous CFO, she also understands programming, and can talk to us about what we're building.

"Sorry I'm late," I say. I set my bag down and take a seat. My skin tingles. I'm not sure if it's nerves or excitement.

"It's fine. We were just about to start," the reporter, Nancy Lang, says. I've watched her on the local news for years, so I feel like I know her well, although we've met only one time in person, when she requested this exclusive interview for the relaunch. "Okay," she says. "We'll do a sit-down with all three of you here, and then individual interviews, followed by some B roll around campus, in your dorm rooms, on the quad and in classrooms and so on," she says. "Sound good?"

"Sure," Sara says.

I nod. I try to remember exactly how messy my room is right now, and wonder if there's time to text my roommate to tidy up. But of course, in front of the camera I just smile, because what am I going to say—sorry, but my laundry is on my floor, we can't film?

"Let's get started." Nancy's crew helps rig me up with a microphone, and then spends a very long time adjusting the lighting in ways so small that I don't notice a difference, although they definitely do.

"Okay, I was thinking you guys could tell us a little bit about the app, and then I'll ask you a few questions."

I nod, and a red light clicks on above the camera.

"So, Roberto and Sara, as I understand it, you were at the helm of one of the fastest-growing dating apps in the world. And then, in what seemed like an instant, you took it offline. Why?" she asks. "What happened?"

Sara looks to me and I nod; she can answer this one. She's had more of a journey answering that question for herself.

"Well…" She repositions the way she's sitting. "We realized that the product we were making was not having the sort of impact we had hoped. Our initial product, which was called Perfect10, hinged around individuals having a ranking of desirability. And we started to see the detrimental effects it was having on almost all our users. When we realized this, and that the problem was at the core of the algorithm, we had no choice but to shut it down," Sara explains.

"What's more," she continues, "the app wasn't doing what it initially promised, which was to help people find love. Finding true love is not about hundreds of people thinking you're desirable, but about connecting deeply with the people who are right for you. No one is objectively more lovable than someone else. It's about finding the right person and building a strong partnership with them. So we set out to build a new product, something that will promote that sort of connection." She turns to me.

"We're in the process of launching our new product," I say. "Which at the moment we are calling ImperfectMatch, since both parties are imperfect, as all humans are, but also implies that when they fit together, they can become something greater than they are alone. We've found that the biggest problem with most dating apps is judgment based on superficiality. The dating profile does not accurately reflect how humans connect in the world. Most people wouldn't meet someone in person and ask them to list a personal résumé for evaluation. Instead, you spend time with someone and see how they treat people, what their sense of humor is like and what their interests are. These things are more important to building a deep connection," I say.

"So the app works like this—when you set up your account, you're given fifty questions psychologists have found to be predictors of compatibility. You then answer questions about what you like to do in your spare time. When a potential match is found for you in the system, you'll get an alert asking you when in the next week you are free to do a certain activity, whether that's going for a hike, visiting an art museum, attending a talk at a nearby university, or trying a new tapas place. Once both parties have compared availability, you'll be told a time and place to meet. But you won't know who you're meeting, or see a picture of them, so you can't internet stalk and prejudge each other. When you arrive at the location, you'll be instructed to meet at a certain point, and when both parties' GPS indicates they're in the same place, you'll be informed who you are meeting, and that you are a match. After that, the relationship is in the hands of the people who have met. Maybe you just spend an afternoon doing something you enjoy with someone you have some values in common with and then part ways, or maybe you hit it off, and something really special begins."

Nancy asks a few questions about the new app, when are we launching again, how much do we expect to grow, how does it feel to have the support of Professor Thomas. And then she gets this glimmer in her eye and says, "Now I have to ask the question that I know viewers will be wondering, given the tech blog rumor mill, and that is about you and Sara." She looks at me. "You are rapidly becoming the young power couple of the tech world, and you're designing an app for dating. I think what everyone wants to know is, how did you two get together?"

Sara and I look at each other. Warmth spreads through my chest. Her cheeks turn rosy.

"I'm not sure we have time for that," Yaz says with a smile. "It's a very long story."

★ ★ ★ ★ ★

author's note

Although exact numbers are hard to come by, the Pew Research Center estimates that around eleven million people currently live undocumented in the United States. Like Robbie's mother, many of these people have close family and friends in America.

In researching this book, I read articles and books, and viewed documentaries about immigration. I also interviewed and discussed details of Mrs. Diaz's fictionalized case with a law student and immigration activist who has worked with numerous clients going through deportation proceedings. I wanted to ensure the information presented in the book was as accurate as possible. That being said, any factual errors in the manuscript are my own.

If you would like to learn more about immigration in the United States, you can find information at: https://www.aclu.org/issues/immigrants-rights.

acknowledgments

The creation of a book, much like a start-up, is a group effort. Therefore, I would be remiss if I did not acknowledge, endlessly thank and scream from the rooftops about all those who were the Robbie to my Sara on this project. (Or the Sara to my Robbie. I'm not quite sure, but safe to say, we were Braden-free.)

First, thank you to my rock-star agent, Nicole Resciniti, and to everyone at The Seymour Agency. Thank you, Nicole, for putting up with a number of time zones and changing schedules and hopping on the phone with me to talk through everything from new ideas to minor plot points. You are my confidant, champion, beta reader and friend. Thank you for taking a chance on me when I was still in high school.

Thank you to everyone at Inkyard Press, and the wider HarperCollins family. To Leslie Wanger, who first welcomed me to Harlequin TEEN/HarperCollins. Thank you to my editor, Natashya Wilson, whose insight on this project was invaluable, as it is on so many things. I owe you a debt of gratitude for helping me cut through the tangents and confusion and find the core of this story, and what it needed to say. Thank you also to Gabby Vicedomini, for your encouragement and insightful notes. Thank you to Laura Gianino and everyone in publicity and marketing, for helping readers find stories.

Thank you to Kathleen Oudit and Laci Ann Shaffer, for a beautiful, thematically resonate and fun cover.

Thank you to the writers who have inspired me with their words. Thank you particularly to Sandhya Menon, Elizabeth Acevedo, Angelo Surmelis, Tiffany Jackson, Misa Sugiura, Caleb Roehrig and Gloria Chao. It is surreal and an absolute honor to have shared a panel or stage with authors I admire so.

Thank you to Joelle Charbonneau, who took the time to give me advice and encouragement, even in the midst of deadlines and a rock-star tour schedule. Thanks also to Hannah Orenstein, whose advice on fiction and journalism has been so helpful, and whose words resonate deeply with me and so many other young women.

Thank you to Christa Desir and Julie Cross. It means so much to receive encouragement from those I look up to.

To the entire YA Lunch Break group, and particularly Beth Fama, who first invited me. I will miss you guys on the East Coast! Special thanks to Evelyn Skye, who gave me so much encouragement during my debut, and who even apologized for not making it to my launch party, even though her conflict was her own wedding!

To my Electric 18s, thank you for joining me on this roller coaster of a year and for making me feel so welcome, both online and in new cities.

Thank you to booksellers. Particular thanks to Anderson's in the Chicago area and Kepler's in Northern California (my two local bookstores) for making my dreams come true when I got to sign my books in your stores.

Of course, none of this would have been possible without the amazing teachers I was so fortunate to have, particularly those who helped me when I struggled to learn to read and fell behind my peers. Thank you to my teachers, from St. Francis Xavier and Nazareth Academy to Stanford. Including but not limited to: Jessica Radogno, Amelia Garcia, Lori Wasielewski, Mary Kate O'Mara, Janine Zacharia, Adam Tobin and Phil Taubman.

Thank you also to those who have mentored me and helped to sharpen my writing outside the classroom, from *The Mash* and *Huffington Post Teen* to the *San Francisco Chronicle*, including: Taylor Trudon, Liz Perle, Morgan Olsen, Michelle Lopez, Phil Thompson and Jessica Mullins.

Thank you to my family. To my parents, for all you have done for me. Thank you especially for taking my dream seriously and treating chasing what I love as a viable career path. Thanks as well to my siblings, who encourage me, take pictures of my book in every store they find it and keep me humble.

Thank you also to my Stanford "second family." To my women in CS and SymSys who inspire this "fuzzy" every day, including Katelyn Jones, Aditi Poduval and the original "code-blooded bitch" Ana Caro Mexia, who has been one of the biggest supporters of my writing and who kindly edited all the Spanish in this manuscript.

To my dear friends of all majors and passions, who inspire me with their drive, including: Nicolas Lozano, Maddie Bradshaw,

Alex Barakat, Becca Rose, Carrie Monahan, Maddie Bouton, Marothodi Ntseane and Kristin McIntire.

And of course, to Graeme Hewett, who didn't just put up with but celebrated my eccentricities. Who comforted and encouraged me when deadlines had me declaring I was turning into "a little ball of stress." And whose belief in my talent and career potential is unwavering, even when I doubt myself.

And last but not least, thank you to my readers. The time since *Frat Girl* has been out in the world has been surreal, and I cherish every Tweet, email and Instagram DM I receive. I am so glad my words have connected with you and started a conversation, and I hope we can keep chatting for years to come.